DISPLAYS OF EXPERIENCE

'Ready for the last three?' I asked.

After the briefest pause, she nodded. I laid the cane back neatly and directly along the centre stripe and her bottom lifted fractionally to greet it.

'Move your legs apart.' She obeyed straight away and I couldn't resist the desire to peer round and see what was now revealed. I could see right through to her puffed-up, downy lips. They were not just swollen. They were glistening; enticingly wet and aroused.

'Amanda? You're so wet down here.'

Her voice was still muffled. 'I know. Get on with it.'

DISPLAYS OF EXPERIENCE

An anthology of short stories

Lucy Golden

This book is a work of fiction.
In real life, make sure you practise safe sex.

First published in 2000 by
Nexus
Thames Wharf Studios
Rainville Road
London W6 9HA

Typeset by TW Typesetting, Plymouth, Devon

Printed and bound by
Cox & Wyman Ltd, Reading, Berks

ISBN 0 352 33505 X

Contents

Gemma's Tale – A Second Order

It was different this time. Barry knew that I was going to the Giffords for a presentation, and knew what had happened the previous time. I'd told him everything – almost. I found him waiting in the hall.

'How do I look?'

'Fantastic.' He wrapped his arms round me and kissed me, his fingers playing up and down my back and then right down to my bottom. I was already nervous, already tense, already excited and I didn't need any caresses from him to make it worse. I pulled away and smoothed down my skirt.

'I must go.'

He reached up to straighten the collar of my blouse, just ironed, and his fingertips trailed down over my breasts. He raised his eyebrows when he discovered I wasn't wearing a bra and pinched my nipple lightly. I backed towards the door.

'I must go,' I repeated.

'Just a minute.' He pulled me back into the hall and slid his hands up under my skirt, lifting the hem. For a few seconds he stood admiring the new knickers and hold-up stockings before suddenly taking hold of my knickers and pulling them down. I backed off again, not wanting him to kiss me there, to discover how wet I had already become, but he pulled the knickers right down to my ankles and lifted each foot in turn to take them off me.

He stood up. 'I don't expect you'll be needing these,' he said, and then he pushed me out and shut the door firmly behind me.

It was well before eight o'clock when I reached the Giffords' house and parked a short distance down the almost empty street. All these houses had their own garages so few other cars littered the road, and there would be no danger of missing Melanie's new bright yellow convertible. I'd see – and hear – that easily enough when she arrived. I settled back to wait.

For no obvious reason, Melanie and I had taken an instant and entirely mutual dislike to each other from the moment we met. She had always scoffed at my serious and professional approach; I never hid my disgust at her frivolous flirtation. Against that background, I could understand why she had been so sceptical when I had sidled up to her at the end of one weekly sales round-up dangling the prospect of half commission on a £25,000 order. When I explained that I had already secured one order for windows from these same clients and now they had decided on a conservatory but wanted her as well, she was even more doubtful.

'Why? Why me?'

'Apparently you took an order from some friends of theirs. Someone called Williamson? A month or so ago?'

Melanie had actually blushed. 'Ah, yes. I remember.' Then the blush had turned to a frown, and her eyes fixed firmly on her cigarette as she tried to decide how much I knew, how much she could safely tell. I didn't like her enough to put her out of her misery.

'Apparently they liked your style.' My remark kept her splendidly off balance. 'It seems the Giffords have similar tastes.'

She had nodded slowly and uncertainly. 'Ah. I see.'

We were circling like fencers, probing for an opening, but reluctant to commit ourselves. Neither of us knew how far the other had gone, and we were each unwilling to divulge too much in case we were mistaken; each afraid of the reaction our revelation might produce in the other. I expect she knew as well as I did that at some stage we would have to disclose everything, but neither of us wanted to be the one to go first.

In the end, she had pushed me into a corner by simply coming straight out and asking the question. 'So, what did they want? What did you do?'

I had still prevaricated. Melanie made no secret of flirting with the customers, but what about the rumours that she sometimes let them go all the way? Was this just jealousy? Malicious gossip? Or was there any truth in it? She was certainly attractive, but she also looked quite innocent. How could I tell her what I had done already, what they would expect of her if she came with me, without laying myself open to the same rumours that circulated about her? Was there any alternative but to trust her?

'Can we keep this just between the two of us?'

'Yes, of course.'

'I had to undress.' I tried to make it sound matter of fact, unexceptional.

'What, completely?'

'Yes.'

'Bloody hell! I've never gone that far!' My disbelief must have shown in my face, because she had reddened again. 'I know people talk, and say I sleep with all the clients, but I don't, you know. I mean I admit sometimes I flirt a bit if it looks as if that'll help, perhaps give them a little flash of my boobs or my knickers, but never more than that.'

She had looked up at me again. 'Honestly.'

I still wasn't sure whether I believed her or not, but if she were telling the truth, then I was way ahead of her. After all, I had allowed Mrs Gifford to touch me. I decided not to say any more until nearer the time but she had taken my silence as either disbelief or disapproval. She looked down at my chest.

'Well, this time they can have an ogle at two pairs of tits.' She had taken a long drag on her cigarette. 'Small and minuscule.'

In truth her breasts did not look to be a great deal bigger than mine, but I had ignored the remark. 'So you'll do it? I can tell them we'll both go?'

She had blown out a great cloud of smoke and smiled at me in a way that was actually quite friendly. 'I've got to admit I badly need another good sale, and I suppose if you can manage it, I should be able to. Anything you can do, I can do better! Let's go for it. We could be quite a team.'

'Yes. That's what Mrs Gifford said.'

So I had arranged an appointment with the Giffords and even posted them the brochures in advance. Now we were due at their house and there was no sign of Melanie. As eight o'clock passed, I started to worry that she had chickened out; it was quite unlike her to be late. I decided to wait until quarter past and then, if she hadn't arrived, go up to the house on my own.

At ten past, my mobile started chirping.

'Gemma? It's Melanie. Where are you?'

'Where am I? Where on earth are you?'

'I'm at the Giffords' house. We're all waiting for you. Where are you?'

'Oh shit! I'm outside. I've been waiting for you!'

I quickly ran up the path and rang the bell. Mrs Gifford ushered me in and received my apologies with

4

the unforgiving patience of a headmistress on Parents' Day.

'Never mind, dear. At least you're here now. I'm just making some coffee; you go on through to the living room.'

I peered round the door, finding Mr Gifford in his usual place on one side of the elaborate brick fireplace, and it struck me that I had never seen him anywhere else but in that chair. He didn't stand up when I first came in nor when I left and I suddenly wondered whether he could stand, or whether that could be the reason for the little displays that his wife arranged.

On my last visit I had sat opposite him on the end of the sofa. Now that place was taken by Melanie, looking greatly relieved to see me walk in. She was smart as always, dressed in a neatly tailored tweed trouser suit. The jacket had four big buttons up the front and beneath that was visible an attractive silky top whose high neck ran straight across just below her throat. The trousers were fitted and slightly flared so that the whole effect was decidedly androgynous and disturbing, but it was also extremely appealing. Her face was big and open with round eyes and a wide generous mouth that smiled at me with such honesty I wondered if I had misjudged her. Her light brown hair was cut to jaw-line length and curled forward with an innocent wildness that was either infuriatingly natural or impossibly expensively styled. Either way, I was beginning to think that the office rumours could be true: perhaps she could seduce anybody of either sex.

Yet she looked calm and serene where I just felt flustered: hot and wrong-footed and I hadn't even been able to check my hair before running up here. I turned away.

'I'm terribly sorry, Mr Gifford. I was waiting for Melanie outside but I didn't see her car.'

'No, she was just saying the garage has recalled it for some modification or other.'

'Yes,' she butted in. 'They've given me a courtesy car for two days. Dark green saloon? Parked opposite?'

I nodded, sickened. 'Yes. I saw it.' I smiled at Mr Gifford again; I couldn't bring myself to smile at Melanie. 'Anyway, sorry.'

'That's quite all right. We've had time for a very interesting chat. I thought you'd said Melanie was away on holiday last week. Apparently she was at work all the time.'

'Oh! Were you? I thought someone said you were away.' It didn't sound convincing and I hate lying so it was a relief when Mrs Gifford appeared with the coffee tray, bustling about like a mother hen.

'Now, we'll get the boring business out of the way first. Mr Gifford needs to run through the order with you. Gemma dear, you sit here next to your friend.' She straightened the cushions and then perched on the arm of the sofa beside me, smiling down at us. 'You two all right there?'

I nodded. 'Fine, thank you.'

She smiled too. 'Not too hot?' It was the way she looked at me, holding her gaze just a fraction longer than was really necessary that gave the emphasis. She was playing the same game as last time. Nothing would be asked for explicitly, just hints and suggestions and a response only after we had volunteered.

I reached up and toyed with my blouse, undoing the top few buttons so that an expanse of skin was visible. I glanced over at Melanie and when I caught her eye, she shrugged and unbuttoned the jacket. As

6

it swung open, her top was revealed as no more than a tiny vest whose shoe string straps looked ready to fall at any moment. Mr Gifford nodded appreciatively and picked up the brochure I had sent him, but he didn't open it, just looked across at Melanie and I knew what he expected. She didn't. She looked puzzled at the delay and then turned to me, a frown creasing her round face. I would have to lead her.

'Shall I give you a hand with that?' I asked and took hold of the jacket to help her off with it. Then she understood.

'Oh no. That's OK.' She stood up and removed the jacket as we all watched her. The movements were just sufficiently exaggerated, just a little too ostentatious, to be entirely natural so that all our eyes were drawn to her. Swaying and rippling as she moved and turned, the outline of her little breasts, clearly braless, was visible through the thin silk vest. Nobody moved or spoke until she had finished and was sitting next to me again.

'Sorry, Mr Gifford,' she smirked. 'Please carry on.'

It was comical the way he smiled so eagerly at her coquetry, but I wasn't sure that I wouldn't have done the same if she had smiled that smile at me.

As he worked page by page through the brochure, he had clearly decided already most of what he wanted. He still had one or two questions and I let Melanie answer; she had been in the job much longer than me. But she also understood his game and took every chance to lean forward so that he could look down the hanging front of her loose top and at one stage stood next to him while she explained the different mullion profiles so that her breasts pressed against his shoulder as she talked. For more than ten minutes I sat in silence watching and listening, as the order form was gradually completed with every detail of every size, shape, style. Yet all the time I was keenly aware of Mrs Gifford perched right beside me, and though I felt her eyes on me, I dared not look round. As they neared the end, Mr Gifford paused and looked up at his wife and over at us.

'Now then. How are we doing?'

His smile was encouraging; his words were ambiguous; his expectation was clear. He wanted us to reveal some more. Yet undoing any more would mean that the top part of my breasts would be exposed and as I fumbled with the remaining buttons, I felt isolated and alone. My confidence was draining away. I had been excluded from the cosy conversation between Mr Gifford and Melanie and I was starting to realise that she was much better than me at this sort of thing. She knew how to be seductive, whereas I no longer felt alluring or even pretty. Compared with her, my clothes felt stupid, my breasts seemed too small and my hips and elbows and knees were all too bony. I knew what they wanted and expected to see, but I couldn't bring myself to show them. Sitting there in a room with three other people, all practically strangers and two of them fully dressed, I couldn't calmly start taking off my clothes.

I was trapped. The more I considered how events would inevitably develop, the tighter the trap closed. A pulsing pressure of fear was building up until I realised that I simply could not participate at all. The previous visit, with only the Giffords, had been difficult enough and if it had been only them again, I might have been able to continue, but not with Melanie there. She changed everything. I couldn't let her see that I had come out this evening with no knickers, nor that our treatment so far and anticipation of more to come was already making me wet. Nor could I open my blouse in front of her, and let her mock my pathetic little breasts, and my nipples, already so tight and hard, so eager and afraid.

Melanie's presence made it quite impossible. It was bad enough that we knew each other and worked together. It was worse that we disliked each other. It was worst of all that now she was in her element, loving every minute of it and doubtless enjoying even more my anguish and the ease with which she had pushed me aside. She probably had no qualms at all about exposing herself to these people, would undress completely in front of them and in front of me if that was what they required. Well, I wouldn't. I couldn't. Even if I lost the commission.

I stood up. 'I'm sorry, Mrs Gifford. I have to go. Melanie can take the order. I'm sure she can . . .' I hesitated, searching for the right euphemism. 'I'm sure she can handle everything you need.'

I snatched up my bag and ran out but Mrs Gifford caught up with me in the hallway, grabbing me by the arm.

'Gemma, my dear, please don't be frightened.'

I don't know why, but I burst into tears. 'I'm sorry, Mrs Gifford, really I am, but I just can't do it.'

I hadn't cried like this since I was a baby, not the deep racking sobs that were suddenly welling up from I didn't know where but were completely taking over everything I said or thought. I didn't care that the two in the living room could hear me. I just stood there weeping as Mrs Gifford enfolded me in her warm arms and hugged so that I buried my head in her great soft bosom. She stroked my hair and patted my shoulder and cooed into my ear as if I were a child.

'There, there! There, there! Just have a good cry and you'll feel so much better.'

She was so comforting as she stroked me, so soothing and reassuring that I found I had wrapped my own arms round her and was cuddling her as if she were my own mother. She even produced her own little embroidered handkerchief to wipe away my tears and held it while I blew my nose.

'There now!' she murmured. 'All better now.'

She still had one arm round my shoulders as she continued gently stroking my cheek with the other hand. 'Don't be frightened, dear. Remember how you were a little bit frightened last time, but you managed in the end, didn't you? I'm sure you can manage now. And you've got your friend with you this week as well, and you don't want to look silly in front of her, do you? What will she say if you run away and spoil everything? And what about me? You and I got on ever so well before, didn't we? Mr Gifford would be dreadfully disappointed with me if I let you go running off now. Hmm?'

Her low soft voice and warm shoulder were so mesmerising that I felt myself being won over. I didn't want to let Mrs Gifford down and I didn't want to look a coward in front of Melanie, but they demanded so much.

'I'm shy!' I finally blurted out.

'Oh, get along with you! You've no need to be shy!' She stepped back to look at me, appraising the picture I presented. 'You're such a pretty little thing and you know how much Mr Gifford likes to look at you. Come along, let's just slip this shirt off and I'm sure you'll find it all much easier after that. You know you have the most adorable little breasts, so tiny and so sweet.' Her fingers had worked down and were stroking through the thick cotton shirt, pulling at the point where my nipple was already hardening under her caress.

10

'Besides,' she said, 'I'll bet Melanie is jealous of these, isn't she?' She had already started unbuttoning the front and I found myself watching her, hypnotised.

'I don't know.' My voice was little more than a whisper. 'I doubt it.'

'Oh, come along now. I bet hers aren't as lovely as yours, now are they?'

'I don't know. I've never seen them.'

'Never?' She was genuinely surprised.

'No.'

But now she had finished unbuttoning the shirt and was pulling it out of the waistband of my skirt. 'There now. Look at you! Such pretty little breasts. Oh no, don't cover yourself up.' She caught my wrists and pulled them away from where I had instinctively reached up to shield my nakedness. Her hands ran across my chest, appearing to ignore my breasts as the palms swept in great arcs across the whole of my body. Yet every time her hands rode up over my nipples, pushing them aside and leaving them to spring up again when they were released, a shiver went through me and when Mrs Gifford leaned down to plant a little kiss on each nipple, I felt myself seeping a little more. I wished I had some knickers to absorb the wetness before it started to leak down my leg.

The woman smiled at my reaction. 'There, you see? Your breasts are so tiny I can cover each of them just with my hand, yet those little nipples just won't stay down, will they? What a lucky girl! Now, let's go back in.'

Still I held back. If I had to stay, if I had to persevere, only one thing would make it bearable, one thing I had to ask. 'Mrs Gifford? Will I be able to kiss you again? Kiss your breasts, I mean?'

She smiled at me, amused but curious. 'Is that what you really want?'

'Yes.' I felt so ashamed of myself, but I had been dreaming about her breasts, about those huge white soft pillows where I had buried my face before and if she would just let me suckle at her nipples again, I felt I could allow her anything.

'Why?'

'I just do. Please?'

Still toying with my nipple, she leaned forward and kissed me on the mouth, just quickly so that I barely registered the little flick of her tongue before it was gone. 'We'll see, child. Maybe.' And she pushed open the living-room door.

Neither Melanie nor Mr Gifford appeared to have moved but as we came in, they both turned towards the door and I saw Melanie's face. She was terrified, on the verge of tears herself. I had completely misjudged her. She was no more comfortable with what we were being asked to do than I was; she was no more relaxed, no more confident. If I had not returned, I don't believe she would have stayed either.

I hesitated at the door, conscious of my nakedness, as Mr Gifford smiled triumphantly to see his wife leading me by the hand.

'She's decided to stay,' she said, guiding me back towards the sofa where I settled down beside Melanie, bringing my arms round in front of me to cover what I could of my nakedness. Mrs Gifford took a seat on the arm of her husband's chair, all the while offering out the same cheerful and embracing grin. 'Melanie? What about you?'

It was a relief that I was not to be the only one to be exposing my breasts, but now that I had seen through the artifice of Melanie's show of courage, I could see that her pauses were not some clever flirtation. She was as nervous and as unwilling as me. For a moment I thought she was going to refuse and perhaps even leave. After all, she had admitted that she had never gone further than an occasional brief flash of her body. Now we were being asked to sit entirely on view and if we were topless at this stage of the presentation, they would doubtless expect us to be entirely naked by the end.

Melanie looked at me and then shrugged her shoulders. A twinkling of black and gold shimmered off her vest as she moved and turned, slowly teasing the hem upwards. She glanced shyly at Mr and Mrs Gifford as the undercurve of her round breasts was revealed, then the dark half-circles of her areolae, her nipples as ripe and red as cherries and finally in a single sweep the whole vest was stripped away and she pushed her chest forward towards them.

Now that they were revealed, I could see that her breasts were only a very little larger than mine, but although they were still small by most people's standards, I was jealous. I've never wanted really huge breasts, but I would have liked hers. They had a wonderful roundness, lifted away from her chest on soft round curves that cried out to be cupped in an open palm. Like me, her nipples were small and like mine they were already erect. I caught her eye and we both smiled. The Giffords were also entranced, both watching intently as she moved and it gave me the confidence to sit up straighter and show off my own nakedness.

'That's much better.' Mr Gifford's delight bubbled over as he glanced across from one of us to the other, sitting stupidly side by side with our little breasts exposed. 'Truly enchanting. Let's continue.'

Within five minutes, the order was completed. Even the price, with no discount asked or offered, was entered and the only box now empty was for the signature.

Melanie closed the brochure and lay the completed form on top, the empty signature space prominently facing him. 'Is that everything, Mr Gifford? Is there anything else I can help you with before we complete any last formalities?'

The man smiled appreciatively before turning to his wife. 'Margaret? Anything else?'

'No, I don't think so, dear. Not on that aspect, but how about you, Gemma? Is there anything you would like to contribute? Anything more to offer?'

I felt the eyes burning into me as everyone waited for my response. 'I'm sorry, Mrs Gifford. What did you want?'

'I think we explained that last time, my dear. I believe you know how we like to do things in this house.'

Her voice was low and cajoling and yet it commanded. I turned to face Mr Gifford and slowly slid my knees apart, allowing the short skirt to ride up my thighs. I still felt their eyes on me and it was when the wide dark band at the top of my hold-ups came into view that I faltered. I had temporarily forgotten what Barry had done, but the minute I remembered, I stopped.

The woman frowned slightly. 'Gemma?'

'I don't have any underwear on.'

Mrs Gifford smiled so gloatingly that I needed to explain; I didn't want her to misunderstand. 'Barry, my boyfriend. He took them. He said I wouldn't need them.'

She smiled. 'So you've told him all about our little games, have you? Well, that's good. You should always be entirely honest about these things. He was right. Why don't you slip the skirt right off?'

I gave in and stood up, found the zip and pulled it down. Then I let the skirt slide down my legs, stepped out of it and lay it over the sofa. I was about to sit down quickly but she stopped me.

'Just a moment, my dear. Let's have a look at you.'

So I stood and waited for her inspection, my nakedness emphasised by the stockings and shoes that were all I now retained. I felt myself blushing as I stood there, all their eyes roaming over me again. Mr Gifford cleared his throat.

'Ah! How lovely!' he said. 'Now why don't you slip those last things off and turn around so I can see you properly.'

Having gone so far, there was no point in stopping now, so I took off the stockings and the sandals and then turned round. I knew from last time that it was my bottom he really wanted to see, so I turned away from him and found Melanie's wide green eyes fixed on me. I don't know whether it was admiration or disdain, but it was an expression that I knew from work when I had voiced any disagreement with her views or failed to equal her sales targets, but most of all when I had shown disapproval of her flirting or flippancy.

Yet now my hypocrisy was revealed. I had plunged to depths even she had never reached, and I was ashamed at how easy it had all been. Even having been through a similar ordeal before, I should have had some modesty, some delicacy, but in the end I had allowed myself to be drawn in with virtually no resistance at all. As I weakened and wilted under her gaze, I remembered that I hadn't warned her what to expect. I'd been intending to give her more details outside the house before we came in, but her arriving first had given me no chance.

I smiled and tried to make it apologetic, but she turned away. Her distrust was not to be mollified by a smile.

'Is that all right? May I sit down now?'

'In a moment, child, but first please turn round again and bend right down. You know how much my husband admired your little bottom before, and it would be lovely to see that again.'

I really had hoped to be spared this indignity. He had seen my bottom when I was standing in front of him and I felt so degraded bending down like that showing off everything, even my lips and my thighs all shiny. Yet I couldn't refuse or object or even let them know I was reluctant; I was determined not to give Melanie another excuse to gloat. So I shuffled my feet wide apart and bent forward and even, because I knew that they'd demand if I didn't offer, reached back and, just briefly, pulled my cheeks open a little further. I heard Mr Gifford sigh, and when I quickly stood up and looked round, his wife was ruffling his thinning hair with great affection. I felt I had acquitted myself well and was glad that at last my part of the ordeal was over. Now it would be Melanie's turn.

I sat next to her, entirely naked now, but still ashamed of what I had done and what I had failed to warn her of. We didn't have long to wait before Mrs Gifford took the lead again.

'Melanie, dear? What can you show us?'

At first she didn't move. I felt the sofa quiver under me and for a moment I wondered if she were crying, but I couldn't bear to look. If I were right, it would be my fault and I couldn't deal with that. Instead I reached out my hand and took hers. Just a light squeeze, trying to pass across some confidence and restore some good faith, and although the pressure wasn't returned, at least she didn't snatch her hand away. Slowly, she released my clasp, stood up, took a place in the centre of the room and stared at the floor.

Yet even now she couldn't bring herself to start. She seemed petrified, her arms hugged round her body as she swayed gently from side to side and I felt a sudden surge of sympathy for her, standing up there alone: fighting so hard the urge to flee when she was faced with a demand to stay. Her pathetically skinny arms so obviously wanted to cover her nakedness, and yet she was waiting there in front of us all because we wanted to see her take off even more.

Slowly she prised off one shoe against the other foot; the second shoe against the first foot. And stopped again. The two shoes, square toed, black leather, lay discarded on the floor like the televised evidence of some foreign massacre. Her toes lifted and writhed inside the neat little white socks, tiny innocents whose time would soon come. None of us said anything. No one helped or encouraged or advised or, I think, even blinked. We all watched and waited as she stood and squirmed. Eventually her right arm, staying across her body, dropped down to her waist and fiddled with the hook and eye on the side of her waistband. The hook popped free. The fingers fumbled for the tab of the zip, gripped it and stopped and hesitated and finally tugged it down.

Mr Gifford sighed.

A wide pale V now appeared at her side and across the top of it, the thin band of black elastic of the top of her knickers. Her arm came back up and gripped her shoulder, squashing her little breasts against her ribs. The other hand dropped down and pushed into the opposite side of her waistband and pushed down but the trousers were too tailored, the zip not completely undone and they caught.

Melanie sighed.

Nobody moved.

I felt responsible for putting her in this position, and although I didn't know whether I was helping or making her torment worse, I finally slid off the sofa, crawled across the floor to her until, kneeling at her feet, I reached up to the waistband again to the last section of the zip. It jerked free and slid down easily to open up the pale V still further. When I glanced up, her eyes were shut tight and her arms were still wrapped round her, protecting her breasts from our gaze, but her face gave no clues. With no resistance or objection to deter me, I gripped the coarse tweed material and pulled. As the trousers came down over her softly rounded stomach, the black lace triangle of her knickers appeared, a tiny triangle, thankfully opaque, suspended from a single strand of narrow elastic that disappeared round her waist. I tried not to look too closely and concentrated instead on easing the trousers down her long slender legs until she meekly lifted each foot and I tossed the trousers over the sofa behind her.

I stayed kneeling on the floor, her crotch at my eye level, mesmerised, I suppose, by the sight. I don't think I had ever been so close to a girl in these circumstances. Yet here I was, entirely naked and kneeling at her feet, while she, stripped now to no more than a single item, a pair of black lace knickers, little more than a G-string, towered over me. My breasts were achingly hard, my vulva running so profusely I could smell my own secretions and I shifted over, no longer caring what kind of spectacle I presented to the couple sitting just behind me, I shifted over to sit more directly down onto the heel of my foot and squeeze it into my crease. Melanie was still unmoving, beyond a gentle figure of eight swaying of her hips. It was almost as if she were in a coma but whether it was a heaven of rapt arousal or a hell of betrayed humiliation, her tightly closed eyes didn't reveal.

I didn't know whether to continue. Which would be easier for her? Which worse? Was there greater dignity in being a willing participant, actively exhibiting herself while we watched than innocence in being a passive victim, powerless as I took her clothes off her? While I hesitated, still looking up for guidance, she briefly opened her eyes and minutely pushed her hips out towards me. I still couldn't bring myself to this final act, but when I didn't move, she reached down and caught hold of my wrists herself to lift my hands up to the thin strip of a belt. She actually wanted me to take them down for her.

So I did, picking the thin elastic away from her skin and drawing it down, peeling away the thin lace triangle that hung so low on her stomach and which, after I tugged it free from where it had become caught right up between her lips, dropped away to reveal a short strip of golden pubic hair no more than an inch wide and pointing, like an arrow, at that place at which we all stared anyway. I had read about girls who trimmed or shaped their hair, but I had never seen it done before and I couldn't decide whether it was stunningly alluring or obscenely gross. What shocked me most was not that the sides were completely shaved away, but that the middle was trimmed short, so short that I could see clearly the indented crease. And down between her legs, on the lips themselves where my own hair is thick, she had none at all. It made her lips much more visible, and they seemed plump and ready, all on display and all more voluptuous than me; everywhere seemed more generous, less inhibited and more available. I was jealous.

Quickly I looked away and pulled the minuscule garment down her legs as she obediently lifted her feet to let me take it off. The instant I did, she

19

swivelled round, turning her back on me and on Mr and Mrs Gifford, to scuttle back to her seat on the sofa and in doing so to show off the enticingly round cheeks of her bottom, entirely naked but for a small tattoo, an ornate rose, which crowned one buttock.

But Mrs Gifford wouldn't let her escape so easily. 'Oh, come along, my dear. There's no need to be so timid. Stand up and let's have a look at you. Gemma managed it, so I'm sure you can!'

Melanie stood up again, her obvious unwillingness almost heartbreaking, and with her hands up to her mouth and her elbows over her breasts, she slowly turned all the way round for their examination. She too was told to wait and to face away from them, and to bend down with her legs apart and she obeyed, and stayed there waiting. But she didn't do the last bit, and I knew Mrs Gifford would not be satisfied until she did.

So I did it for her. As she was bending forward so close to me, I reached up to her neat round bottom, rested my palms on her cool skin and eased the cheeks apart just enough for Mr Gifford to see right in to the little dark star in the centre. Seeing it presented there, I began to understand how Mr Gifford felt. It all looked so sweet and delicate with the tiny folds stretched tight around the minute opening in the centre. It was all so intimate and so private; to see that, was to see everything.

Moreover, from where I was kneeling so close to her, my eyes were a little lower down, so I was treated to even more than that. I could see through to the smooth hairless puffed lips of her vulva, and smell an aroma at least as strong as my own and see unmistakable streaks shining on her thickly puffed lips, shining with proud declarations of her hunger.

While I was kneeling there, Melanie stood upright and quickly sat on the sofa. I was about to do the same when I felt a warm hand slide across my shoulders and run down my chest to rest on my breast, the fingers playing and teasing at my nipple. Mrs Gifford bent down and whispered in my ear, a whisper loud enough for everyone to hear, 'You remember what you asked to do, sweetie?'

'Yes, oh yes!' I scrambled to my feet, turned to her, earnestly in need of some comfort after being so disturbed by Melanie's performance.

'And what was that?' As her fingers strayed down from my nipples and came to rest in the short curls of my hair, twisting and tangling, before pushing right down between my lips, her voice sounded low in my ear.

'I wanted to kiss your breasts,' I breathed.

'Good girl. Well first, why don't you kiss your little friend's breasts? I'm sure she'd like that.'

'Oh no, Mrs Gifford. I don't want to do that, please, and I know Melanie wouldn't want it either. I just wanted to do it to you.'

'Nonsense, dear. Look at Melanie's lovely bosom. Much nicer than mine. You play with her.'

Melanie was staring at us in total horror, her hands flattened defensively across her breasts, and her knees pulled up protectively towards her, but Mrs Gifford released my breast and half patted, half pushed me towards where Melanie was sitting. She sat down herself on the sofa and pulled me down into the middle between her and Melanie.

This time Melanie appealed to her. 'Excuse me, Mrs Gifford, but Gemma's right. We really don't want to do anything like that. I just thought you were going to want to look at me.'

'Nonsense, child!' Mrs Gifford's mild tone did not hide her determination. 'It'll be fun. You'll see.'

When I sat down, my bottom touched Melanie's hip and the intimacy of the contact, the touch of bare skin, frightened me; it emphasised so clearly our complete nakedness. We both jumped and tried to pull away, but there was no room. Mrs Gifford was still there, with one hand on my shoulder while the other reached over to Melanie's wrist and hauled it away to uncover the soft little breast and round ripe nipple. And Mrs Gifford's hand on my shoulder was guiding me down, pressing me lower and lower until Melanie's breast was presented right in front of me. Then she pushed me the last bit and my mouth touched skin. I was left with no choice but to open my lips and draw the nipple in. The girl sighed underneath me, an extended sigh as I felt a second hand, this time on my other shoulder, pulling me down as she rolled and pulled my head closer to her breast. When Mrs Gifford finally released my shoulder, I felt her hand running right underneath to my own breast: touching me, holding me and pulling at my nipple.

I was half turned towards Mr Gifford and from the corner of my eye I could see him watching us avidly. He could see what Mrs Gifford was doing to me and he would see the reaction it was causing. My breasts are so sensitive and her fingers insistently squeezing and pinching at the nipple were making it so hard I felt it would burst. I kept my thighs together, clamped tight together, to try to hold in the juice that I could feel building, because I didn't want him to see that. I didn't want to betray the arousal that was overtaking me as his wife caressed me while she made me suck on the other girl's nipple.

Finally Mrs Gifford let me stop and sit up, but her fingers crept over my thigh and squeezed down between them, pushing one leg hard up against Melanie and pressing the other against the thin material of the dress that covered her own legs.

'There now.' She smiled at me. 'That wasn't so bad, was it? Kissing her breast? It seems to me as if you really rather liked that, didn't you? Besides,' and here she reached right across me to Melanie, 'she does have such sweet little breasts, almost as tiny as yours.' This time she reached up and gently pulled at Melanie's nipple, squeezing out the little pink peak between her fingertips.

Then she looked over at her husband and as she did so he reached down beside his chair, pulled out a carrier bag and handed it to her. She came back to stand in front of us.

'Now then, girls, we've got something here for you.' The bag was being dangled in front of both of us and when Melanie didn't move, I took it from Mrs Gifford's hand.

'What is it?' I asked, but she just smiled and settled back on the end of the sofa.

Curious, and more than a little wary, I peered inside to find a tangle of straps and a length of white plastic, but nothing identifiable. As I pulled it out of the bag, it appeared to be a very large bra, but Melanie gasped.

'What is it?' I repeated, and then I realised and I too gasped. I had heard about things like this, but I had never personally seen one.

Mrs Gifford chuckled. 'Now you see! Have you ever worn one? Either of you?'

'I did once.' Melanie's admission was so quiet that Mrs Gifford had to ask her to repeat it.

'I did once. Just for some photographs. I mean I've never, you know, used one with anyone.'

'Are you telling me the truth?' She was genuinely surprised.

'Yes, honestly, Mrs Gifford.'

'But I take it you two have made love together before, haven't you?'

'No! We aren't like that, Mrs Gifford. Really, we don't do that kind of thing.'

The glances of puzzled surprise she exchanged with her husband suggested she was unsure whether to believe us and they looked from one to the other as if expecting one of us to break down, to admit we were lying. Instead we sat like a pair of innocent children, side by side in front of them, completely naked and holding up this grotesque toy. They had asked us to their home because we were supposed to be young and wild and adventurous, and yet there we sat, utterly naive. I felt so stupid.

'Well, I must say I'm surprised. I thought you young girls nowadays were into all sorts of different things. Anyway, now's your chance. Mr Gifford and I thought it would be fun to see you with it. Here, I'll help you put it on, then you can try it with little Gemma here. Stand up, child.'

I watched in dread and horror as Mrs Gifford untangled all the belts and made Melanie stand in front of her as the thing was strapped on. The woman explained how it fitted, pointed out the small hollow nub that would fit over the clitoris and Melanie stood there and allowed it to be fastened around her waist. Neither of us spoke, neither of us protested although we both knew what was happening and that the whole situation was spinning away out of our control. Yet as I watched the preparations being made, I was hypnotised. Mrs Gifford wrapped the straps carefully round Melanie's thighs and buckled them tight. She made no secret of sliding her finger carefully under the base to check that the nub was positioned correctly over Melanie's clitoris and that the straps were arranged properly between the girl's legs, smearing her fingers across Melanie's lips several times as she did it.

When she was finished, Mrs Gifford made Melanie turn round in front of us so we could see her from all sides. From the back, the incongruous straps digging into her soft body looked faintly ridiculous but from the front it was different. From the front, she looked pagan and wild. If the phallus had been thicker or longer or more brightly coloured, it might have seemed frivolous, as if she were only wearing it for show. Instead, it was slender, curving up from her hips in an obscene arc: gaunt, mean and determined. And it was pale as ivory; like a corpse; like some alien creature that lived its life in the darkness, whose strength stemmed from its obscurity.

Melanie stood in the middle of the room with her fingers wrapped around the shaft as if in wonder, stroking it gently up and back as if she were a man and her erection were real. Her eyes were fixed on me: staring, bestial and cruel.

Mrs Gifford sat back down on the sofa arranging me sideways on her lap until finally she had me the way she wanted me: sitting nervously across her thighs with her arm round me so that I was supported partly against the sofa but partly against her glorious bosom. The false buttons down the front of her summer dress dug into me, but it was short sleeved and with a scoop neck cut low so that in places I was touching her, touching her cool skin. I longed for her to take the dress right off, to be as naked as me, but in my heart I knew she never would. I knew that in my memories and fantasies it would always be that way: she would always be dressed: I would always be naked.

She leaned over, cuddling me against her breast and kissed me again, her tongue reaching in to find mine and her lips sucking and nibbling at my mouth. Her hand ran up and down the whole of the exposed front of my body, across my breasts, pinching at my nipples, down to tease at my curls, and then back. As the sensations built unbearably in one place, she moved to another, finally ending down in my lap again. She eased my legs wider and wider apart, even stretching my lips open, seeking out the wetness and the softness and the small hard bud that was aching for her caress. I could feel the juice running freely down my lips and when she pressed her finger right against the entrance of my vulva and then pressed far in, my body swallowed her even as I felt her nail scraping up the sensitive wall inside. She smiled down at me and planted a light kiss on my mouth.

'I think you're ready for Melanie now, aren't you?'

I turned away in shame as I felt the sofa moving beneath me as Melanie climbed on. But I had to see. Humiliated or not, I had to witness with my own eyes everything they did to me.

Melanie shuffled up the sofa towards me, squeezing between my legs. Mrs Gifford pushed my knee aside, opening my legs further to give her more room, but also pressing my other leg out of the way so that her husband could see more clearly, see my vulva, and see how wet and ready I was. Then Melanie's thighs were pressing right against mine and she looked at me with such sadness and apology in her eyes that I wanted to hug her, to kiss her and tell it would be all right. I reached out to her and cupped her breast, stroking my thumb across her swollen nipple. Maybe she did hate what she was doing – maybe she hated herself for doing it – but she was no less excited than me, no less eager.

Mrs Gifford reached down again with her fingertips to draw up the skin at the top of my crease, opening me wider still. Melanie pressed the phallus down into the wetness and for a few seconds its head ran round the entrance, butting up and over my lips and across my clitoris before she centred it between my lips and its hard unyielding shaft slipped deep, magnificently deep, inside me. I sighed a long deep moan of total surrender as it pushed in and Melanie settled down and let me get used to the feeling.

She leaned forward, resting her hand on my shoulder, but Mrs Gifford silently lifted it off and placed it instead on my breast, where Melanie automatically stroked over my nipple and I smiled up at her as she did it. I could no longer imagine why I had disliked her before. We were so much alike in age, in appearance and, as it now transpired, in our lack of experience. When Mrs Gifford intercepted the smile and hooked her hand round Melanie's neck, just letting her thumb stroke briefly at her cheek, it clearly didn't take much pressure or persuasion before Melanie leaned down until she was so close to me that the kiss became entirely natural and inevitable.

And Melanie didn't taste of bitterness or arrogance or boastfulness. She tasted sweet and kind and concerned, maybe even afraid. She tasted like me; she seemed like me; she smiled like me and when she finally relaxed her body even further down, her little breasts touched mine and nestled down on mine, just as soft and pathetic and embarrassingly minuscule as my own have always seemed on the chest of every boy across whom I have ever lain.

I was almost in love and I chased her agile tongue all round my mouth as she kissed me with an energy and a passion that was for me, not for the couple watching us. Yet even while we kissed, I felt the slight easing of pressure inside me as she pulled the phallus back a little. Then she pressed forward again, and it filled me right up to my cervix before she pulled back once more. Her movements continued slow and gentle but the phallus was long and unyielding and touched parts far inside me that had never been touched before.

If I looked across the room, I encountered the intense gaze of the man sitting motionless opposite, so I shut my eyes and tried to forget him as Melanie thrust slowly and gently and beautifully inside me. Mrs Gifford's fingers were still running slow circles round my clitoris but occasionally her hand lifted away and I guessed she was touching Melanie. In the middle of one gentle slide, Melanie suddenly gasped and thrust right into me hard and painfully and when I screamed out and struggled up, I saw why: Mrs Gifford had her fingers inside Melanie's vulva, where she was sliding in and out steadily.

We settled back, although Melanie was still flinching and twisting from time to time as Mrs Gifford's hand worked away inside her but when that stopped, I felt the fingers return, slippery now with Melanie's juices, to slither across my skin and back to my clitoris. I lifted my head up to Melanie's mouth this time, and our tongues touched before our lips did as we settled into another glorious kiss and she returned to the gentle but unbearably stimulating movement of her pelvis. I could hear her breaths shortening as mine were too and her mouth, lips and teeth had an additional fiercer urgency as she crushed me down harder. Her thrusts were becoming much less gentle and each ended with a final twist as her end of the phallus pressed down on her clitoris. Deep inside I felt myself filling with a torrent of juice that I knew was going to pour from me when I came and this time I didn't care. This was for Melanie's benefit, not for Mr Gifford; this was my present to her.

However, Mrs Gifford was still in charge. Her hand pulled away from my vulva and she may even have lifted Melanie's head up off me; certainly she was watching closely as our lips were finally dragged apart. Then Mrs Gifford's mouth came down on mine again, but I moaned at the interruption so close to such ecstasy.

'Now then, Gemma my dear, this will be something quite new and special for you, I expect, and something rather lovely for Mr Gifford and me so I want you to trust me and do as I ask. Will you do that?'

'I'll try, Mrs Gifford, but what do you want?'

She didn't answer directly, but instead reached down my body again and stroked agonisingly slow and light circles round my clitoris and hooked her finger round the back of the phallus still lodged deep inside me.

'Will you do that for me, Gemma? Will you promise?' Her fingers were so bewitching, her voice so gentle and her breasts so soft, how could I mistrust her? I knew she would not hurt me.

'Yes, Mrs Gifford. I'll do what you want.'

She smiled. 'Good girl.' She kissed my mouth again, the briefest flurry of her tongue, before she turned to address Melanie.

'Now then, Melanie, my dear,' and I felt her fingers encircling the phallus and drawing it away from me. 'I think Gemma's had enough like that, so you can pull it out of her now.' With a last slurping sigh, the tip pulled out, leaving a cold, lonely emptiness that had me practically sobbing in frustration.

'Now, dear, push it in again, but this time into her bottom.'

My world collapsed as I felt the slimy wet tip tracing small circles around that tiny delicate opening, and I immediately started up.

'No, Mrs Gifford. You can't do that. That's not right. I'd never let anyone do anything like that. It's not right.'

But she ignored my protest, seemingly entirely unconcerned, and stroked my cheek as if she were humouring a petulant infant. 'Nonsense, child. If you just relax, it'll slide in as easy as anything. Besides, you promised me you would.'

'But you didn't say you meant that. Please, Mrs Gifford? Please don't!'

Melanie was sitting up on her heels, looking horrified at what she had been asked to do. Her eyes were fixed on Mrs Gifford's hand holding the phallus and running it up and back along my sopping wet crease but always returning to the little hole behind, and pressing each time against the closed ring, pressing each time just a little harder.

She released the phallus and patted Melanie on the hip. 'There you are, my dear. It's beautifully slippery already. Just slide it up into her bottom. And for you, Gemma, here's a little treat for you.'

She settled back herself now and at last reached round to unfasten her own dress and pull the elastic neck right down over her shoulders. She slid each arm out, revealing a huge white bra like my mother used to wear and although she did not pull it right off, she pulled the straps down off her shoulders and tucked me in against her so that I could reach up and ease each of her glorious breasts out of the thick cotton covering.

As I finally touched her great round nipple again, another jab at my bottom stabbed me. I know I cried out as I turned and buried my head in the warm expanse of her bosom and tried to relax.

The tip of the phallus pressed against the cramping muscles that guarded that tiny entrance and I just could not make them loosen to allow so foreign an object in so private a place. Then the tip slid away and in its place came a finger, a small, agile and slender finger, Melanie, not Mrs Gifford, that traced round the syrup seeping down my crease and spread it over my bottom. The finger returned and, just briefly, pushed up inside my vulva, circled and withdrew and then I felt it touch on the sensitive little entrance of my bottom and finally worm its way in. I sighed as it squeezed inside and, once past the narrow entrance, slipped further up into my bottom.

When she pulled it out again, the feeling was entirely different. I had a terrible sensation as if I needed a toilet but also a wonderfully deep caress along sensitive nerves that I had never known existed. The minute her finger was right out, she pressed the head of the phallus to my bottom and pushed. I could not help resisting, but the resistance was now only half-hearted. Then she pushed harder and though I gasped and cried out, she pressed more and finally it was through and pushing deeper and deeper inside me. I cried out again as she pulled back and pushed in again; pulled back and pushed in again and I had to look down and see.

Melanie's sweet green eyes were tight shut and she had thrown her head back as if lost in some dream. She was hugging my thigh with one hand and the other was pressed between her own legs and curling down underneath to her own sex. Her breath was coming in great pants as she pumped in and out of my bottom, each stroke ending with a little upward flick as she pressed her clitoris down hard against the base of the phallus. She had forgotten me now, was concentrating only on her own pleasure as she plunged with increasing urgency into that most tender place. I tried to keep from crying out, but the pain was unbearable and I could feel the tears welling up and running down on to Mrs Gifford's breast as she cuddled me against her and then eased my head

31

back to plop a huge nipple into my mouth. It was almost enough, but I still needed a little more and reached down to my own clitoris at last, full and hard and familiar, and I squeezed and stroked the way I like to be squeezed and stroked. Mrs Gifford fondled my breast, pinching fiercely at my nipple and the juice was welling up in me again, but this time unstoppably.

I no longer knew whether the rasping thrusts so deep in my bottom were pleasure or pain but they were there and my breasts were being twisted and pulled and that might have been pain too, but I had a glorious, massively ripe nipple filling my entire mouth and Melanie was screaming obscenities and the flood gates within me opened and I was utterly lost, utterly possessed and utterly overwhelmed. I hadn't warned Melanie how much I spurt when I come and this time I could feel cascades pouring from me as I lay back there so totally naked in front of the couple whose sofa I was drenching in my fluids while Melanie, sweet Melanie who I had always loathed, plunged the plastic phallus deep, deep, deep into my virgin anus.

We stood just inside the front door when we were leaving, and Mrs Gifford kissed us both. She kissed Melanie on the mouth, a light peck, but me she hugged to herself and kissed warmly, even licking at my tongue for a second before pulling away. She seemed genuinely sorry to see me go, and her fingers reached up to stroke my cheek and my nipple for one last time, because we both knew there would be nothing more. That was everything and we would never see them again. Twice now I had come to that house; been humiliated, stripped and abused; watched and violated and I knew I would miss them and could never repay them for the heights to which their abasement had lifted me.

As Melanie and I crossed the road over to our cars, I knew we were still being watched from the kitchen window, and I reached out for Melanie's hand and ran my own hand down her back to cradle her bottom as she put her arm round my waist. She turned her face to me, her eyes blazing with excitement, and our mouths met in a long, wet, glorious kiss. I think Melanie and I both knew at the same moment that for us this was just a beginning.

The Giffords may have run their course, but we would find others, once word got round.

Charlotte's Tale – My Bequest

Stephen Blake had great difficulty tearing his eyes away from my chest but I'm used to that. Finally he picked up the file in front of him. 'There are just one or two formalities before we can proceed. May I first confirm that you were nominated this year's Head of School of the King Edward II School, Chichester? You don't happen to know the date of nomination, do you? Well, no matter. I need to ask the headmaster to provide a certificate confirming your nomination; I can ask him then. Anyway, I take it you are Charlotte McRae?'

I tried to keep a straight face but sitting on that glorious summer day in the office of a London solicitor, particularly one as dry and dusty as this (I include both room and occupant), it was all too much like something from an ancient black and white film. 'Yes, I am Charlotte McRae.'

'And am I right in saying that you are not a minor? That is to say, you have passed your eighteenth birthday?'

'Yes, months ago. I'm practically nineteen.'

'Good. Good.' He stared at me, hesitated, was momentarily distracted by my breasts again but recovered himself, fiddled with the papers, took a deep breath and then charged on. 'Then it is my duty to read to you the following extract from the will of the late Clarence Wallingham. Before I do so, I should explain two points.

'First, the Wallinghams are a very fine family who lost their money in the depression but King Edward's School admitted Clarence on a scholarship and he subsequently restored the family fortune. He always wanted to repay what the school had done for him, but on one occasion during his time at King Edward's he was, most unjustly in his view, severely caned by the Head of School in front of the entire assembly. He vowed that he would be avenged for that.

'Second, I do not imagine the deceased considered for one moment that his alma mater would ever become co-educational and even less that there might come a time when the title Head of School would be taken by a girl. I am quite certain I speak for all the executors when I say that, in the circumstances, if you were to accept the bequest, the condition regarding the manner of dress would be waived.

'Having explained those two points to you, I will proceed.' His embarrassment was rather sweet and he cleared his throat with some difficulty before he could at last 'proceed'.

' "I, Clarence George Monmouth Wallingham, being of sound mind . . ." '

I drifted away, stared out of the window, counted the buses going past, looked idly at the pictures on his walls and was starting to assemble a birthday party guest list when I realised that the words he was reading affected me. I sat up and started to pay attention.

'Good God!' my friend Amanda squealed down the phone at me when I recounted the whole thing to her the second I got home.

35

'Well exactly!' I replied. 'And the joke is, he claimed in his will to be of sound mind! He must have been totally barking!'

'Yes, but why? Why you?' Amanda was probing already.

'My name just happened to fit their criteria.'

'Well, my God! You lucky thing!' she went on.

'What? Amanda? Have you been listening to a word I said?'

'Yes I have! Bloody hell! You're set up for life!'

'What on earth do you mean?' I couldn't work out which of us had gone mad. 'I'm not going to agree!'

'What? Why the hell not?'

'Amanda! Did you hear me? Allow some pervert to whack me with a cane in public just so as I can inherit some money from someone I've never met? Certainly not!'

'No, Charlie, not "some money": fifty thousand pounds. And not in public: in a posh private gentlemen's club. And not "whack you with a cane": this is six smart strokes. Picture it!'

'I have, which is why I have no intention of doing it.'

'Well, you're crazy. I'd jump at it.' Amanda's sincerity was beyond question.

'You would?'

'Of course! Imagine it! All those people!'

'I have.'

'God, Charlie. You'd be up there with all those old buffers staring at you, dribbling and drooling. Where else could you get a chance like that? And then, bent over, show off your bare bum. And you know you've got a magnificent bum.'

'Thank you, Amanda. You're too kind.'

'You're welcome. No, but they'd love it! Not a dry seat in the house, I'll bet you.'

'But it'd hurt!'

'Perhaps.'

'Perhaps?'

'Well, all right, yes it'd hurt a bit, but think of the reaction! Half of them will have heart attacks and die on the spot. The other half will want to marry you. You're set for life! I know what I'll be fantasising about come bedtime tonight!'

'Amanda, you're nothing short of a pervert!'

A deep sigh trickled down from the other end of the phone before her soft but crushing reply. 'Yes, Charlie, but so are you.'

Her words came back to me as I undressed for bed that night. As I lay in my narrow solitude, I pictured Amanda, thirty miles away, lying alone but almost certainly naked in her own bed, and I knew what she was doing at that very moment. I knew that the images that were inciting her were images of me, half naked before a crowd of men, bent over a stool and receiving six strokes of a cane. As far as I knew, I had never been the subject of anyone's sexual fantasy before, and the knowledge that I was now the subject of hers was amazingly stimulating. It gave me a pride and a self-assurance I had never known.

I wondered, too, about poor shy Mr Blake. Could he be having similar thoughts? Was it now my face he saw as he kissed a chaste goodnight to Mrs Blake? Was it my bottom he visualised when he snuggled up to her?

Yet, stirring though all this was, I had to acknowledge that I was a coward and even if certain parts of the scenario were beginning to appeal to me, I did not think I could ever stand the pain of six strokes with a cane and couldn't see how to find out without agreeing to the punishment. The solution came to me during the night.

I drove over to Amanda's first thing in the morning and we climbed up to her room right at the top of her house.

'So?' she asked. 'What's this favour you want to ask?'

I took a deep breath. 'I'm thinking of agreeing.'

'I should bloody well think so!'

'Yes, but I'm scared it'll hurt too much and I won't be able to stand it. Supposing I just can't go through with it and chicken out halfway? I need to know if I can bear the pain, so I want you to cane me. Just a couple of strokes. Just so I know what it's like.'

'Me? I can't do that.' Her eyes shone with a sparkle that betrayed her lie.

'Yes, you can. For heaven's sake, Amanda, who else can I possibly ask? Does your dad still have that cane?'

'Yes.'

'Right. He's not in, is he? Go and get it.'

I squirmed nervously on her bed until she came pounding back up the stairs.

'Right, here we go. Now then, how do you want to do this?'

'Amanda, it wouldn't do any harm for you to be a bit less enthusiastic, you know.'

'Sorry!' she trilled.

'Let me see it.' I turned the ageing yellow stick over in my hand. Amanda's father had been at King Edward's himself, but it had been during his time there in the 1960s that the school had abolished corporal punishment. As a celebration at the end of that year, he and a few friends had raided the headmaster's study and stolen all the canes. He still kept one in his study as a souvenir, although it hardly seemed a fitting trophy for a bishop of the Church of England.

Now, as I turned it over in my fingers, I saw it for the first time as something other than a memento of a schoolboy prank. Now it was an instrument of punishment: something to be used to inflict pain on someone. And that someone was me.

I handed it back to Amanda and, after a short hesitation, turned and unbuttoned my jeans. They were tight across my hips because, as Amanda had already reminded me, my bottom is pretty full and as I wriggled them down to my knees I was embarrassed, knowing that she was watching me. What with showers after sports, sharing a dormitory and everything else, she must have seen me naked hundreds of times, right from when we both joined the school at thirteen, but this was different. This was just me undressing and not her. And this was in a bedroom, and private and furtive and somehow all the more thrilling for that. The fear of the pain, the awkwardness of asking her to cane me, the embarrassment of taking my jeans down in front of her, all agitated and stirred me. Yet there was still another feeling; something peculiar and deeper: a bizarre pleasure in the whole dreadful predicament.

I pushed down my knickers and bent over the end of her bed.

'Right. Just do one.' I shut my eyes and waited.

'Um, Charlie? How hard?'

'I have to be prepared for the worst. Do it hard.'

'OK.'

I felt the cold thin length of the cane laid across my bottom and pressed my head right down into the mattress.

The cane lifted away, there was a second's pause, half a second's wail through the air and then I felt the impact as it hit me. The sound of the bamboo striking my skin was horrifying. Instantly the blazing sting spread across the whole of my bottom as if I were sitting on red-hot steel. I yelped and buried my face in the bedding to keep from screaming out loud. When I eventually lifted my head, Amanda was standing beside me, the cane dangling uneasily from her hand as she nervously studied my face. She reached out to wipe my eyes with her fingertips.

'How was that?'

I started to push myself off the bed and then stopped. The initial shock had been terrible, but it was quickly subsiding into little more than a warm glow that suffused the whole area.

'Bearable, actually.' I stayed there a moment and then flattened down on the bed again. 'Do it again, harder. Hard as you can.'

The blow came quicker this time, and it certainly was harder but I was ready and bit down into the bedding to muffle my cries. Within a few seconds, the immediate agony had passed and the glow was warmer but still not unbearable. I turned my head to the side.

'One more.'

Again, I gritted my teeth through the dreadful shock that tore into me, but it receded quickly to a general radiance and energy through the whole of my bottom. Every nerve in my body was awakened and invigorated and I felt a glow like the effect of diving into the cold sea: shattering, yet so stimulating. I knew then that I would be able to stand the full six. I was lying there, unmoving, assessing the effect when I remembered Amanda was waiting.

'Shall I do the rest?' she asked with an almost innocent enthusiasm.

I had established what I wanted to find out, what it was going to feel like for me. Now I needed to know the effect on the other people who'd be there, what it was going to look like to them.

'No,' I said and struggled up. 'It's your turn now.'

'What?' She took a step back from me. 'I'm not letting you do that!'

'Oh yes you are, Amanda. It was your idea that I agree to this thing, so you can damn well learn how it feels. Besides, I need to know what it'll look like to all the old men there. If I can stand it, so can you. Take your jeans off.'

'Off?'

'Yes, off. You'll find it easier.' I didn't specify what it would be easier for and didn't honestly know, but I had already taken the cane out of her hand and was pulling my own jeans back up again.

'I can tell you what it looks like,' she said, although she had already started to unbuckle her belt. 'It looks incredibly red.'

'I need to see for myself.'

She stretched herself over the bed just as I had done, her legs straight out and her bottom lying offered up to me, round, pale and entirely unmarked as she waited for me to colour it red and disfigure it with crimson stripes.

'Are you going to do it hard?' Her frightened voice was half muffled in the bedding.

'Yes.'

'How hard?'

'As hard as you did.'

'But that's not fair; you've got more padding than me.'

'You'll get an extra one for that.'

Then I laid the length of the cane right across her so that the tip came just to the fullest part of her right cheek, lifted it back over my shoulder and thwacked it down as hard as I could.

She shrieked and bit at the bedclothes, her legs kicking out impotently behind her and a succession of stifled moans coming up to me as she squeezed handfuls of blanket in her fists. I wasn't listening. The speed and strength of reaction were gratifying but I was concentrating on her bottom, where a disappointingly pale pink line had appeared. I lifted the cane and struck down again, trying to hit the same spot but it landed much lower and she screamed again, kicked again and her knuckles turned white where she clutched the blanket. I felt the same surge of power but also disappointment at the insignificance of the mark the stroke had created. For the third stroke, I lifted the cane back even farther and threw it down with every ounce of my strength.

Even smothered by the bedclothes, I feared her scream would bring her mother running. Amanda released her grip on the bedding and reached back to cover her bottom, squeezing and pulling at the cheeks as she kicked and sobbed. For a few moments I let her lie there. I had applied the strokes much more quickly than she had done and so maybe she was not having time for each one to subside before the next came.

But I still longed to know what it looked like, so I lifted her hands away to inspect the marks. This was much better. A broad band right across her bottom was entirely red and within that a cluster of dark red weals was rising rapidly. Her legs continued quivering lightly, scissoring up and down while her hips pressed against the mattress in a way that suggested pleasure much more than it suggested pain.

She did not resist when I unambiguously moved her hands back up beside her head. Instead she silently twisted her fingers into a knot of bedclothes and waited.

'Ready for the last three?' I asked.

After the briefest pause, she nodded. I laid the cane back neatly and directly along the centre stripe and her bottom lifted fractionally to greet it.

'Move your legs apart.' She obeyed straight away and I couldn't resist the desire to peer round and see what was now revealed. I could see right through to her puffed-up, downy lips. They were not just swollen. They were glistening; enticingly wet and aroused.

'Amanda? Your slot's absolutely dripping.'

Her voice was still muffled. 'I know. Get on with it.' She shuffled her feet even further apart.

I was so relieved to find that I was not alone in having this reaction to the pain. Not only did it prove that I was not as perverted as I had begun to fear, it also meant that the minute her six were over, Amanda would insist on giving me the last three of mine. Best of all, it meant I no longer needed to hold back.

I laid the cane between her stripes, lifted it back and then whipped it down on to her skin. Her whole body shook and she cried out but I counted the seconds in my head as I recalled the initial shock and then the gentle seductive slide into that enervated glow of arousal. When I calculated that stage had been reached I gave her the fifth, and after a similar pause, lashed it down with all my strength for the final time. She lay weeping into the mattress as I stood hypnotised by the quivering glory of her proud red bottom. The central band was wider now, covering almost half the exposed curve of each cheek and the weals rose up tight and livid, one from each stroke on each buttock, twelve angry ridges ploughing through the scarlet plain. Her slender hips were still moving, lifting and sinking, but also rotating in a slow tormented circle, grinding her pelvis down into the mattress on every turn.

I sat beside her, stroking her hair until she pushed herself up off the bed and grabbed the cane out of my hand.

'Right, you cow!' She was blinking away the tears and trying to sound angry. 'Time to finish your six. Take your jeans off, and I mean off.'

It was no surprise she demanded this too, so I didn't argue, just unbuttoned them again and pulled them right off, tugging off my trainers as well, and then my knickers.

I hurried to take up my position over the end of her bed, anxious to be ready and available for now there was something much less innocent in our game. Not only the fact of our semi-nakedness but also the disclosure of Amanda's arousal had started a different current running. I did not yet know how it might end, or how I wanted it to end, but I knew it was different, that we had crossed into new territory.

Amanda made me open my legs and I felt the tip of the cane running down and prodding between my sloppy lips. 'I don't know what you were complaining about,' she said. 'You're just as wet as me. Now, take a deep breath, because you deserve this.'

She barely gave me time to turn my head away before the cane tapped two or three times on my hot skin, lifted away and then came crashing back down three times in quick succession. She knew better what she was doing now, and deliberately gave me no chance to recover between each one. The effect was like a single stroke, but drawn out into an extended torment, one prolonged searing agony that burned through me in a continuous rampage. It cut through my bottom and seeped out through every nerve so that as the pain dulled, just the awakening of my senses remained, coursing through me, flowing and building.

Through my tears, I felt the muscles in my thighs and bottom tensing and flexing and I realised this was the quivering that I had seen on Amanda. Also like

44

Amanda, my sex was flowing like a river with the intensity of all I had suffered. I struggled to my feet, wiping away the tears still seeping from my eyes, and turned to face her. She had dropped the cane to the floor and was now standing in front of me, her hands digging unashamedly between her legs but her eyes glazed.

'God, Charlie, that was . . .' She closed her eyes and her words died away into a shuddering sigh as her fingers worked furiously in the groove of her sex. Then she opened her eyes again.

'Quickly, turn round again, I want to be able to see your bum while I come.' I turned away and kneeled across the bed, reaching down myself to the fire blazing in my sex. We had tacitly acknowledged that we both masturbated occasionally, but never discussed it openly and certainly never actually done it in each other's company before. Yet this was something glorious. I felt a bond between us in what we now shared. It was not just that we had each suffered the appalling pain and experienced the exquisite pleasure, we had also each inflicted them both. We had been the instruments of the pleasure, been the instruments of the pain; received the pleasure, received the pain; witnessed the effect on each, seen the glowing red of our beating and the glistening wetness of our joy and each enjoyed vicariously the effects on the other. I felt closer to her than ever and tilted my hips up so that Amanda, in her moment of orgasm, could take in the sight presented by my bottom and my lips, and my fingers thrumming in my own sodden slot.

The instant I heard her cries swell, burst and begin to fade, I made her change places so that at last I could see the clear evidence of the stripes that I had created across her slim white bottom and the shining pinkness of her thick swollen lips and I could hold that picture in front of my eyes as I dived into the deep comfortable release of so intense an ordeal.

When I went back to see Mr Blake a few days later, Amanda came with me for support, but I made her stay in his waiting room. Close as we were, I couldn't let her know all the details of the inheritance.

Mr Blake showed me back to the same chair, took up his same place and again struggled to keep his eyes above the level of my breasts.

'Well now, Charlotte, I am pleased to say that we have been granted probate on the will so all that can proceed. On the other hand, some other news is not so good. I am sorry to have to tell you that I have spoken to one of my co-executors, Colin Harris, and he does not agree that we can waive the requirement regarding dress; he considers that the deceased's instructions on this point are quite explicit and we have no right to alter them. The matter is not yet resolved, and I am confident that the third executor, who is herself a lady and in fact the deceased's daughter, will agree with me.' He faltered again and fiddled with his papers before continuing. 'However, I consider it my duty to warn you that Mr Harris does not share my views on this aspect and feels that it is necessary for that part of your anatomy to be, er, unclothed while the, er, procedure is carried out.'

The poor man was almost melting with embarrassment, surviving only by sheltering behind a catalogue of euphemisms. It would have been cruel to ask him to be more specific.

'I'm sorry, Mr Blake. Could you be more specific? Do you mean he suggests I should be caned on the bare bottom?'

'Er, well, yes. Regrettably, Charlotte, that is the position.'

'Not even my knickers?'

'No, not even your ... er no. I must say I have made it perfectly clear to my colleagues that I personally could take no part in any proceedings if such a distasteful condition were to be applied.'

'I see, and who exactly would cane me? If I agreed to this, that is.'

'One of the three executors. We have not considered who that might be and I'm sure it's not a duty that any of us could relish. Of course the question only arises if you should decide to go ahead with this. Have you, in fact, made a decision?'

'I have considered this very carefully and, distasteful though it obviously is, I feel I should go through with it. If I refused, I really feel I would be letting down not only my school but also Mr Wellington.'

'Wallingham.'

'Yes, sorry. Mr Wallingham.'

On the day, I decided to go up on my own. I did wonder about taking Amanda, but there remained aspects to this that I did not want her to know. Besides, I was still not totally convinced I could go through with it. I had been running the thing over in my mind for days and sometimes the excitement outweighed the humiliation but often it didn't. Although I now had some idea what the pain would be like, I was not fully confident that I could stand it. So if, when it came to the crunch, I needed to pull my excuse out of the hat and escape, I would rather do so without anyone around to jeer.

The club was easy enough to find, just off Piccadilly in one of the little streets that lead off north towards real wealth. The white stucco front towered up over my head and huge columns either side of the wide steps bore matching brass name plates, both highly polished. I was half an hour early, and retreated to a small café for a comforting cup of hot creamy chocolate.

When I returned, I didn't hesitate. I strode up the steps and pushed open the intimidating wooden door into a cool, dark hallway. As I stood waiting for my eyes to adjust to the darkness, a voice behind me, like something from a crypt, made me almost jump in the air.

'Can I help you, miss?' A man's severe and wrinkled face peered out from the little porter's office.

'That's all right, Watkins. She's with me.' I was greatly relieved to see Mr Blake advancing from the cluster of seats in the gloom at the back of the hall. Although I had tried to envisage the progress of the day's events, one aspect I hadn't considered was how I would explain myself to the porter: 'Yes, I've come to be caned, probably on my bare bottom but I'm waiting to hear on that aspect.'

It was comforting to feel Mr Blake's hand resting lightly on my shoulder as he steered me back towards the seats. However, even by his usual bashful standards, his timidity had reached a new depth.

'Er, Charlotte. Yes. How good to see you.' The man was terrified, and I resented that. After all, I was the one who had reason to be afraid, not him. Then he added, 'I'm afraid there's a bit of a problem. Come and sit down.'

The minute we were settled in the huge leather chairs, he jumped up again. 'Can I get you anything? Coffee? Coca-Cola?'

His hesitation was laughable. 'Mr Blake, I am over eighteen.'

'Are you? Oh yes! Yes, of course you are. How stupid of me. I mean you wouldn't be here otherwise, would you? Well, er, would you like something stronger then? Wine or, er, gin and something?'

'No, thank you. I'm fine.'

'Sure? Right.' He sat down again and fiddled with his leather folder. 'Well, the fact is this, Charlotte. This morning I met the other two executors who, as I think I told you, are Mrs Dyer, who is the deceased's daughter, and Colin Harris, so we could, well, you know, finalise the arrangements. Are you sure you wouldn't like a drink?'

I put him out of his misery. 'No, really, but please you go ahead if you like.'

'Er, well, yes, perhaps I will.' He craned round to call. 'Watkins? Could you ring through and ask them to send me down a gin and tonic?'

'Certainly, sir. Club?'

'Yes, I think I'd better.' He turned back to me. 'Sorry. "Club" means a large one. Some people are embarrassed to ask for . . . well, anyway that doesn't matter. The thing is, it's about the terms of the will. What the clause actually says is that the bequest is . . .' He opened the folder, rummaged through the papers, finally found the place and started reading. 'The bequest is subject to the beneficiary [that means you, my dear] accepting on behalf of King Edward II School, a punishment to be administered by my three executors equal to that which I suffered so unjustly, that is to say six strokes on his posterior with a cane, the strokes to be taken bare.' There then follow various provisions regarding where it is to be done and who is to be there, etc.

'Now I have to say, and I hope I am not being unprofessional in this, that I am somewhat disappointed in the attitude being taken by my co-executors. I had assumed they would agree, in deference to your sex, to waive the requirement that the punishment be taken bare. I'm afraid they don't agree. However, it is worse than that. They take the view that the terms require the punishment to be six strokes from each of the three executors and that by being "bare", the intention is that the beneficiary should in fact be entirely naked.

'Naturally, I have argued strenuously that this is a most harsh reading of a provision that is, I have to admit, a little ambiguous. Had I been drafting the document, I would have ensured that the terms were more clearly stated. However, our difficulty is that the will does say "a punishment equal to that which I suffered" and it is clear from Mr Wallingham's own autobiography that he did receive eighteen strokes in all and that, in accordance with the custom of the time, he was indeed naked while the punishment was administered. We are therefore not on very strong ground in trying to persuade the other two of our view. Furthermore, there is regrettably the fact that the will named three executors because it sets up discretionary trusts for various charitable purposes and it also provides that in the event of any disagreement on any aspect, the majority view shall prevail. In simple terms, therefore, we are outvoted.

'In the circumstances, I can only recommend that you decline the bequest. I am not going to suggest that my co-executors are acting out of self-interest, but it is a fact that in the event of the bequest being declined, the sum returns to the remainder, and therefore passes to Mrs Dyer. Please take a few moments to consider, but I strongly recommend that you decline. I am only sorry that Mrs Dyer will benefit so handsomely.'

I hadn't said anything throughout poor Mr Blake's long-winded explanation; I was not exactly struck speechless, but having spent so long preparing myself for the event, it was hard adjusting to the complete change. The way the man spoke was so formal and impersonal that it had been difficult to remember that we were not considering some hypothetical situation, but that it was all about me. I was the one who was actually affected by all this, and I knew what my answer was going to be. I had been prepared to tolerate six strokes. I knew I could not take eighteen. I cleared my throat, preparing to tell him so, when Mr Blake interrupted my thoughts at the same instant as the waiter arrived with his drink.

'Honestly,' Mr Blake muttered, almost wistfully, 'nobody should be asked to suffer so severe a penalty and no young lady should be expected to expose herself in such an obscene manner. It simply does not bear thinking about.'

He twisted awkwardly to sign the drinks chit held out by the waiter, who bowed in the manner of all the best club servants as he murmured softly, 'Excuse me, Mr Blake, but Mrs Dyer asked me to enquire whether you have explained the situation to the young lady and if so whether the young lady has confirmed her rejection and Mrs Dyer may now leave.'

'Yes, I think so. I think you can tell her that is the case, is that right, Charlotte?'

But during their brief conversation I had noticed two things. First the waiter's eyes as he approached us had run swiftly up and down me; he knew what I had come for and the sparkle in his eyes betrayed his enthusiasm for my mission. Second, in spite of Mr Blake's assertion that such public exposure did not bear thinking about, the poor man clearly had been thinking about it; the evidence was apparent from his awkward movements and the substantial bulge in the front of his suit. Amanda had been right. I would have dozens of men in the palm of my hand; I had two already. Of the rest, half would die of heart attacks on the spot and the other half would want to marry me.

'No,' I said. 'I'm damn well not going to let this woman frighten me out of my inheritance. If this Mr Wallingham could stand the punishment when he was just a boy, so can I.'

A brightness glittered in Mr Blake's eye as he swivelled round to face me, an almost breathless excitement and a new admiration in his tone. 'Are you quite sure about this, my dear? I mean this is your decision but you should not underestimate the severity of the ordeal.'

'Yes, I am.' At that moment, I meant it.

Mr Blake turned to the waiter with sheer glee. 'Kindly convey our reply to Mrs Dyer. She's lost, damn her.'

I was led up the swirling marble staircase to the first floor where, Mr Blake explained, a room had been put aside for me. It was sparsely furnished with a drab desk, two or three hard chairs and an armchair. In the corner, another door led through to what Mr Blake called 'the usual offices' and turned out to be a toilet with a wash-hand basin.

'Where will it happen?'

'Ah yes. That will be next door, the Spencer Library. Would you like to see it?'

He led me out into the corridor and through a pair of double doors at the end that opened into a magnificent room, lined from floor to ceiling with glass-fronted bookcases. It extended the full width of the building, so was twice the depth of my room next door and its walls soared up to a vaulted ceiling high in the roof.

As we were standing there, Mr Blake beginning to recount who had donated the library and when and why and what for and I wasn't listening to any of it, two of the waiters came in. They glanced at Mr Blake, looked more searchingly at me and then turned to him again.

'Excuse me, sir, Mrs Dyer has asked us to prepare the room.'

'Ah, yes. Go ahead. Did she indicate how many people might be attending?'

'We have been asked to provide seating for thirty.'

'I see.' Mr Blake looked over to me. 'I'm sorry, my dear. I had asked that we try to restrict numbers as much as possible. It might be worth my going to speak to them again. Would you excuse me?'

Left alone in that oppressive room with just the two staff working silently and efficiently on the preparations, I was already losing courage. I felt like the prisoner in a Hollywood western watching through the bars as a scaffold is erected outside his cell. Although neither of them spoke, they kept looking at me, and their expressions revealed that they were already seeing me stretched naked. I realised then that the reaction from some club members would not be admiration; from some it would simply be bare lust.

The tables had all been moved away to one end of the room and the chairs arranged in a circle. In the middle, one of the staff was now placing an elegant padded piano stool. He glanced up at me as he arranged it carefully in the very centre of the circle and then slipped back out into the corridor.

As soon as the door closed behind him, the room settled down into absolute silence. Not even the sounds of traffic could reach me and the windows set so high up in the two end walls gave pictures only of sky. I was alone. The small stool, set out just for me, so forlorn in the centre, echoed my loneliness.

It was the silence, the overbearing seriousness, of that room that crushed me. The whole club had been sombre, but I had expected that. The staff had been businesslike, and that was no surprise either. What I had not expected was the dismal solemnity of this setting. Talking with Amanda, the whole scheme had seemed somehow more jolly. It was a bit naughty perhaps, but frivolous; just a prank.

The reality that I now faced was entirely different. This was cold and earnest. This was shameful. Under these oppressive conditions, I could not hope to survive the embarrassment of appearing naked in front of a room full of men, let alone withstand the pain of eighteen strokes with a cane. I was sickened at the prospect and although I tried to recapture the pride in seeing the effect I had created on the waiter and on Mr Blake, it was gone. This all seemed an utterly stupid thing to have embarked upon and I started to plan how I could get out of it. The first thing was to get out of that room.

I returned to my little anteroom and found that while I had been away someone had placed the most beautiful embroidered white silk dressing-gown on the table. I was holding it up, resting my cheek against the smooth sheen and wondering whether I could try it on, when Mr Blake strode in. He looked aghast at seeing me there holding the gown; he couldn't have been more mortified if I had been stark naked. In a cloud of apologies, he hurriedly and belatedly knocked on the door.

'Well, they are assembling now, Charlotte. I am overjoyed to report that Mrs Dyer is most put out by your decision. You are a great credit to your family and your school. Congratulations. Now, I will make sure that all is ready and then come and fetch you. I asked for that robe so that you can undr – er, change in here rather than having to do so in front of everyone in the library. I'll be five minutes. Will that be enough?'

My escape was cut off with the closing of the door. I should have spoken the instant he came in but missed my chance and although I could understand his feelings about Mrs Dyer, he was so elated at thwarting her that he had not even considered what I would have to suffer to complete the victory.

I laid the silk gown back on the table and kicked off my shoes.

Five minutes, Mr Blake had said. In five minutes he would come back and lead me through to the other room. To be caned. To be led out to the centre of the room and bent over that stark wooden stool. Naked. Before they caned me, they would make me take off the dressing-gown. I would already have been deprived of my own clothes and given a thin, semi-transparent dressing-gown in their place. Then they would take away even that. Nothing was to be allowed to obscure their view of my breasts and my genitals. They would make me expose myself to them all. I was not a virgin, but I could count on the fingers of one hand the men who had seen me naked. My heart fluttered and my armpits felt clammy but there was also an appeal, an anticipation, which was not exactly the same as when I was waiting for Amanda to return with her father's cane, but was more like that than it had any right to be.

I pulled my sweater up over my head.

They would all sit round in a contented, comfortable circle, all neatly buttoned up in their suits and ties while I was displayed in the centre. What memories and fantasies would be churning through their minds as they stared at my breasts, at my bottom and at my pubis? Who would be there? I pictured all old men. Like Mr Blake. Like my own father. Respectable, dull and now restless. But also Mrs Dyer, so would there be other women? Young? Old? My age? Could there really be thirty people? Could so many have arranged to be here that afternoon, assembling to watch an eighteen-year-old girl being stripped naked and caned?

I unzipped my skirt, pulled it down and laid it on top of my sweater.

Would they give me a break between each batch of six? If they did, would that be better, or worse? Would it be better just to get the whole thing over in one swift horrible go? Would I be able to stand it? I had screamed when Amanda gave me six. I had cried, and I wouldn't want to do that in front of so many people. Worse. I had got wet. Suppose that happened. Could I stand such shame?

I unhooked my bra, let my breasts tumble free and dropped the white cotton down on top of the pile. For a brief moment, I cradled myself in my hands, stroking lightly with my thumbs at my nipples, nipples that pushed out disgustingly erect.

When I next put that bra back on, it would be afterwards. After I had exposed myself to them all. After three of them had taken up a long cane and beaten me with it. Six times. Each, in turn. Deliberately brought it down hard on my skin in order to hurt me. Aiming stroke after stroke at my naked skin. Watching me shake, tremble and ultimately, inevitably, weep.

I hooked my fingers into the waistband of my tights and knickers and pulled them all down together, adding that bundle to the heap on the table. After a moment I added my wristwatch.

I stood naked. As they had directed.

Voices echoed out in the corridor; footsteps passed the door. Quickly, I pulled on the dressing-gown and tied it up tightly, but even as I did so the gesture seemed utterly pointless. Why attempt such modesty now when I would be allowed no modesty so soon? The voices died away and I straightened the pile of clothes, untangled my knickers from the tights and buried them at the bottom. I didn't know who might come while I was in the other room. I heard voices again, steps slowly approaching down the corridor and then a knock at the door. When I called, Mr Blake nervously slid into the room.

'They are assembled, Charlotte. Are you ready? I am sorry about this, you know.' He glanced round again, starting momentarily as his eyes fell on the jumbled pile of my clothes. 'They have asked me to go first, then Mr Harris and Mrs Dyer last. I'm sure that they'll understand, I mean, they won't be too . . .'

'Thank you, Mr Blake. I understand. I'm ready.'

'Right. Well then. Let's go.'

He led the way and I followed barefoot down the polished corridor behind him. At the library door, he stood back but when I hesitated he led the way in.

The low murmur of voices died to total silence as we entered and I felt myself the subject of intense scrutiny from a wall of eager faces. There looked to be many more than thirty people there. Most were as I had expected: old, dull and respectable but there were one or two younger faces, including three women. Two sat together, close together, but the third, a thin staring woman with an angry earnestness in her face, was obviously Mrs Dyer. The piano stool stood in the middle of the room and a cane lay across its seat. A dull, yellow stick with a curled handle, just like the one Amanda had used on me. Just like the one whose six strokes, in the hand of a friend, had caused me such pain. Now this one waited to give me eighteen, and at least twelve of those were from no friend.

Mrs Dyer and the man sitting next to her advanced towards us as Mr Blake quickly made the introductions.

'This is Miss Charlotte McRae; Charlotte, this is Mrs Dyer and Mr Harris, my co-executors.'

I felt their eyes slithering down me and Mr Harris licked his lips, but the bitterness and hostility on Mrs Dyer's face were worse. I knew that look from other women. I had seen that resentment of my youth, of my smooth skin, thick blonde hair, my full round breasts; all these badges that they themselves had worn so proudly twenty or thirty years before and now had been forced to relinquish.

She plucked disdainfully at the collar of my dressing-gown. 'I can't imagine why you have bothered with this thing. We will all get a good look at everything you have to offer quite soon enough. Anyway,' she turned back to Mr Blake, 'let's get started, shall we? I'm sure Charlotte does not want to prolong her ordeal any longer than necessary. You are going first, Mr Blake?'

They retreated to their seats and Mrs Dyer folded her arms with an obstinate animosity that chilled me. I may have won the battle, but I had antagonised someone who would soon have the chance to exact her revenge to the full.

Mr Blake picked the cane off the stool, glanced round at the silent watching figures and his voice was little more than a whisper.

'Shall I take your, er . . .? I'm afraid you need to remove the, er . . .'

I reached down and tugged at the knot. It was tight and my fingers trembled as I pulled at the thin band of silk. Finally it came free and I pulled the knot undone. I was conscious of all the eyes fixed on me, waiting for my next movement, waiting in a silence broken only by the slow wheezing breath of one eager spectator.

I took a deep breath and pushed the dressing-gown off my shoulders, handed it to Mr Blake and stood proudly naked in the centre of the floor. I held my head up and stared defiantly round at them all. If I had to be naked, I didn't need to be ashamed and, looking round, I felt confident that I had more justification for pride than anyone there. I pushed back my shoulders further; my breasts were bigger, firmer and fuller than any of the three women there and probably better than any of the men had known in many years.

In the far corner, a small door was pushed open and three club waiters sidled in to press themselves surreptitiously against the wall, their eyes wide, their grins broad as they saw me watching their arrival.

Mr Blake had deposited the dressing-gown and was standing nervously waiting for me. I walked up to the stool, bent down and rested my hands on the seat. In the total silence, Mr Blake came up beside me. The cane rested briefly on my bottom as I stared down at my hands, spreading out my fingers so that I could count the strokes off. It would be only one hand's worth plus one extra. I could stand that, and I didn't have to think about the second six just yet.

I felt the cane lift away and from the corner of my eye I saw Mr Blake moving, then the first stroke landed. It was light, easy and I almost grinned, but in the silence I heard a snort of disgust from behind, where Mr Harris and Mrs Dyer were sitting. The second one came, no worse than the first and I counted this off on my forefinger. Then the rest: middle finger, ring and little finger. One more, this last perhaps a little harder than the first five, and Mr Blake was already moving away.

I stood up and although I was conscious of so many eyes staring at me, staring at my proud breasts and thick blonde bush, I didn't try to cover these, but reached round to place my palms over my bottom, feeling no more than a dull warmth. The first part had been easy, and although I had expected this from Mr Blake, it was still a relief to have the first third of my ordeal out of the way.

The cane was passed to Mr Harris as he strode up to where I waited by the stool and Mr Blake took the empty chair. I bent down again and waited.

He tapped the cane across my shoulders. 'Right down, girl. Elbows on the seat.'

I lowered myself further, my heavy breasts sagging down until the hard nipples were almost scraping on the seat and horribly aware how this pushed out my bottom and would expose me even more blatantly to those sitting directly behind me. A few seconds later there were a few light taps with the tip of the cane as he gauged the distance, a short silence then a whistling swoosh through the air and the fire swept across my buttocks. I screamed.

Behind me I heard gasps from several in the audience and Mr Blake called out in protest. This was worse, far stronger, far harder, than anything Amanda had given me and, as I fought to gulp in air, I heard the second whoosh and another stream of fire blazed across my skin. I screamed again. The third followed as swiftly and I understood the agony that Amanda had suffered when I caned her as swiftly, giving her no time to prepare. After three, Mr Harris paused and walked round in front of me.

'Up!' he called. 'Turn round.'

At first I didn't understand what he wanted but then he made me move round the stool and face the other way, so that now when I looked up, it would be

Mrs Dyer and Mr Blake I would see, while my burning bottom would be displayed to all those on the other side of the room. Right at the back I heard the shuffling of feet where the club waiters moved to get a clear view of my new stripes. My thighs trembled. The cheeks of my bottom quivered and I blinked back the tears.

I leaned down again, right down on to the stool, pushed my bottom back towards the seated watchers and waited. The first seepings of wet desire were building inside, slipping down my vagina and I clamped my thighs tighter together.

The fourth stroke whistled through the air and I yelped as it seared across my skin, but there was a longer pause this time, and the pain had dissipated to a smarting exhilaration by the time the fifth whipped down. He paused again before the sixth, maybe to give me time to dread what was coming, maybe because he relished what he was doing but then came two light taps with the tip as he measured the distance and then the final resounding smack echoed like a shot round the room. I heard myself scream again. The sound was undignified, I know, but this was as painful as the first one, a permeating spread of fire across skin that was already so bruised and inflamed that I could not have stood another stroke from him.

Stiffly I pulled myself back up and stood nursing my raging bottom as he turned back to his seat and the last of the three executors stood up.

Mrs Dyer practically snatched the cane from the man's hand and advanced to where I shivered, waiting. For a moment our eyes met and the triumph in hers was unmistakable. She intended to enjoy her time.

'Mr Harris,' she called without looking away from me, 'kindly remove this stool. I shall not require it. I shall have the girl bending in the traditional posture.'

Once the stool was out of the way, Mrs Dyer pointed with her cane to a spot in the centre of the floor. 'Stand there, girl. Legs wide apart, bend right over and grip your ankles.'

I tried to do as she said, but found I could only reach my ankles by shuffling my feet wide apart, much wider than Amanda had done so that I knew that my whole bottom, even my bottom hole and right through to the thick wet lips of my sex would be plainly visible. Everything I have, everything I am, was now exposed to those sitting behind me. Thankfully, I was facing Mr Blake so his view was less revealing, but looking backwards between my legs, I found a wall of staring eyes, all earnestly studying every intimate part of me, all spread open before them. Several men were dangerously red faced and looked about to burst, but the two women were even closer together, and now holding hands.

Mrs Dyer paraded round and paused behind me, craning forward to peer closely at the marks criss-crossing my cheeks. For a moment her fingers traced along the tender ridges, the long nails gouging the swollen weals. When she was directly behind me, so close that her skirt brushed my legs, her hand even slid down right between my legs until her fingertips were grazing between my sopping lips and the sharp pointed tip of one nail stabbed at my swollen clitoris. She sniffed in disgust at my undeniable arousal.

Then she straightened up and walked round me again, flexing the cane and repeatedly whipping it through the air as she walked. She stopped again by my head and, unable to see more than her legs and feet, I held my breath and waited. Just once, just briefly, just hard enough to sting, she flicked the tip of the cane up against each of my hanging breasts. The room fell into total silence.

At last she completed her circle and stopped by my side. The cane was pressed against my stretched skin and deliberately scraped up and back across the raw raised weals of the first twelve strokes.

I bit my lip, determined not to admit any pain, not to allow her any victory and although I was trying to clench the muscles in my vagina to hold back the growing trickle that I could feel running down inside, I was also trying to relax the muscles in my bottom. I failed.

She was determined too, and from the moment the first stroke flicked out and back with the speed and ferocity of a snake strike, I knew I was lost. I cried out at once and started to leap up but for her shouted command.

'Stay down!'

After a short pause to examine the effects of her strike, she stood back and prepared for the second stroke. Grunting like a tennis champion serving an ace, she whipped the cane down once and then immediately again. I lifted my head as the tears ran down and sobbed out towards the wide staring faces sitting in front of me, faces utterly absorbed in the humiliating spectacle I presented.

Mrs Dyer paused again after that, sauntered right round me again, whipping the cane through the air in a succession of vicious and terrifying strokes. She stopped in front of me and grabbed my chin to yank up my head and smile proudly and smugly as I tried to sniff back the sobs.

'Three more, my little pet, and I'll make them count. However, I do think Colin Harris had the right idea; we'll turn you round for the last set. Let's let those who've seen your tears see your stripes.'

I stood up, shuffled round and bent down again as Mrs Dyer returned to her place. Now my bottom was pointing directly towards Mr Blake. My legs, my cheeks were spread open, my lips were hanging wet and thick and heavy, and my condition was disgustingly evident. Glancing back between my thighs, I could see his revulsion as his eyes focused on that spot, but whether it was at the marks of the beating inflicted on me or my reaction to it, I couldn't tell.

Mrs Dyer took up her position again, laid the cane back across my tortured skin and then slid it steadily down the curve of my cheek into the fold at the top of my thigh. The stroke landed with total accuracy and my whole body trembled with the shock of such ferocity in so sensitive a place. The fifth followed on the same target and I cried out again.

Yet again she paused. Yet again she sliced the cane brutally down through the air next to me so that I heard the whistle, felt the wind and anticipated the stroke. Yet again she stood back and two short taps on the fullest, the roundest and the most bruised part of my bottom told me she was preparing the last one.

She threw everything into it, every ounce of rage at my clinging on to my inheritance, every scrap of jealousy at my youth and my victory. I screamed out a final time as the stroke landed, spreading stinging tongues of fire across the whole surface of my skin: spreading pain, spreading exhilaration, spreading desire.

It was over and I slumped down to my knees, clutching my hands to my bottom as I knelt on the floor. I didn't stand up. I couldn't stand up. I collapsed on to the floor crying and clutching the swollen cheeks of my poor bruised bottom and desperate for some privacy to ease not just the pain but also the fire that now blazed uncontrollably in my sex. I was only dimly aware of Mr Blake helping me up, wrapping the dressing-gown round my shoulders and guiding me back down to the little adjoining room.

'I'm sure you'd like to be left in peace for a while, my dear. Is there anything I can fetch you?'

'No, Mr Blake, but please don't go. I wonder if you could do something for me?'

'Well, of course, my dear. What is it?'

I shrugged away the useless dressing-gown and let it drop to the floor. He tried not to look, but my breasts were heaving with every sob, my thick nipples were eagerly pushing out towards him and when he tore his eyes away from my bosom, they were drawn automatically to my pale golden bush, the hairs unmistakeably damp and matted. He blushed.

'Could you get some cold water on a towel and dab it lightly on my bottom? I think that might help.'

He hurried out to the little adjoining washroom and I took the opportunity to sink my fingers into the quivering running crease between my thighs. When he returned with the damp towel in his hand, and I leaned forward over the table to present my naked bottom to him for the final time, his face still struggled between mortified embarrassment and yearning lust.

He dabbed lightly at the burning weals, wiping carefully and softly at the tender bruises and soothing the blistered skin. It was wonderful, but not enough. I spread my legs apart.

'A little lower, if you could.'

He dropped down to the few lower stripes where Mrs Dyer had aimed into the fold at the top of my thighs.

'Could you go a little lower still? A bit further forward?' I was whispering, ashamed of asking him for this, but I needed so much relief after so much

65

pain. He slipped the bundled towel down between my spread legs until it was just touching my lips.

'Here?'

'A bit further.'

Now that he was in no doubt as to my need, he pressed the towel far in against my opening lips, right up to my clitoris and pressed firmly against me. Through the thick cloth, I felt his fingers quiver and dig at my delicate nerves and that tiny direct contact was all I needed. With a wail that must have been clearly audible to all those still dawdling in the library next door, I climaxed, clamping my thighs shut on to his trembling hand.

Two weeks later I called on Stephen Blake for the last time. Again, Amanda came with me and waited outside. He was clearly very uneasy in my company.

'Yes, well, Charlotte, my dear. I expect you're highly relieved that distasteful business is over. May I say that you bore the trial with fortitude and admirable courage.' He stirred uneasily in his chair and adjusted the front of his trousers as he recalled the event. 'Now. Let us move on to happier matters. I imagine you are here to ask when you may expect to receive the inheritance. Regrettably, I cannot let you have that today because I am still waiting for the headmaster's certificate of your nomination. I don't know why it has taken so long. You are sure you forwarded the form to him, I take it?'

I cleared my throat. 'I think I may have misled you rather, Mr Blake. In fact no, I didn't forward the form to him because there would have been no point. You see, although I was nominated to the position of Head of School, I declined it. I am not therefore entitled to the inheritance.'

Mr Blake stared. For a couple of seconds his jaw lifted and dropped. 'But, Charlotte, what on earth are you saying? Surely you must realise what this means! You can't have thought ... You must have known ...'

'The person who was actually appointed Head of School,' I hurried on before I was shamed any more, 'is my friend Amanda Williams. I asked her to come with me today and she is waiting outside so you can explain what will be required of her. I think you'll find her quite willing.'

For a few seconds, I really thought Mr Blake was going to pass out.

Rebecca's Tale – Expectations

We stopped for petrol on the way to Mr Cathart's house and as I walked over to the office to pay, Beckie called out after me.

'Could you get me something to drink? A bottle of water?'

Back in the car, she unscrewed the top immediately and drained half the bottle. I assumed it was nervousness, and looked for something to say, anything to break the silent tension. 'You're thirsty!'

'No, not really,' and she took another long draft, then looked round at me. 'He wants to watch me pee, remember?'

Her quiet words, the picture they evoked, the flat resigned tone of her voice: it all hit me in the stomach like a fist.

It had been Beckie's idea to apply for the job as a photographer's model, even though she had never done anything remotely similar before, even though she had never before let another person so much as see her topless on a beach. However, for a reason I still could not fathom, she had given in to Mr Cathart's Svengali voice and step by step, item by item, she had allowed herself to be persuaded until finally she stood naked in front of him. The first time, last week, he had taken some test shots and now wanted her to go back for what he termed the real thing. But what did he mean by that? What would he expect? He knew she was shy and completely inexperienced. He knew she was mortified at having to undress in his presence but he knew too that in the silent privacy of his study, she had eventually succumbed the previous week; had stripped completely, revealed the soft pale curves of her beautiful breasts, her smooth white stomach with its sweet brown curls and even bent over at his command to display the gentle cheeks of her perfect round bottom.

But had he also realised that, hateful though it had been, it had left her unquenchably excited? And if so, what was the real thing? What would he ask? What had he meant by suggesting just as we left that he wanted to photograph her while she urinated?

He rang one evening in the week: a brief conversation that I couldn't hear because Beckie pushed the kitchen door shut but she emerged to say that he wanted to put the appointment back to late on Friday evening.

She was on late shifts that week, and went up to change as soon as she came home, saying she wanted to have a long bath and get ready. It was over an hour before she came down for her tea and then we sat in almost complete silence, though I found myself carefully studying her movements in eating and drinking. She made no reference to Cathart's instruction, but she fetched a large glass of water, drained that, and then drank three cups of tea afterwards. Every sip that I watched her drink, I pictured that man watching her expel later. Seeing her there, I was hypnotised by the demure elegance she presented: the immaculate make-up, the neat hair, the delicate earrings that quivered and sparkled with every movement of her head. Nor could I forget the grotesque images I had conjured in my mind while I crouched like Caliban outside the half-closed door of that man's studio less than a week ago.

We set off in good time, stopping at the usual garage for petrol except this time Beckie had also wanted a drink. The rest of the trip passed in silence.

The evenings were still light, but as we turned down Cathart's road a single street light was beginning to offer the first tentative orange glow, discolouring the bleak house as we parked outside. We were early, but we were here again, six days after our first visit, obeying the summons we had received. I switched off the engine, turned to kiss Beckie on the cheek and felt like Judas.

Unlike last time, I knew now what would happen once we stepped inside. I knew that over the threshold I could do nothing to help, and that the whole burden would fall on her. I knew how loathsome it would be for her, and I was beginning to have an inkling (that Beckie in her innocence did not) of how depraved the man could be. I knew that although I would stay with her for as long as he let me, my support was worth nothing: my witnessing her humiliation did not reduce it one ounce. I knew all of this and did nothing. I needed only to start the car and I could have taken her home to safety. I did not move.

We watched the small red figures on the dashboard clock until they flicked over to 9.00. I glanced across. 'OK?'

She nodded and we got out and walked up to the front door. I rang hesitantly at the bell. Although lights were shining behind the curtains of the massive front bay, they did little to brighten the towering porch, dismal in the fading dusk. Beckie shivered beside me, and shuffled from one foot to the other so that I reached out for her hand in the shadows. She laughed nervously.

'I don't think I did need that water after all.'

At last the door was opened, spilling light out on to the porch.

Cathart seemed unsurprised to see me there again but did not try to welcome me. Indeed, he ignored me entirely as he turned his attention to Beckie.

'How lovely to see you again, my dear; do come in. We'll go into the drawing room first. I have a few friends here this evening who I am sure would be interested to meet you before we get down to work.'

I followed them into the gloomy hall until, halfway down, Cathart stepped aside, pushed open a heavy wooden door and ushered Beckie through. As she passed him, his hand dropped down momentarily to rest protectively, perhaps only politely, in the small of her back, but it did not rest there long before slipping down over the swelling of her skirt and his hands curved underneath her rounded cheek for an instant.

Inside the room we found four men, smartly dressed in suits and ties, at ease on the chairs and settees that formed a semi-circle round the stone fireplace. A huge chandelier hung from the centre of the ceiling and between this and several wall lights, the room was lit as brightly as a stage. A fire burned low in the grate, logs glowing with an ominous red light beneath the cream marble mantelpiece; a glass-cased carriage clock took pride of place over the fire but its pendulum was still, stopped at twenty minutes to nine. Littered around the room on tables and chair-arms stood coffee cups and half empty brandy glasses, the scattered leavings of a rich dinner.

The guests were much the same age as Cathart, at least fifty and one perhaps as much as sixty, and as each was introduced to Beckie (but not me) they stood politely, smiled and shook her hand. Although I had initially worried what Cathart intended, it was reassuring to realise that this had not been planned; they were quite as surprised by our arrival as we were to find them there.

During the round of introductions, I was ignored entirely, although a couple of the guests looked at me inquisitively. At the end of the circuit, when Beckie had been brought back in front of the fire and to the centre of the half circle, Cathart noticed me again and pointed dismissively to the window seat.

'Stay there, please.' I took up my place, outside the semi-circle, behind the others, but able to see between the chairs to a space where a small low stool stood on the hearth rug.

Cathart firmly closed the door and took up a position in a high-backed library chair near the fire, close to where Beckie was waiting. In her simple white blouse and neatly pressed long black skirt, she could have been a dutiful waitress and though it was disloyal, I wondered what made her take such care in selecting her clothes when she had known that within a couple of minutes of entering this house, she would be taking them all off.

'Now then, I should explain to you, my dear,' and he nodded to Beckie, 'that these gentlemen are here because it has become a tradition for the five of us to assemble on this date each year for a dinner together. And I should also offer an explanation to you,' and here he turned to address the four men sitting patiently, silent but curious. 'This charming young lady visited me last week to see if she was suited to doing a little modelling for me. Isn't that right, my dear?'

Beckie nodded and mumbled a nervous acknowledgement. Revelation of the details would be embarrassing for all of us and it would be better if he moved on as soon as possible.

'Yes indeed. And explain to our guests here, how exactly do you model for me?'

Beckie glanced up. She swallowed with difficulty and then looked down to the floor again. 'It depends how you ask me to.'

'Well yes, of course.' Cathart laughed lightly, picked at the crease of his neat trousers and, in a sudden intuition, I saw through him. He was deliberately taunting her by eking out a full explanation and dragging it from her own lips. Just as on our first visit, when he had asked her to reveal intimate details about herself, now he would do the same, making her recount to strangers every aspect of what she had been made to do. 'But what I mean is, describe what you were wearing to model for me?'

Beckie's head jerked up. This was nothing to do with any of them, but a purely private matter between him and Beckie. She turned away again without a word.

He smiled again. 'As you see, gentlemen, she is wonderfully shy. But please, my dear, do tell them. What did you wear for your modelling last week?'

Her single word answer fell out into the silent room: 'Nothing.'

'Well done! Quite right! Nothing! Now then, I thought that this evening it might entertain our guests if they could witness your work. I should tell you, my friends, that although she is a very timid little thing, she can also be quite uninhibited in many respects so I am sure you will find the evening most entertaining.'

He turned back to address Beckie. 'So now this evening you have brought your little friend back to visit me again. Is that right?'

I grasped his meaning immediately, with a sick lurch in my stomach, but Beckie did not. She looked

73

across at me, puzzlement clouding her deep brown eyes.

'Yes, Mr Cathart. My husband is here.' Her voice was so soft and uncertain that she was almost whispering.

The man smiled. 'Oh no, I can see that. No, I mean the little fellow you have hidden away inside your little panties. I have been waiting all week to see him again, so don't let's waste another minute! Slip your clothes off and let me have a look at you.'

It was an utterly blunt instruction that made no pretence of being given for any reason other than the man's desire to see my wife's naked body again. She blushed deeply, now understanding exactly what he had meant before, but she did not move. For several long seconds the room was completely still; completely silent. Beckie remained stiffly upright, her hands clasped in front of her, fingers entwined and her mouth pressed tight. Finally Cathart spoke again.

'Do not be concerned about our guests, my dear. I just feel it would amuse them to witness the proceedings, but I assure you that everything will be just as before and you will not be asked to do anything that you would not have done anyway.'

Beckie squirmed, twining her hands again, but she made no move to obey the request. Indeed she looked to be on the verge of tears so that I was about to step forward and rescue her when Cathart cleared his throat and spoke again.

'If you really don't feel you want to, my dear, then of course I shall not insist. You and I can simply go through to the studio as before. It is up to you entirely.'

Beckie looked up, searching round the circle of faces and even over at me for a support that I could not give. She had said nothing about anyone else being present, and I guessed from her reaction that she had been given no warning these other men would be here. I did not know what she would do, how far she could bring herself to go. Sickened at the thought of her letting these men see her naked, I despised myself for wanting so earnestly to watch her do just that. I should have been protecting her, but I sat silently passive while this man picked away her defences. I should have been shielding her and now meekly watched him goad her down a path to her degradation.

I hoped desperately for a chance to make amends, yet was overjoyed when I saw the first signs of her acquiescence. Her hands meekly stretched up to her collar where she unfastened the top button of her neat white blouse, then the next, the third and steadily right down to the waist. She slid it off and let it drop down at her feet.

It was a very flimsy little bra that was now revealed, whose delicate white lace cups encased but did not conceal her full round breasts. The small pointed nipples were offered out towards us all, dark points pressing through the thin cotton, and again I wondered what factors had influenced her choices earlier. Knowing that Cathart would soon be making her take off her outer clothes, what had made her choose these underclothes? Had she studied her reflection in the mirror when she selected that bra? Had she considered the image it presented, the way it displayed and enhanced her breasts and had she decided that this was an effect she wanted to achieve? That this was the image she wanted to show the man?

She quickly sat back on the little stool and hunched over so that her breasts were mostly hidden from our view as she slowly and methodically unfastened her shoes, and unzipped the side of her skirt. She stood up to slip this off, followed by her shoes and knee length stockings and then she froze.

Standing now in only her knickers and bra, she stared round at the assembled circle, a rabbit cornered and terrified. Yet I knew now that it was more than fear that made her tremble and brought the bright crimson flush to her cheeks. Although her underclothes were perfectly modest, still her hands came up over her breasts and her crotch and she stood for a moment examining us all, almost hypnotised by us, until finally Cathart broke the silence in his coaxing, wheedling tone.

'Continue, my dear.'

Slowly, she reached up, pushed the shoulder straps of her bra down and then, as the two lacy cups slipped and then hung, promising at any moment to bare her breasts to the world, she stretched round and unfastened the back, letting the whole thing finally tumble away and reveal the glorious fullness of her sweet breasts. A sigh whispered round the room as the men were treated for the first time to the sight: her nipples already puckered and half erect, their areolae darkening as we all watched. In breathless silence, her fingers reached up to the elastic waistband of her knickers and then fell away, her hands clasped together in front of her, unable to continue. She was searching anxiously round the room for someone to save her, someone on whom she could rely, and she looked to me and passed on. Ultimately it was to Cathart that she turned.

'I didn't know there would be all these other people.'

The man smiled, a genial, accommodating smile. 'Don't you worry about them. They understand that you are shy; that is perfectly natural. They are all old friends of mine and very respectable and understanding. They know what a young lady fears and what she wants – sometimes perhaps better than the lady herself. So, don't be afraid, my dear. Let's have your knickers off, shall we?'

Two weeks ago I had been the only man in the whole world who had seen Beckie's glorious naked body. Two minutes ago, that experience had been shared with just one other person. Now it was not enough and he was asking her to expose herself to four strangers.

Still Beckie did not attempt to continue but her lips quivered as she fumbled for the right words. 'I did what you asked.' She glanced guiltily at me but spoke only to Cathart.

'Excellent.'

Still she faltered, glanced round nervously at us all before facing Cathart again. 'They will be able to see everything.'

'Yes, dear. Indeed they will. That is the point.'

For a moment I thought she was going to protest again, but then, still facing out towards us all, her fingers crept back up towards the waist of her white knickers, and after another tiny pause when she first gripped the thin elastic, she slowly eased them away.

Beckie had known what to expect; Cathart had known what to expect. But the four other men didn't know; and I didn't know although I had seen her naked many hundreds of times. As the waistband slipped down below her delicate round navel, slipped below the line of her tan to the pure white of her stomach, it should have reached the dark triangle of her pubic hair. But no hair appeared. As it continued to slide down, the top of her vulva finally came visible, a slim vertical crease in her pale skin that curled down between her thighs as the knickers were pushed further down to reveal her cleanly shaved pubis and the very tips of her labia. She finally bent down, carefully disentangled each foot and the last item was added to the pitiable pile of clothes.

I had never seen her looking so utterly naked, so purely exposed and defenceless. I found myself thinking back to the time a couple of hours before this; while I had been breezily fiddling about with plates and cups of tea, she had been upstairs preparing for this. She had spent the time working carefully with a razor to make herself more open to examination. With nothing left for her to hide behind, Beckie bowed her head and allowed us to stare as we liked while she silently awaited our verdict.

Cathart broke the silence. 'Lovely, my dear. Truly lovely. Now, before we go any further, I do think you ought to introduce our guests to the little fellow hiding away down there. You know who I mean by that?'

Beckie blushed at the reference; her huge brown eyes were rimmed pink as if any moment she would break down in sobs; her fingers writhed together. 'My private parts.'

'Oh, come now!' He was affectionately scolding a naughty child. 'Rather more specific than that; try again.'

She swallowed, and finally almost whispered. 'My clitoris.'

'Yes indeed. Your clitoris. Tell me. Do you have a name for him?'

She hesitated too long in the denial.

'Ah!' Cathart was jubilant. 'Tell us his name! Quick!'

'Pip,' she muttered. It was a silly, childish name, but being the shape and size of an orange pip, the name had stuck.

'I'm sorry?'

'Pip. Pip, sir.'

'How lovely. Now, show us where Pip lives. Sit yourself down on the stool and then we can see you better. No need to be shy! After all, we aren't strangers; I've met him before, haven't I?'

She cautiously lowered herself down on the little round stool, and opened her legs wide before looking up. Then, peering out under her brows at the silent staring circle, she gripped the edges of the stool, arched her back until her belly was pushed out directly towards us, opened her legs even wider and finally reached down and pulled apart her lips. She looked so exquisitely naked, utterly vulnerable, without the slightest trace of hair to hide the swollen welcome of the open crease that was so deliberately thrust forward towards us all.

Already she was glistening wet, with dew shining all round the plump puffy lips themselves but also gathering at the little crease where her lips joined. A tiny droplet looked ready to break free and trickle down into the shadows beyond. Her forefinger brushed gently down the length of her lips and then pulled back on the fold of skin at the top so at last we could all see the sleek smooth surface of her clitoris itself. Her fingertip grazed gently across its surface, so that for a moment it seemed she might lose all inhibitions and, without any provocation, start to masturbate in front of us all. However, after a few seconds she seemed to collect herself and suddenly pulled her hand away and clamped her legs shut.

The spell was broken. All the men quickly sat up straight, shuffling their feet, and some trying surreptitiously to make unambiguous adjustments to their clothes. Cathart smiled.

'I think it would be polite if you were to introduce your little friend to our guests, don't you? Perhaps you could introduce him to each of us in turn.'

Hesitantly, Beckie rose to her feet and walked over to the first chair where the eldest of the guests was sitting, a thin, grey-haired man who smiled most kindly at her approach. Close in front of him she stopped and stood with her legs apart so that her damp inner lips were clearly visible to me and even more so to him. He grinned, smugly and stupidly, but Cathart was not satisfied.

'That's no good, dear. We can hardly see the little fellow like that. Let's meet him properly.'

Gingerly Beckie took hold of the wall for support, lifted her foot up on to the man's chair beside him and rolled her leg out to open her vulva completely. Although the action peeled her lips apart fully, her other hand still dropped down and I watched as her fingers pulled up and back at the lips even further so that her clitoris was now fully revealed to the man sitting in front of her.

Cathart was pleased at last. 'Good. Now, Alec, pat his head if you want to. And Rebecca, introduce him.'

Beckie frowned momentarily and then looked down at the man who was now leaning forward between her legs. She licked her lips, searching for words.

'This is,' and she paused again, glanced across at Cathart before finding the courage to continue, 'this is my clitoris.'

As she said the word, the man in front of her looked up and smiled and then tentatively reached out his hand and ran it gently through the sleek smooth crease of her vulva. Beckie flinched at the touch, and for a second she pulled away, but then she shuffled closer to him and pushed herself even more blatantly towards him so that she rubbed the length of her crease along the edge of his hand. I saw her shiver, and the man grinned at her.

'Very pleased to meet you, little fellow.'

So it continued. Beckie moved steadily round the circle, exposing herself to each guest, inviting the caress that they all bestowed. As she reached the fourth, who sat directly in front of me, I could see over his shoulder how swollen her lips had become, how wet, succulent and ready. Her voice was starting to sound strained and her fingers trembled as she repeated the action of peeling open her lips to display herself to this, the fourth in the circle. Immediately he withdrew his shining fingers from her crease, Cathart interrupted, making it clear that I was not to be included in the circle of introductions.

'Thank you, dear. Please return to your seat. Well, gentlemen, now that you have been introduced, I wonder if any of you have any particular requests?'

One of the men crossed and re-crossed his legs self-consciously. 'Actually, Charles, I have to say that I am something of a bottom man myself, you know. I wonder if we might ask her to turn around and show us that particular part of her anatomy.'

'Certainly! I was actually thinking earlier that we have rather ignored your sweet little bottom so far. Rebecca, my dear, would you oblige?'

She took a single step towards the man and then turned her back on us all, but carefully kept her eyes lowered so none of us would see whatever fear or excitement there might be. Her hands rested on her hips and for a man who, by his own admission, had a particular leaning towards this area, the presentation of her slim young figure and unblemished round cheeks, displayed practically at eye level, must have been heaven. He was clearly delighted.

'Lovely, my dear, simply lovely. Charles, I am most obliged to you for this unique demonstration.'

But Cathart was more demanding. 'Bend right forward, please.'

Beckie leaned forward, but still not enough for Cathart. 'Further than that, my dear, I'm sure we would all like to be able to see right up to your little botty hole.'

She leaned a little more, her hands still on her hips and practically toppled forward. She straightened up and stared up at the ceiling for a few seconds.

Cathart waited for a moment, before his voice, a little cracked, came out again. 'Come along, my dear. We are waiting.'

Beckie turned round to him. Not to me. To him. 'Please. I'm shy. I don't want to show them that.'

Cathart's smile was almost kindly. 'Of course you're shy. That is why I have asked you here this evening.'

'Please?' Her eyes were full and shining again, and her voice so low I could barely hear her.

Still Cathart said nothing, and slowly Beckie turned away from us all again. She took a couple of deep breaths and then shuffled her feet apart again and bent right forward, pushing her bottom out towards the eager spectator. For a moment she stayed there and then, without any instruction being given, she reached back to spread her fingertips across the smooth pale round cheeks and she pulled them apart. The entire room was silent as Beckie waited in front of us. But as she stood there, displayed like a museum piece, she must have known that the neat multi-wrinkled brown star of her anus was fully exposed to us, and beneath that her plump lips were presented, full, pink and enticingly damp.

'Excellent, my dear. Now, push a finger inside for me, would you?'

At this Beckie started to straighten up again, but then she changed her mind, and her fingers slithered forward until her forefinger touched right on the very centre of her bottom. She pushed and twisted it, but her body's instinctive revulsion to so obscene an action prevented her.

Finally she stopped. 'I'm sorry. I can't do that. It won't go in.'

'A bit tight, are you? Well, not to worry. Up in the bathroom I have got some vaseline that might help you. Straight at the top of the stairs, and you'll see the medicine cabinet directly in front of you. Try rubbing a little of that on. I think you'll find it helps. You might bring the whole jar down.'

Beckie merely nodded and, with apparently no concern for her nakedness, marched straight out of the room without a glance at any of us. We heard her feet padding rapidly down the hall and up the stairs, then footsteps creaking across the ceiling above our heads as we all sat below in expectant silence, like strangers in a doctor's waiting room, discreetly ignoring each other's presence. I knew nothing about them; they knew nothing about me. My only connection with Cathart was that it was my wife who, just a few moments ago, he had ordered to strip naked, and who was now upstairs greasing her bottom at his direction.

I tried not to listen to the sounds from above, tried not to picture what she must be doing up there, but I was not alone in feeling the pressure of the expectant silence. Eventually, one of the other guests started speaking, although I was still excluded from the conversation, isolated both physically and socially, outside their circle, watching and listening furtively as the events unfolded.

'What an absolute treasure, Charles! Well done! Shaved as well! That is a treat! How on earth did you get her to do that?'

Cathart acknowledged the appreciation. 'Oh, I phoned her in the week and asked her to shave. By nature, she's actually quite a hairy little thing and I thought we would like to see clearly what was what.'

'Does she never object to your requests? Never refuse?'

'Oh no. Never. It's curious because she has never done anything like this before and she is really quite a chaste little mouse. As you could see tonight, she's deeply torn between profound natural modesty and a powerful exhibitionist urge. Even now I can never be entirely sure which will win at any particular moment, but it is pure joy to witness the struggle.'

At last the feet came padding back down the stairs, across the wooden hallway and Beckie reappeared with a huge jar of vaseline in her hand. She returned to her position in the centre of the semi-circle, but her face was scarlet and her eyes stayed demurely towards the floor.

'Find it all right? Good. Well, let's see if that has helped.'

She turned her back on us again and bent over but this time she did not wait to be told. Her hands came round to pull open the cheeks of her bottom, revealing her tightly puckered brown rose glistening with vaseline and shining streaks smeared right across both cheeks.

'Ah, that looks better. Is that easier for your finger now?'

We all stared as her hand reached back further and a fingertip wormed its way tentatively round the entrance of her bottom before it slipped in as far as her knuckle.

'Good. That's the way; I am sure that with a little more practice you will be able to manage even further than that. For now, I think we should go through into the studio and start, shall we? Bring the vaseline jar with you.'

Beckie looked over to me, agonized humiliation on her face; I think she had assumed, as I had, that there would be no photographs tonight. Cathart intercepted the glance and seemed suddenly to remember my presence. Whether he misunderstood her meaning, or understood it perfectly, I have no idea, but he turned to address me.

'Ah yes, young man. I hope that you won't mind if I ask you to excuse us for a few minutes. Perhaps you could wait out in the hall and I will send young Rebecca out to join you when I've finished with her.'

They all, Beckie included, looked round at me in silence as I digested his dismissal. Finally I got to my feet and made my way out to the hall where I perched on a low bench. Soon afterwards the drawing-room door opened again and they all trooped out: Cathart shepherding Beckie naked down to his lair, and the other guests following behind like so many wolves, hungry for whatever titbits they could snatch from the feast. Once they had passed, I hurried after them into the study, so that I should not be cut off entirely.

I had been determined that this time I should not humiliate myself by waiting and listening outside the door, that I should not betray Beckie by stealing erotic pleasure in her degradation and shame. But I did. As soon as the door swung to behind them, I scuttled over and waited. As last time, the door had not latched and I wondered whether Cathart knew this, maybe even intended it, to increase my torment and his pleasure. I was already erect.

'Perhaps you gentlemen would like to settle yourselves on this side, and I think we'll have you, Rebecca, under the window. Make yourself comfortable on the rug there. That's good. Lean back against

85

the cushion, no need to keep yourself all huddled up; we don't have any secrets, do we? Arms behind your head for me, and legs nice and wide apart. That's better. Now then, did you have plenty to drink as I asked you? Good girl! I could get you something more if you think it will help. No? Sure? Excellent! Well, you won't have to hold it in for long, but there are a few more shots that I would like to take of you first.

'Now then, stay like that, but lift your bottom up a bit. That all helps to open you up for me, and with your pussy so delightfully bare, it is a truly exquisite sight. Now, open your lips again and let's get your little friend to come out and join us, shall we? He's not going to play shy, is he? Ah, there he is.'

Then I heard Beckie's low soft voice interrupting. I could not make out her words, but I gathered the meaning from Cathart's reply.

'Well, yes all right, if you really think you can't wait, but I had thought to leave that until the end. You're sure you couldn't hold on a little longer? All right then. We'll do that first. Spread that plastic sheet out and then lay the towel over the top of it. That's the way.

'Stand in the middle. Bit further forward and if you bend your legs just a little . . . that's it! A sort of half squat. Now then, I'd like you to hold this glass under you as you go, and see if you can fill it right up with your own special champagne. Ready? Fine! Off you go, then. Just try to relax and let it all go. Bit difficult, is it? Take your time, just forget about us all being here and try to relax. No need to be shy. It'll get easier with practice. Ah! A little trickle! I do hope there'll be some more. Is there any more? Oh yes! Lovely! What a pretty little fountain! See if you can fill the glass right up! That would be lovely. Oh splendid! Goodness, you certainly will fill it. Don't worry if it overflows, just let it run over. Oh excellent! Just do as much as you can. Quite delightful! Any more for us? A few little dribbles. You have done well! You must have been absolutely bursting! That's it. Lovely, really lovely!'

Huddled outside, all my composure was evaporating. I even had so little self-control that I did not try to rub my penis through my jeans: this time I slowly, quietly, unzipped them and reached in to extract my erection and caress myself directly. Still the odious voice came through to me.

'Finished? Fine, no stay there like that. Let me take a couple with you just like that. A couple close up with a few little glistening drops.

'Now then, hold the glass up in front of you. Good! Hold it straight up; you can be proud of producing all that. Lovely, and look at me, give me a smile! There now, and lift the glass to your lips. Good. And how about a little sip? How is that? Quite warm, is it? Wonderful. Well then, a little more. That's lovely, and again? Drain it all down. That's a good girl. Last few mouthfuls. Excellent! You really are a wonderful girl, aren't you? I can see we're going to have a huge amount of fun together over the next few weeks.

'Now then, you are still all rather wet down there; have you got anything to wipe yourself with? Perhaps you could run and get your brassiere, or those sweet little panties you were wearing.'

I managed to stuff my penis back into my jeans and pull away before Beckie appeared through the door. She looked frightened to see me, as if she had forgotten that I was still there, but her face was electric, shining both with desire and excitement. And more than that. I pulled her to me and kissed her, tasting the strong acrid flavour of her own urine as my tongue swirled round her mouth. I tried to hold her, to rub myself against her, but she pulled away and darted out of the room.

From behind the closed door, I heard another voice sounding both eager and worried. 'I say, Charles, is this all right? I mean are you sure she doesn't mind doing all this?'

'Mind? Oh, Bernard! Of course she minds! She hates every minute of it; hates not only the fact that she does all this, but hates herself for indulging so willingly! That's what makes the whole event so thoroughly enjoyable!'

As I digested his comment, I realised Beckie herself had returned, may even have heard Cathart's words, but before I could reach out, the slender hairless figure scampered past me and disappeared back into the studio. Cathart greeted her.

'Ah, here you are. Does that feel better? Yes, I bet it does. You had obviously been holding all that in for quite a while. Still, all nice and clean now, are you? Shall I have a look? Oh yes. Not bad at all. Still a few little trickles just around here though, aren't there? In fact quite a little flow from inside! You are the most wonderfully moist little thing, aren't you? Look. You've made my fingers all wet and sticky now! That is your fault, that is. I think you should lick them clean for me, don't you? Go on then. That's the way. And this one. Good girl!

'Right now, Rebecca. I promised you a little present this evening, didn't I? Well, I haven't forgotten. There it is, on the chair behind you. That's the one. You may open it now, my dear, it's a little something for you to play with.'

There was a long rustle of paper, and then silence.

Cathart's voice sounded, proud of his gift. 'There now! What do you think of that? Do you have one already?'

Beckie's answer was inaudible.

'Oh! But you have used one, I take it?'

This time I did just catch her reply: 'No. Never.' She sounded ashamed of the failure she was confessing, but I could not work out what it was, although I was beginning to understand Cathart and had a suspicion.

'Well then! I'll have to help you, won't I? Hand them both to me. Shall I put the batteries in for you?'

The reference to batteries seemed to confirm my fears: Cathart must have produced a vibrator, and was now going to ask her to use it on herself while he watched. More than that, while he took photographs of her doing it, others would watch her as well. There was an unmistakable low hum, a sound that I remembered from a friend's stag party, but Beckie, I knew, had never heard it; had never seen or handled a vibrator at all. She had refused to answer when I once asked if she had ever actually masturbated in her life, although whether this was shame that she had, or shame that she hadn't, I could never be sure. She would certainly be horrified to be faced with something like this at any time, and in these circumstances, in front of these strangers, she would be terrified. I dreaded to think what agonies she must be suffering but I reached inside my jeans to grasp my own erection as I imagined them. Cathart's voice broke my reverie again.

'There now. Here we are. Right, now stretch yourself out on the rug so we can all see you and off you go. No, no, turn round so that your legs are pointing down this way, then we can all see you nicely. That's better. Nice and wide apart. Wide as you can. Let's see your little pussy opened right up. That's the way! Goodness, you are a slippery thing, and so wet already, aren't you? Let's really have a look at you this time. Show us everything! Where has your clitoris gone? Disappeared again. Let's have him back out. That's the way, lovely little thing. Pull him right clear and let me see his little gleaming head. Lift your legs up too, so we can see down to your botty. Oh no, no, no! Don't stop playing with your clit. We like to see that. I want a good few more photos of that. Yes and closer still. Pinch him right out between your fingertips. That's lovely! Excellent. Couple more. Good! Fingers right in there, right in deep. Excellent!

'Now I think it's time you were allowed to play with your new toys, but before that, I want you to do something else. Where did you put that vaseline? Yes, get that and put some on your bottom. Roll yourself over on to your hands and knees, no, down on your elbows would be better so that we can all see you clearly. That's the way. And smear it all over. All round your pretty little bottom hole. And push some up inside as well. Good. Now turn a bit more and point that exquisite little bottom straight at me, that's the way. Good! Now here's your special new present. Shall I turn it on for you? There you are. I know it's quite big, but I'm sure you can manage it all the same. You're a willing girl and nice and slippery, aren't you? Push it in, right in, as far as you can. And for this one, I'm going to give the honour to Bernard, because I do believe he is rather taken with you. Bernard, come here and push the little one into Rebecca's bottom for her. Here you are; spread plenty of grease on it. Oh, come along, man, don't be shy. She's not made of glass, you know, you can push a little harder than that! Get hold of her bottom and push it in there. She's quite slippery enough for it. Ah, excellent. Let me get a picture of that.

'Right now, Rebecca, my dear, you just ignore us and play with your toys and play with yourself as you like. Still, no pretending now. We want to see you really enjoying yourself! So, make yourself come! We want to hear you come and we want to smell you come. Just let yourself go.'

I heard little more talking after that. A few words of encouragement from Cathart, sometimes from one or two of the others, egging her on, directing her to some new indignity, a new humiliation or to repeat some particular obscenity. I finally dragged myself away. I could no longer tell what was going on in there and it was too sickening to imagine what she was going through, what they might be making her do. Sitting outside, my own frustrated erection in my hand, I listened to the muffled grunts and cries, some low, some high-pitched, and sometimes rustles of clothes and rasps of zips. But I knew that whatever was happening and however many times they made her bring herself to her own climax, either with her hands or any of the objects they had in there, whatever she was required to do for them, I knew she would still be ready for me when she got out, and all the readier and all the more exhilarated for what she had endured.

Finally it all went quiet, and I heard Cathart again taking control as he announced the end of Beckie's ordeal. 'Well, I think we should call it a day for this evening, gentlemen. We mustn't wear her out or she'll be in no state to come back! Perhaps you would return to the drawing room and I will join you in a moment.'

I hurried back out to the hall and sat there innocently as the four filed by. Three of them glanced down at me, ashamed and embarrassed; one could not even bring himself to do that. The instant they were back in the drawing room, I scuttled back to the studio door. Cathart's voice was coming through again.

'Well, I must say you have done extremely well, Rebecca. I really am very pleased with you, and I am sure that my guests are as well. We are nearly done, but now that it's just the two of us on our own again, I have got one last little surprise for you. You know I asked you to have lots to drink so that you could perform for me? Well, shall I tell you a secret? I have had several drinks this evening too, so that I could join you. So, what I want you to do now is lie back on the sheet again, I know it's all rather wet but not to worry. Now lie down flat on your back. Oh, no, open your legs up again, my dear! There's no need for you ever to have your legs together when you're with me. That's the way! Now, move up a bit further so there's room for me to stand beside you. Oh no, I'll just stand here. Good girl! Ready?'

I heard the splashes that followed a second later and was sickened as my mind pictured the man standing over her, the stream cascading down between her open legs, soaking her neatly shaved vulva and running down between the cheeks of her bottom. Possibly even worse; maybe he would direct the flow up her body and on to her perfect white breasts. Even as that appalling thought hit me, Cathart spoke again.

'Now look up at me, and smile. Nice smile, and open your mouth for me. A little wider. Here we go!'

All my restraint was destroyed; all my resolutions mocked. I pulled wildly at my pounding erection and instantaneously erupted into a cupped hand that let the sperm pour down my fingers, down my erection and my clothing. So overpowering was the climax that I practically collapsed, and fell against the door. Of course it was still not latched, so that I half fell through into Cathart's den, this secret chamber which I had never before entered.

Spread before me lay Beckie, my own sweet innocent Beckie, lying in a spreading pool, her breasts and belly awash both with urine and the unmistakable white spatters of semen. Beyond her, Cathart stood with his stubby pink cock in his hand, barely half erect but still spurting the last few jets of urine on to dear Beckie's perfect face, a face as shining and besmirched as her body. But Beckie could not see me, for though her mouth was opened wide to receive Cathart's stream, her eyes were tight shut and her hands were gripped around the thick black vibrator clamped between her thighs as she grunted herself to one last slow crushing orgasm.

Leanne's Tale – President of the Committee

I was nineteen when I went to university and during the first week I attended the usual Freshers' Fair when all the clubs and societies set out their stalls and try to recruit you to go canoeing, learn Esperanto or save your own or someone else's soul. Within minutes I was swamped with leaflets, flyers and posters for concerts, outings and meetings that would have filled every hour of the next two hundred years. As I was browsing through with some friends from my hall, a shy, timid, little girl came sidling up to me, almost sheepishly, and pushed a leaflet into my hand before she scurried off. I muttered thanks, stuffed it down on top of all the others in my carrier bag and thought no more about it.

Until I got back to my room and started spreading out all the leaflets on my bed, to see whether any were likely to interest me. And there was the girl's flyer, proudly headed The Itty Bitty Titty Committee.

Now I accept that I'm not just slim. I'm flat-chested. I'm a 32AA if I bother measuring myself, but that is something I very rarely do. I never wear a bra, I don't even own one, and always buy children's sizes of clothing. I don't mind being flat; I've always had plenty of boyfriends who have clearly loved my shape with a fervour quite equal to that which others show for the Pamela Andersons of this world. Even so, I am a little self-conscious and I suppose I was somewhat indignant at the highly personal nature of the comment in this flyer. I was about to throw it straight in the bin when my eye was caught by the words 'Please don't throw this away. Please don't be offended.'

So I read on.

The Itty Bitty Titty Committee was apparently just a social group of girls who are all, as they proudly boasted, utterly flat-chested. Some girls, they recounted, could be embarrassed or ashamed of their lack of bosom and would often go to great lengths either to increase it, or conceal it or even, worst of all, conceal themselves out of a sense of inadequacy. The Itty Bitty Titty Committee was established to help and provide mutual support. In short, I had been assessed as potentially eligible and was invited to join.

I tore the leaflet into several small pieces, stuffed them into the bin, and continued sorting through the rest.

At bedtime, I undressed, pulling off the baggy sweater and T-shirt to stand in my room half naked. I looked at my reflection, at the deep dark nipples that projected a good half inch from my chest. But for them, I could have passed for a man. Even with them, you would have to look carefully. I passed my palm up over my skin and my nipples, always highly sensitive, immediately sprang up to a firm erection. I am proud of their sensitivity and I really am not ashamed of my lack of breasts, but sometimes I do wonder what it might be like to have a huge bosom thrusting out in front of me. It would just be so different.

I fished out the pieces of the flyer again. The first meeting of the year, to select a new President, Vice President and Secretary, was that Friday; new members should assemble at eight o'clock in the bar of the next door Hall. I threw it back in the bin, vowed not to go, and knew that I would.

There was no doubting that I had found the right venue. At eight o'clock girls started drifting into the bar; girls of all heights and colours, but all on their own and all with one thing in common. We smiled shyly at each other as we recognised others who had been similarly invited. We introduced ourselves, discussed where we came from, which courses we were studying, where we were living. None of us mentioned what we were doing there. At ten past eight, an older girl strode into the bar, introduced herself as Hannah and announced that we would now all move across to where she had booked a seminar room for the meeting.

Once we were all assembled in the stuffy little seminar room, the curtains had been tightly drawn, the door firmly shut and locked, I looked round at the circle of apprehensive faces. There were nine or ten of us, of whom all but two, Hannah and another, were clearly 'Freshers'. Hannah stood up again.

'Right, girls. Welcome to the first meeting of this year's Itty Bitty Titty Committee. As you will know, assuming you have read the invitation flyer, we have first to select the three officers of the Committee, so Angela here is going to pass round the voting papers. Before that, we have something much more important to do. We are all here because we are proud of our Itty Bitty Titties, so let's not hide them!'

Without any embarrassment, she simply peeled off her sweatshirt to reveal a chest as braless as mine and almost as flat. The other girl standing with her immediately followed suit and one by one most of the rest of us gingerly started to take off our own tops. I figured I had nothing to lose and so quietly slipped off my sweater and turned back to face the others. Eventually we had all stripped off and were sitting back in the circle of chairs with our tiny breasts on display. The room was warm – presumably Hannah had arranged for the heating to be turned up – but even so, I felt myself hardening as I became conscious of being so displayed in this circle.

Hannah took over again, smiling round at us all. 'That's it, girls. We are flat and we are proud! Now while the voting slips are passed round, I will explain how we select our officers in this Committee. It is very fair, very democratic and very simple. Since this club exists to celebrate our breasts, we choose our officers the same way. The one judged to have the smallest, cutest, sweetest boobs is President, second is Vice President; third is Secretary. In a moment we will go round and each state our names so that we can all enter a vote. First, please examine the contenders displayed all around you and make your decision. You are quite free to vote for yourself if you want to, but remember, we are principally selecting the smallest.'

I'm sure I wasn't the only one who blushed as we realised that all the other girls were now going to look at me and examine me. Better than that, we were all permitted, we had been instructed, to study the breasts displayed all around us. I glanced at the girl beside me and just failed to avoid catching her eye. We both blushed and quickly looked away, but her breasts were puffier than mine, with nipples so pale they were almost nonexistent. Hannah spoke again.

'Personally, I think mine look their best when my nipples are erect!' and with no shame, while we all sat round her and stared, she reached up to her own breasts and squeezed and turned the tiny nipples between her finger and thumb until the little buds became pointed and tighter. Even then, she continued gently caressing herself in her fingertips.

I found I was shivering inside, and before I knew what I was doing, I had reached up myself and palmed across my own breasts again and recognised my own nipples responding to the exposure, to the caress and, as I looked all around the circle, to the appreciation of the others watching me. I squeezed myself again, relishing and exalting in the admiration of everyone around me. Even Hannah was smiling across broadly at me, nodding.

'That's right. We should all be proud of ourselves, and proud of the very special assets we have. Now, for the nominations. I'll start. My name's Hannah; I am a 34A.'

We went round the circle introducing ourselves. As each girl spoke, we all looked at her face when she said her name, and we all looked at her breasts when she told us about them. When it came to my turn, and I knew everyone was concentrating on me, on my skinny chest and proud nipples, I was filled by an incredible urge to show them more. I wanted to strip off all my clothes and have them examine me entirely, fully and in exquisite tiny detail. I felt myself trembling and deliberately prolonged the moment by caressing my breasts again while they were all watching.

In the end, although many other girls had very attractive breasts, most of them were larger than mine, and only one other girl was a 32AA.

'Well,' Hannah continued when we had completed the circle. 'Now take a last look at the candidates and then cast your votes for the neatest, smallest, prettiest little breasts in the university.'

So we all again looked round us. Celia, the other 32AA, was blonde and sweetly angelic and I decided to vote for her. Her breasts were just as sweet as mine and her nipples looked so soft, round and pink that they should have belonged to a doll. If I had been that way inclined, I would have reached out to stroke them. Her thick blonde hair reached down below her breasts so that when she turned her head, it cascaded in a curtain across her chest covering her completely. On most girls, the breasts would have poked through the hair; with Celia they didn't and it was hypnotising to watch the way she kept shyly sweeping it back again and her almost childish breasts reappeared. She saw me watching her, staring, admiring and considering and she smiled with such sincere sweetness that I knew she would vote for me and I knew I should vote for her. Even so, I took the opportunity to consider all the other choices, and since Hannah set the lead by making no secret of her deliberations, indeed she blatantly walked round the circle, looking closely at all the other girls, I followed suit. It just seemed too good an opportunity to miss, since they were all there, waiting to be assessed and examined and until then I had never found an opportunity to compare my own tiny swellings with anyone else for fear of the mockery I expected. When I came round in front of Celia, I even reached up and touched her lightly, and felt warmed by her smile as her feather-like fingertips reached up to stroke me.

When all the votes were in and counted, Celia and I were tied for first place with three votes each, and two of the others had received one or two. I was wondering what would happen, but Hannah took charge again.

'As the outgoing President, I have a casting vote in case of a tie. So could Leanne and Celia come up in front.'

We stood up side by side and Hannah came round to examine us both. First she produced a tape and measured us each. She did Celia first, but with both of us, she took great care to lay the tape directly over our nipples and several times her fingers brushed against us as she worked. Twice she slipped her fingertips in under the tape and then slid them round against me, smiling as she felt my nipples' response to every tiny caress. Satisfied that we were both the size we claimed, she then turned her attention to our nipples. Again she started with Celia. However, this time she made no secret of squeezing, twisting and finally stroking and caressing her nipples as they steadily hardened under her fingers. By the time she was done, Celia's breath was beginning to sound laboured and little sighs were escaping from her slightly parted lips. Hannah's eyes softened as she watched the reaction that she was producing, and I saw her own legs twisting and her thighs unconsciously clamping together. Finally, with a last gentle stroke, she leaned forward and softly kissed each little pink peak before turning to me.

I was already aroused, not just by the exposure, the caresses I had given myself and the sensuality of being in an environment devoted solely to admiring our breasts, but on top of all that, by seeing the treatment that Celia had just received and knowing that I would get the same. I also knew that my breasts are exceptionally sensitive and it would not take much for me to climax. I trembled as Hannah stood up in front of me.

She smiled into my eyes and watched my reaction as I felt her soft cool fingers brush along the skin around my nipples and then simultaneously her fingertips drew the whole little point out into an achingly erect peak. She twisted gently and squeezed at me almost as if she were milking me, repeatedly drawing her fingers along the nipples as they swelled and darkened and ripened for her. I trembled again and felt a stirring deep down within me that she noticed too, and she smiled again. Then she pulled away and for a terrible moment, I thought she was done. However, she only moved round behind me so that her body was no longer concealing me from any of the others sitting in silent concentration round the room. Now she reached round to my front, giving herself full access to my breasts again as she lightly took hold of my nipples in her fingertips.

'You see, girls? The power contained in the smaller breast is many times greater than in those over-stuffed unsensitive pillows that we are told to admire.'

Then she ran her hands back up my chest, her thumbs gently rocking my nipples to and fro with each caress. Her fingers returned to pluck gently at the lengthening peaks and I twisted my legs together, desperately trying not to disgrace myself in front of so many people. It was no use, and Hannah was determined that I should reveal the full extent of my arousal. Her hands rippled across my skin, traced circles round the dark areolae, rubbed pleasure into my nerves and kept returning to pick teasingly, enticingly and gloriously at the very nipples, squeezing, turning and drawing them out. I struggled to keep my hands at my sides, though I desperately wanted to rip open my jeans and fill up the pleasure more directly. But Hannah would not leave me, would not let me, and though her action was now quite blatantly a caress, slowly she drew me on and on. Out of the corner of my eye, I saw Celia now openly stroking her own breasts, as she stared avidly at Hannah, at me and always at my thick dark nipples, shivering and trembling in the first small tremors. Seeing her watching me, seeing her arousal feeding off mine, was all it took to ignite the charge that had built with such power throughout the evening. The tremblings grew up somewhere deep inside me and washed up over me until I finally reached down to grasp my hungry sex, clutching at the sodden crotch of my jeans while a circle of girls watched me, and Hannah caressed me, teasing at my tiny breasts, flattening them against my ribs as the whole ecstasy engulfed me and rocked me and controlled me.

Eventually, Hannah came round and gently kissed each of my dark nipples as she had with Celia, but with me, she drew each momentarily into her mouth and I felt the tiny tip of her tongue swirl round for a second before I was released.

'Well, girls, my casting vote goes to Leanne for President.'

Malcolm's Tale – The Alvis

'Come on, mate. Fair's fair. You've been looking over the love of my life, haven't you? Now I get to have a little look as well, at the love of your life. I don't see no harm in that.'

'But that's ridiculous!' I protested. 'I was only looking over your car! Now you want to examine my wife! It's hardly the same thing!'

'It is to me, mate; it is to me. Still, don't worry; she won't be touched.'

I have always liked cars. Not the modern ones whose only aspiration is to greater economy, efficiency and safety. I like the classics, the real cars of the 1920s and '30s when motoring was new and exciting and exuberant; when people really knew what life was for. Sarah, my wife, shares my passion, and enjoys being admired when we drive out in an open sports car. She likes to dress for the period of the car, and when we bowled out in my 1937 MG TA across Salisbury Plain one Sunday last September, during a wonderful final touch of dying summer, Sarah was stretched out beside me looking radiant. She is slim, and in a short dress, with wisps of her thick raven black hair escaping from under the little cloche, she looked every inch the 1920s flapper. Her make-up was light but immaculate, her clothes perfectly arranged and every head turned as we drove by.

I know some husbands get jealous when they catch other men looking at their wives, but I don't. I know what they are all thinking as they ogle her, and I know what they are dreaming, but they'll never know and they'll never see, because she's my wife and we are utterly faithful to each other. What they don't know is that for all the demure innocence she radiates then, sometimes when we are in bed she likes me to use the crudest language imaginable and to treat her so roughly it's almost brutal. The contrast is inexplicable, and when it is over, she is sweetly and devastatingly embarrassed and refuses to talk about her behaviour. I love her all the more for her inconsistencies.

We stopped for a long slow lunch at a village pub lost somewhere in the narrow lanes and when we started off again, I pulled in at the little village garage for some petrol. They're thirsty beasts, the 1.3 litre MGs.

An attendant was there to work the pump, almost as rare as the car itself, and I could see he was working up to a comment. I'd have been disappointed if he had said nothing. 'Nice car. Don't see many like that these days.'

'No, they're getting quite hard to find.'

'Collector then, are you?'

'Not exactly a collector, but I have a few of the great classics and am always ready to snatch up another.'

'Oh. Right.' He watched in silence as the ancient dial clanked round another gallon. 'You might be interested in that thing young Jerry is selling. An Elvis or some such.'

'Alvis?'

'Yeah. Could be. Something like that. Not cheap mind. He wants a grand for it.'

'Ah. Is it a fairly new one?'

'No, mate. 'Fraid not. Bloody ancient. Used to belong to his dad.'

'Really?' My pulse was racing. 'Well, I suppose I might still be interested.'

'Hold on. I've got the details somewhere. He stuck an advert in the parish rag this week.'

The lad replaced the nozzle, wiped his hands on a cloth from which the frayed remnants of sleeves were still dangling, and I followed him into the workshop, picking my way between half a Land Rover, less of a tractor and some vast unidentifiable piece of agricultural machinery. My heart was beating a little faster. An Alvis? Could it be? For a thousand pounds?

'Yeah, here we are. Alvis 12/50. Don't mean nothing to me.'

I handed over my credit card for the petrol. 'Could I see?'

'Sure.' He offered me the paper. 'Sorry, mate, we don't take credit cards. Boss says the bloody banks charge too much. Have you got cash?'

This wasn't the moment to start explaining about the costs involved in credit card distribution or the massive fraud losses we had to stand and so I hurriedly pulled out some notes instead as I read through the small advertisement with growing excitement: 'Old car for sale. 1947 Alvis 12/50. Needs work. £1,000 or near offer.' This was even better: they had stopped making the 12/50s in 1932, so either the owner had got the type wrong, which was unlikely because it is emblazoned across the back, or the car was much older, and much more valuable, than he thought. I handed back the paper.

'Do you know where I might find this Jerry?'

'Jerry? Oh yeah. He keeps The Barleymow. Right at the next crossroads, and straight on past Lower Farm. He'll be there. Huge bloke; you can't miss him.'

The description was right. The pub too was impossible to miss. Once an appealing country inn, it now displayed banners outside offering 'Quiz Nites' and wide-screen sports. Inside, its original character had been smothered with artificial horse brasses and country utensils. As for Jerry himself, well, admittedly there were only three other customers in the pub, all of whom turned to stone and stared as we came through the door, but even if there had been a hundred, Jerry would have been unmistakable. He was well over six foot tall and almost as much broad. Yet his voice as he took our order was soft and mocking, as if he knew that he did not need to be polite, that his size and strength gave him the right to behave exactly as he pleased.

While he poured Sarah's wine spritzer, I asked him about the car, whether it was still for sale, whether I could have a look at it. He displayed little interest in my request, but led me out to a dilapidated timber barn at the back of the pub. The huge wooden door was not even locked, and he pulled it open with one hand, allowing shafts of light to pierce the dismal interior. The dust was thick and swirling, the contrast between the bright autumn sun and the fetid darkness was blinding, the few beams of light were totally inadequate but the moment I stepped through the door, I had seen enough. I had to have the car. I almost screamed out my acceptance at him at once but managed to control my enthusiasm sufficiently to ask a few questions whose answers I already knew or already knew to be irrelevant. After an age of examination of the bodywork, of the engine, of the upholstery, of the whole glorious vision of engineering wonder, I told him I'd take it if we could agree on a price.

'Well all right. Only there's this bloke from Reading, see? Said he'd come out today and take a look. Sounded very keen, he did. Said he'd pay the price in full, without even seeing it, he did.'

I hid my expression in an examination of the magnificent proud headlamps; the glass wasn't even scratched. I could well imagine he would pay the full asking price. So would I. I'd pay five times his price, and I would have guessed my rival would as well. I saw Jerry's eyes narrowing as he considered the lie of the land. It was tempting to offer double, but that might have made him suspicious, and I decided on caution.

'Look, Jerry. I'll be fair. I'll pay you twelve hundred on the nail.'

'Cash?' He was quick on the uptake.

'All right. Cash.' I offered my hand to seal the deal but he was not completely in the landing net, and he looked down at my outstretched arm with suspicion.

'You show me the money. Then I'll shake your hand.' He started to head back towards the back door of the pub.

'Well, I don't have it here.'

'Ah!' Jerry seemed to have been expecting that I would turn out to be just talk, and having no cash immediately available was obviously a major crime in Jerry's eyes.

'I'll go and get it straightaway. I can get down to Amesbury and get cash from the machine.'

'You can get a grand out of a cash machine?' His disbelief was undisguised and I could feel my status crumbling by the second.

'I can!' I cried. 'I work for the bank and I have a special card. Just don't sell the car till I get back.'

I was calling desperately at his huge broad back as he pushed open the back door into the narrow passage that led through to the back of the bar. I trailed along behind like an obedient puppy.

'And if the gent from Reading turns up?' Jerry asked over his shoulder. 'What do I tell him? That I might have sold it to a bloke who might have the money but has gone off to get it and might come back?'

'I'll leave a deposit.' As we reached the bar and returned to our respective sides, I vaguely took in the same three customers there. Two were now playing darts and the third was perched on a stool up at the bar, his backside overflowing it on all sides, but the stillness and studied casualness in their manners reminded me of guilty schoolboys. Sarah had taken a seat at a small table in the window, and although her drink looked to be untouched, yet she looked flushed, so that I wondered for a moment if she had already finished one and was on a second.

I dismissed all this and turned back to Jerry. I fished out my wallet and flashed it open, seeing immediately the solitary ten-pound note that was all it now contained. His hawklike gaze missed nothing, but I flustered on.

'Plus,' I added, 'plus my watch.' I took this off and laid it on the bar. He picked it up, sniffed at it and laid it back down again.

'You telling me that this tenner and a second-hand watch is worth a grand? 'Cos they don't look like it to me. Nowhere near.'

'No, I mean this would just be a deposit. Just to show I'm serious.'

'How serious, though? Eh? A tenner's worth?'

'I'll see what my wife has with her.'

I didn't have high hopes and these dropped even lower when she offered up the dainty period handbag. She had no more than a little loose change.

'Look,' I said, and turned to Jerry again, feeling a thousand eyes staring as Jerry reached up casually to help himself from one of the optics ranged behind the bar, 'my wife will leave her handbag here, as security. You can hardly think we wouldn't return if she left that.'

Jerry peered down at the little black leather bag sitting forlornly on the bar; it was smaller than his fist. 'What would I do with a handbag?'

'All right, and her coat.' I picked it up from the chair and laid it on the bar. 'That's real fur, worth several hundred pounds!'

He shook his head slowly. 'Not much call for fur coats out here, mate. Not even if they're real fur, worth several hundred pounds.'

I had nothing else to offer, but Sarah piped up, 'I could wait here. Just to show good faith. I mean then you'd know Malcolm was going to come back.'

Jerry looked up then, as a horrible leer started to seep across his face. He peered over at Sarah, even craning across the bar to get a better view right down to her shoes. 'OK,' he said finally. 'OK, you're on. Leave her. As a deposit.'

'Right,' I said, trying to keep the jubilation out of my voice. 'I won't be more than forty-five minutes; an hour at the most.'

I turned to go when Jerry called out again. 'Here! You can take all this.' He nodded down at the watch, the handbag, the coat all lined up along the bar. 'I don't want none of them. Just leave your wife. Yeah, just her.'

I gathered all our things off the bar but Jerry stopped me again. 'You can take all the rest of her clobber, too. Just leave her.'

The whole bar fell silent as I tried to work out what he was getting at. The two darts players stopped their game and walked slowly up to the bar, like cowboys in an old western when a gun fight has been challenged. They clustered round the third one, the oldest of the three, on his stool.

Jerry picked up his glass again, drained it and turned back to his range of optics. 'Just her. You can take her clothes with you.'

'What do you mean?' But I had a sickening feeling that I knew.

'Come on, mate. Fair's fair. You've been looking over the love of my life, haven't you? Now I get to have a little look as well, at the love of your life. I don't see no harm in that.'

'But that's ridiculous!' I protested. 'I was only looking over your car! Now you want to examine my wife! It's hardly the same thing!'

'It is to me, mate; it is to me. Still, don't worry; she won't be touched. Least, not unless she asks us.'

The outrageousness of his suggestion left me groping for an adequate response until the silence was broken by the phone behind the bar. I watched mesmerised as Jerry answered it, the receiver no more than a toy in his huge hand. He turned to face me as he spoke to the caller.

'Oh yes. I remember. Well, yeah, I think it's still available. There's a bloke here just thinking it over but I don't think he's serious.'

I interrupted. 'I am serious. Very serious.'

Jerry sniffed. 'Well, to be fair, he's serious, but he don't have no money with him and don't seem able to leave a deposit.' He was staring at me, challenging me, as he spoke and I racked my brain to come up with some way of clinching the deal.

Jerry was still speaking. 'Yep, that's right. Well, this bloke said he'd give twelve hundred, but I want cash.'

I was suddenly aware of Sarah standing up. Without a word, she drained her white wine and placed the glass down squarely in the centre of the bar, directly in front of where Jerry was standing. Then she leaned down, took off one shoe and placed it next to the glass. The other shoe joined it and then she slowly unwound the long scarf from her neck and laid that out across the polished surface of the bar.

Jerry's eyes did not leave Sarah as he grumbled slowly into the phone, 'Sorry mate, it's sold,' and replaced the receiver.

'Sarah? What are you doing?' I choked out.

She turned her gaze on me, calm, almost serene. 'Don't you want the car?' and she reached round to start tugging down the zip at the back of her dress.

I have watched Sarah reveal that glorious slim figure hundreds, maybe thousands of times in the years we have been together, and I suppose some of the novelty has gone. However, never before has there been anyone else in the room with us while she undressed, and never before has there been such an atmosphere of tense anticipation. This time was utterly different and I was watching her with as much rapt attention as any of the other four. I was no longer her husband. Now I was just one more in a crowd of leering men, watching as a beautiful woman took off her clothes in a public bar, as one by one, her coverings were stripped away, laid out on the bar and more of her was revealed.

There was an intake of breath as the short dress was slipped down over her shoulders, revealing a little pale cream slip and below this the tops of her stockings.

There was silence as each stocking was peeled down her long legs, shaken out and then stretched across the bar.

There was an uneasy shuffling of feet when she paused after that, standing terrified in the centre of the circle of probing, devouring eyes. The others all assumed there were still several articles of underwear, but I knew she had only two items left, knew how much would be revealed when she took the next step. The three customers had started creeping closer, but still she faltered, and in total silence we all watched and waited with her. I began to wonder if she had changed her mind, if she would be able to go through with this at all, and I honestly didn't know whether I wanted her to continue or not.

Finally her fingers twitched and then reached down to the hem of her loose slip. She inched it slowly up her legs and when it was at her waist, bunched up the whole thing and swept it up her body. Not until she started to lift it over her head, did her eyes turn to me and I saw the trembling terror in that instant before her face was lost in the folds of material. She turned to the bar as she laid this on top of her dress, and then stood straight, turning to face the three men at the other end of the bar, turning so that the gentle swelling of her tiny breasts was briefly silhouetted against the light.

After a second's pause, one of the darts players burst out laughing: 'Bloody hell! Look at her! She ain't got no tits at all. Here, Jerry, you've been done, mate. She ain't a woman at all!'

Sarah blushed crimson. It is true that she has only the smallest, sweetest breasts, little more than proud nipples on a slightly swollen chest, but I have always loved her for them, loved their sensitivity and resilience and the readiness with which they erect under the lightest caress. Now she pulled her shoulders in, hunching up to protect her beautiful little breasts from the derision of the grinning man.

Her eager brown nipples pushed out hard and erect as she withstood the scrutiny of the surrounding eyes.

Jerry smirked and made his way round to our side of the bar.

'Now, now, Trigger. That's no way to speak to a lady. Besides, we'll know if she's a real woman soon enough, won't we? Once she takes off those knickers. Then we'll see, won't we? You *are* going to take off your pretty little knickers for us, aren't you, love?'

In the short silence Sarah glanced round the circle of impatient faces before she nodded slightly.

'That's a good girl. Well then. Come on. Don't keep us waiting.'

Sarah licked her lips, her head held high, and then her hands moved up, hooked into the waistband of her knickers and she pushed them down her legs, bending right over and lifting each foot in turn before standing proudly naked as she laid the minute garment on top of the pile. She turned to face her critic again and he could not doubt her sex now. I was glad that her pubic hair is so dark and thick that she could retain some semblance of modesty.

Not a word was said, but when Jerry craned round to get a better view, Sarah brazenly turned to face him full on, giving him the benefit of an uninterrupted view of her body. His eyes narrowed, and he shook his head.

'Bit difficult to tell, really. Hell of a lot of hair down there. Could be hiding anything. I think we'd better have you up on the bar, so as we can get a proper look.'

Without another word his huge hands circled Sarah's slim waist and he lifted her up bodily as if she were no more than a child to sit her on the bar. The fat darts player was still dwelling on his disappointment.

'Nice enough arse, but pity she's got no tits. I like a woman with a decent pair of tits.' His mumbles were almost lost in the beer glass he held to his mouth.

His former opponent, a much younger man, barely into his twenties, tall and skinny with long lank hair hanging down his back, pushed his way to the front. He came up right in front of her.

'Oh, I don't know. I like all sorts and I have always had rather a soft spot for flat-chested girls. These are really quite cute in their own way. What's more,' and he glared defiantly at Sarah, 'I'll bet they'd perk up damn quick if I stroked them, wouldn't they?'

Jerry quickly stepped in. 'Now hold on, Danny. You know what we said. We wouldn't touch the lady. Unless she asked us.'

The third man slid off his stool and started up the bar towards us. 'Oh, she's asking for it. Clear as day, she's asking for it.' He turned to face Sarah. 'You wouldn't mind if young Danny had a quick feel of your lovely little tits, would you?'

We all waited silently while she fumbled for an answer, waiting to hear how she would react to this. Still, the man was entirely confident what her answer would be and when she finally nodded dumbly, he pressed on.

'You sure that would be all right? If he has a feel of your little titties? Pinch your nipples perhaps? That all right with you, is it?'

Sarah did not raise her head but she nodded again and we all heard her whispered 'yes'.

The man was triumphant. 'Good. That's very good, my dear. Only will you do something for me? Will you ask him to feel you? Because Jerry did promise your husband that we'd only touch you if you asked, so it'd be best if it was you that asked, not me.'

Sarah raised her head, glancing round at us all for an instant, but finally her attention came back to me, and although she said nothing, I could not mistake the desperate craving in that expression. Her gaze held mine as she spoke to the man.

'Yes, please. Please feel my breasts. Please pinch my nipples.'

'There you are, Danny!' said the man as he stepped back to let the lad through. 'She's all yours.'

Danny said nothing, just grinned eagerly as his long scrawny fingers lifted up and covered her tiny breasts. I heard her suck in her breath as he pressed down on the tender flesh and squeezed, massaging slowly and deliberately in steady circles over her chest. At last the long firm nipples were allowed to spring out from between his fingers and he smiled at her, as he rolled the tips of her nipples in his finger and thumb. Finally he released her, as Jerry finished his drink and almost elbowed the young lad aside.

'Very nice, my dear. Very nice indeed. Still, the question that Trig was worried about was if you really are a woman? I think we really need to get a better look at what you might have hidden away under all that hair. Because frankly, my love, we can't see a fucking thing, if you'll pardon my language.'

Amid the low laugh that greeted this comment, Jerry looked round the bar, surprised to see me still there. 'Right, my friend,' he said. 'Your wife has kept her side. Now, off you go and hurry back with the money. All right? Oh, and don't forget to take these,' and he picked up the pile of her clothes and held them out to me. 'That'll remind you not to take too long. Don't worry. We'll look after her.'

I automatically accepted the bundle he handed me, but could not move, simply could not make my muscles react. I just stood, rejected and powerless, watching this appalling scene unfolding in front of me.

Jerry had turned to Sarah again without waiting for my response. 'Now then, where were we? Oh yes, we were just going to have a little look between your legs, weren't we? Now then, spread yourself open for me, and let's have a look at this little fanny of yours, shall we?'

She did not look up, and although she hesitated a second, I soon saw her inch her thighs apart.

Jerry rested his huge fists on the bar either side of her. They were so close that he could, if he'd wanted to, have poked out his thumbs and touched her thighs. Yet he didn't touch her, didn't press or force her; he just advised, persuaded and cajoled.

'Oh, a bit more than that, love. You could show us a little bit more than that, couldn't you? Tell you what. Shove back a bit and bring your feet up on to the bar. That'll be easier for you.'

He moved those huge hands back up to her slender waist again and pushed her back across the polished surface of the bar. She seemed to need no further encouragement to raise her feet either side of her, and then, with a sound like a low sloppy sigh as her lips peeled apart, allowed her thighs to fall open.

We were all drawn to the glistening pink crease that was at last revealed. For all of us, the sight was hypnotic: for the other four men because they had never seen her puss before: for me, because I could not remember ever seeing her so wet, so swollen and so utterly ripe. Her thick full lips were round and puffed and the glistening beads on her soft black down proof of her arousal.

Danny was craning over Jerry's shoulder all the while and as Sarah's legs were finally drawn apart, he could see her full beauty revealed. The young boy had never seen anything to equal her.

'Bloody heck! Take a look at this, lads! Piss flaps like barn doors, she's got! Bloody enormous!'

'Ah, my dear. Very lovely. Quite the prettiest thing I have seen on my bar since I don't know when. Now then, you won't mind if I just probe inside there a little later on, will you?' Even as he spoke, his hands were slipping down her thighs but they stopped when his fingertips were just touching the soft ends of her hair. 'Well, my dear? Are you going to ask me to do that?'

'Yes,' she whispered, her head hung in shame.

'Go on, then. Ask me.'

'Please will you probe inside me.'

'Inside you? Inside where?'

She didn't look up but answered obediently. 'My vagina. Inside my vagina.'

She blushed at the jeering laughter of the men listening. Even Jerry joined in. 'I'm sorry, lady, but we're not all posh round here, and we don't use words like that. Not round here we don't. I reckon you mean your cunt, don't you? 'Cos if so, that's what you ought to say.'

Sarah didn't move at first but then took a long breath. 'Please will you probe inside my cunt.'

'Good girl!' and Jerry took his hands away from her. 'In a minute I will do just that for you. Seeing as you asked so nicely.'

I could still not fathom what was happening, still struggled to find a base, a course, a solid ground to reconcile the unbelievable turn that events had taken. Finally I turned to Sarah for help. 'Sarah?'

Her words tumbled thickly from her mouth, as if she were drunk. 'It's all right, Malcolm. I'll be fine.'

Jerry grinned at me, then he stretched over for the wine bottle and started to refill Sarah's glass. 'Of course you will, my love. Of course you will. Here, have one on the house. As for you, mister, you might as well go and get the money. The sooner you get it, the sooner you can have the little lady back.'

He turned to argue again with the fat darts player, who was still complaining about the size of Sarah's breasts, and the older man, who was now wanting a better look at her bottom. I heard Jerry talking to her again.

'Come along then, love. You wouldn't mind doing that for old Charlie, would you? Just turn round, kneel across the bar and open your cheeks up. Let him have a good close look at your arsehole. Bit of a pervert is our Charlie, but he's harmless really.'

It was too late for any of us to turn back, but I could stand no more. I grabbed the bundle of clothes and made for the door, frantically locking out Jerry's soft mocking voice as he taunted my sweet wife still further. I threw the clothes down on the passenger seat and jumped into the car, determined to be back within the hour. As I roared out of the pub car-park and down the narrow lanes, my horn sounding at every bend to warn any others on the road that I was coming through and would give way to no one, I contemplated my revenge. Once I had the Alvis, once it was mine, properly registered and all the paperwork completed, then I would go back and tell the man what it was really worth. Then he could sneer if he wanted to, once he knew how many thousands of pounds he had lost.

As I threw the MG out in a wide turn on to the A303, the pile of Sarah's clothes tumbled off the seat and lay accusingly on the floor. I closed my mind to thoughts of the humiliations that she must have been enduring, focusing only on getting into Amesbury as soon as I could. All the same, visions kept flashing through my mind; horrifying pictures of the torments and abuse that she might be subjected to, so that I had to concentrate on the driving to avoid an accident and also to try to prevent myself being tortured even further by my own imagination. What could they do, with her left so nakedly available? What would they *not* do? What would any man do, presented with such a rare and unforeseen opportunity?

In the centre of Amesbury I found the bank and pulled up on the yellow lines in front, not bothering to turn off the engine or close the car door as I stuffed my card into the machine and drummed impatiently on the front while it read the embedded chip and asked for the PIN number. I tapped this in, the full six figure version which lets me access the special privileges.

'Please wait . . .' the screen said. Then 'Please refer to your local branch' and the security screen slid down over the keyboard.

I shouted at the machine, pounded on the wall, hammered at the screen, but dimly behind the scratched glass the display alternated between offering me cheap holiday insurance and asking the next customer to insert his card. I practically wept.

What options did I have? I had no other bank cards with me, knew nowhere I could get that much cash from my remaining credit card. If I returned with nothing and offered Jerry a cheque now, he'd laugh in my face. If I went home I could fetch Sarah's card but she didn't work for the bank; her card only allowed her £250. All I could do would be to go back to Jerry, suffer his mockery and beg him to take £2,000 tomorrow. Surely he'd take that. And I hadn't even thought about Sarah. I couldn't leave her in that place with those foul men for another minute. I jumped back into the car and pulled it through a squealing U-turn.

The pub door was locked, although the orange glow of the bar lights was visible inside and I could hear music and roars of laughter. When I hammered furiously on the door, Jerry finally appeared, his casual smirk even broader than before, and opened the door to me.

'Ah! Back again. Somehow I thought you wouldn't be long.'

I didn't answer but pushed straight past him into the bar, expecting to see Sarah still sitting where I had left her on the bar. She was not there. Instead, just where she had been sitting, stood a wine bottle and glasses and some other stuff that I neither noticed nor cared about.

'Where's my wife? Where's Sarah?'

The man they had called Trigger craned round from one of the little booths. 'She's a bit busy just now, mate. Got her hands full, as you might say.'

I stumbled round to the booth and there she was, kneeling on the floor between the man's thighs. As I approached, she pulled away from him, settling down on her thighs, and revealed the man behind her.

He was sitting on a low bench against the wall, his coarse shirt unbuttoned to the waist exposing a huge sallow beer-belly speckled with greying hairs. His thick corduroy trousers were unfastened and these, together with a baggy pair of off-white underpants were pulled down almost to his ankles, revealing his vast white flabby thighs. Yet he was entirely unashamed, uncaring that his erect penis was fully visible and making no effort to cover himself up. If anything he was proud of the sight, and as I looked down at his groin, it was all too horrible, too sickeningly clear why he showed no guilt.

Rearing up out of the thick forest of ginger pubic hair was the biggest penis that I have ever seen on any human being.

Not only long, at least half as long again as mine, but so thick that I found myself wondering whether he could get his hand round it. Yet even as I watched, he took hold of Sarah's hair and used this to rock her head against his erection, then took hold of his cock in his own huge fist, knowing I was watching him, and rubbed the thick round end against her cheek before he pushed her head further down against his scrotum. Her dainty pale hand was resting on his thigh, and although she moved up and gripped the base of his erection, her fingers curled barely half way round it. Her face was half buried in his thick ginger curls, but I saw her tongue emerge and lick at his heavy testicles, round and pink and as large as eggs. He continued to hold her there, lapping obediently at him while he gripped her hair and grinned up at me, mocking the horror that must have been so utterly plain in my face.

When finally he released her, she turned to me again, an expression of shamed penitence on her face but behind that, simmering and about to burst out, was a look of almost pure ecstasy in her eyes.

I finally tore my eyes away from her face, the smudged make-up, the bedraggled hair and was even more appalled by the sight of the rest of her.

She was kneeling on the floor, facing into the corner, but as she saw me staring at her, she shuffled round until her round bottom was facing directly towards me. Her skin, so fair and pale, was smeared with dirt, with soot and streaks of mud. Her bottom, her glorious creamy bottom, was creamy no more. It was glowing pink, clearly marked with two huge prints of a man's hand, one covering the whole of each round cheek. But worse even than that, a glistening wet trail was smeared incriminatingly down the back of her thigh, a trail which started not from her pussy, but from her anus.

Jerry called to me from behind the bar. 'Come and have a drink, mate. On me. You look as if you could do with one. Trig's just finishing his second turn, then she'll be done. Give 'em a minute and have a drink.'

In a daze, I groped my way back to the bar and collapsed on to a stool next to where the other two men sat grinning while Jerry began clearing the space in front of me.

He delicately picked up a ball of black fluff from off the bar. 'Sorry about that,' he said, holding it between finger and thumb before dropping it into a bin behind the bar. 'We had to give her a bit of a hair cut, as you might say. Hope you don't mind, but young Danny there couldn't see a thing.'

It was only then that I took in fully the implication of the clutter in front of me: a pair of scissors; a video camera; an empty wine bottle whose elegant brown neck glistened in the bar spotlights. Jerry glanced sheepishly down at the other two men as he picked that up. 'Yeah, that was Danny as well. For a young 'un, he's got quite an imagination, that lad.'

This left only a lager glass, with quarter of a pint or so left in the bottom.

'Oh yeah, that's hers too. She had a bet with Charlie that she could fill it right up. 'Fraid she lost; it's not even halfway.' He emptied the glass out into the sink. 'Now then. You were drinking Export, weren't you?'

He pulled the pint and handed it across to me. 'We were just about to watch a film that I think you might enjoy. You'll know everyone in it, specially the star.' He turned towards the darker end of the bar where muffled sighs and slurps were still coming from the booth.

'You not done yet, Trig? Get on with it, mate, we want to watch this film and it'll be time to open up again in a minute.'

A minute or two later, the man called Trigger came sauntering down towards us and perched himself on a stool at the end of the bar. He was followed by Sarah.

I have never seen her looking worse. As she walked towards me, the most obvious thing was the loss of what had always been such a pride to her, her thick neat triangle of pubic hair. Instead, her belly looked like a badly plucked chicken. A few straggling tufts still remained, but the thick crease was visible, and her long floppy inside lips, hanging down between her thighs. Her thighs themselves were spattered with wet flecks that I didn't dare try to identify. Her tiny breasts were pink and bruised, with deep red finger marks all round the nipples. Her face was shining and similarly spattered, as was her hair: bedraggled and hanging loose round her shoulders. I had never known her look such a mess, nor so radiantly alluring. I didn't know whether to kiss her or push her outside and turn a hose on her.

'All set, then?' Jerry asked brightly, turning to push a cassette into a machine behind him and the huge screen above the bar flickered into life and then settled down to a scene, dark and shaky, of the inside of the pub.

'There!' said the young lad next to me proudly, and he actually nudged me. 'That's me!'

The camera pans down to show Sarah on her knees in front of him, and although we can see only the back of her head, it's obvious from her movements that she has his cock in her mouth. She looks up and, in response to a barely audible call from off screen, turns to face the camera. Her whole face is splattered with semen, not just across her cheeks, but right up to her forehead, and dripping down into her eyes.

'God, she's filthy!' Jerry's voice sounds very close; he is obviously the one holding the camera. 'Just look at her! Running with the stuff.'

123

In the background, the oldest one, who I had worked out is called Charlie, drains the last of his beer and stands up, hitching his tatty grey trousers round his belly. 'You know, lads? I think I can help her out there. After four pints, I think I know how to hose her down.' He leads her out through the rear door and the screen goes blank.

When the film restarts, it shows Charlie reappearing through the same door. He is followed by Sarah and, as she emerges from the back of the pub, the camera homes in on her face, clean now, but still visibly wet. In fact her hair is drenched and matted against her head, her skin is shining in the bar lights and so too are her eyes: shining with an intensity that I have never seen before. As the camera pans down her body, we see that her pubic bush is already gone.

'That's better!' crows Charlie. 'And at least it wasn't all wasted. Now, who was next? You've only had the one go, haven't you, Jerry?'

She is lying on the floor when Jerry comes over again. Slowly he unfastens his trousers, lowers them to his ankles and then carefully stands with his feet either side of her head. He slowly squats down directly over her face.

'Can you see all right from there, love?'

Sarah's whispered confirmation is only just audible.

'Can you see my arse?'

Again she whispers that she can.

'Well, give it a nice licking then, love. I like that.'

Sarah's disgust was evident, but she did not hesitate for long before extending her tongue and lifting her head a few inches until her nose and mouth were lost in the crease of his backside.

I glanced away from the screen and over to Sarah, who looked over to me at the same time, waiting anxiously for my reaction to this obscene display of her degradation and willing acquiescence. I knew only one way to express my feelings and I called her over to my side. She stood up, and walked across, watched by me and watched by the other four as well.

Then I turned her round, and made her bend over the nearest table, squashing her plump nipples down on the wooden surface. I stood up, took down my own trousers and, despite the four men watching us, pushed my erection deep into her soaking pussy. How much of the thick lubricant that still ran from her was her juice and how much had come from one or even several of the other men, I neither knew nor cared. Instead, as the others watched us, jeered and mocked, I rammed into her. I reached round to grip her beautiful tiny breasts and reached down to feel the stubbly nakedness of her roughly shorn belly and the thick erect nub of her clitoris that was now so accessible and practically visible. It was all too good and too much.

My own climax was pathetically soon, miserably weak and clearly quite inadequate for her, for as soon as she felt me ejaculate deep inside her, she let out a low moan of disappointment and pushed me away. I was left standing alone in the middle of the floor as the last few forlorn spurts dribbled out onto the pub floor.

I was utterly dejected. And when I looked up, to see Trigger again making his way down towards us, his monstrous thick penis poking out of his trousers and waving excitedly in the air, I was shamefully excited to know that he was going to take my place and fill her to the brim, stretching her sweet young body to the limit.

We all watched as he turned her over and stretched her face upwards over the table. He caught both her wrists in his left hand and held them above her head while he pushed her legs wide apart again with his right. His erection was bobbing at the top of her thighs, its great round head knocking for entrance between her loose puffy lips and he took hold of the thing and fed it inside her. We all watched. The others even cheered as a strangled cry was torn from her when he pushed it home and then started a slow steady thrusting that shook her slim body. Sarah's wrists were still held tight but the man brought his free hand up to smother her little breasts and to paw at her nipples, as he grunted and battered his way into her.

Glistening tears ran down Sarah's cheeks with every brutal thrust of the man's hips but her real reaction to being so completely filled was betrayed by her flushed cheeks, her sighs and half-stifled sobs. 'Oh God! Oh God! Oh God!'

Suddenly her persecutor stopped and pulled back, almost withdrew from her entirely and paused. Though she lifted her hips up to him, squealing for more, still he paused a moment and then rammed himself back home in a swift ferocious plunge that tore another scream from her lips before her whole body shuddered under the onslaught of his pounding thrusts, her head shaking from side to side like a dog and she let out a single long wail as she climaxed. Satiated at last, Trig pulled away, wiped the glistening end of his cock against her leg and then stuffed it back inside his pants. He returned to his stool at the bar, refastening his corduroys and buckling his thick leather belt as he went. I followed and climbed back on to my stool.

'Right then!' Jerry was as bright and cheerful as ever. 'Just let's sort out the money and then you can have the car. In fact I'll even throw in a copy of that video for nothing. Can't say fairer than that, now, can I?'

His words brought me back to earth and to the dreadful sordid reality of our situation. I took a deep breath and explained the business with the cash machine. Initially Jerry looked angry, but then he started to grin and recited all the sarcastic comments I had anticipated during the long drive back: the advantages of having one of these special cards from the bank, and how wonderful the cash machines are. I listened in silence.

'Well, never mind, mate,' he said at the end. 'Nothing's lost. I've got that video, and it'll be a big hit with the lads on quiz night, that will. And there's still that other bloke wants to buy the car.'

This was the final straw. To have suffered so much and then not even get the car was too much. 'Oh no! You can't do that. I'll have the money tomorrow. I can be here by ten o'clock with fifteen hundred pounds in cash.'

He considered me a moment and shook his head. 'Yes, but will you? That's the question. I mean tomorrow's tomorrow, isn't it? You might decide not to bother.'

'Believe me. I'll be here. You can bet your life on that. With fifteen hundred pounds.'

'Well, I dunno. I suppose maybe I could agree to that.' He was still not entirely convinced. 'But you'd have to leave a deposit. Just overnight until tomorrow. Now then, what did we decide you had worth leaving as a deposit?'

Naomi's First Tale – Stags

The sharp gravel dug into the soles of my feet as I
pelted across the car park; I did think they would
have allowed me shoes even if nothing else. My lungs
were on fire so that however deep I tried to suck in
air, there was no oxygen; my thighs felt so tight that
I was sure the muscles would never relax again; the
stitch in my side was threatening to split my skin wide
open at every step; my breasts, ample even at that
age and not used to being unsupported let alone
naked, were bruised as they shook and bounced with
every jarring stride; my ears burned with the jeers
and calls of the onlookers, filling the alleys, hanging
from every window that I passed and, as I finally
came in sight of the entrance to my own block,
crowding so thickly round the doorway that I had to
fight my way through them, pushing past several
cameras, brushing aside the hands that reached out to
pinch, slap or simply grope at my sweaty nakedness.
Up the last few stairs, lined on either side with
grinning leering faces, not all of them male: some
from my hall, some from my classes, but mostly
people I had never seen before but who had now seen
me, seen all of me: people who had heard about my
dare or seen the notice that Gary had put up in the
Student Union Bar. My own door came in sight and

I pushed through, slipped the catch and slammed it shut behind me.

Finally I could stop, could collapse on the bed and let my chest heave at the blessed air, every muscle quivering with the exertion. I clapped my hands over my face and ignored the gleeful pounding on my door.

'Naomi? Bet you can't run back!' Their laughter was childish.

Yet the bet itself had been childish, and I should have known that at the time, probably would have done if I had been a bit more sober. A bit less sober and I could have brushed the whole thing aside as a drunken joke, but I had been in that dangerous middle ground between the two, where I knew what I was doing, but not why I was doing it. Too many people had heard my boast for me to be able simply to back out. Gary had done his streak; done it in daylight, with witnesses, all as we had agreed. However, he had done it at 9 a.m. on a Sunday morning, for heaven's sake. How many people are around at that hour? Accusing him of cheating was foolish, because it meant I could not now do the same. I had to play by the spirit, to emphasise how he had only played by the letter.

And I did. I did not chicken out, even after all that publicity. I slipped my hands down my heaving sweaty chest, across my erect nipples and down to the damp hair at the top of my legs: hair which only that morning I had, in a last defiant act of brazen exhibitionism, trimmed disgustingly close to my skin.

And as my teenage years passed I met Alec, who was wonderful and loved me and respected me and treated me well. I fell in love and got married and settled down and had a good job and although I kept

129

on my little furnishing shop, I found someone else to run it while I concentrated more on designing and worked from home.

And Alec was a careful, attentive and considerate lover.

And still the memory of that summer evening stayed with me, and I told nobody about it, certainly not Alec, but I fantasised about it and tried to find ways I could re-create the whole atmosphere: the nakedness; the taunts of the onlookers; the humiliation of being the only one; the glory of being the centre of attention. I tried to relive it; tried all the usual corny tricks. I let lorry drivers in traffic jams see my underwear; I would still be in my dressing gown when the postman called, and a few times, when the need was particularly strong, I would accidentally lean forward to let him see down my dressing gown. It was all so pathetic and wimpish and cheap and nowhere near enough.

And even though I had failed, I was still utterly ashamed of myself afterwards, so disgusted and humiliated that I found silly ways to punish myself. I made myself wait all day before I permitted myself to go to the loo. I made myself have cold baths. Once, after watching a programme about medieval monasteries, I whipped myself across the bottom with a belt.

And then the fancy dress party, when I persuaded Alec to go as an Arabian prince, and he joked that if he did, I would have to go as a harem girl. And I had got our costumes ready and mine was so sheer it was magnificent, and then at the last moment Alec's mother was ill and we couldn't go.

And then Alec came home from a conference a full day early and found me. In the living room. On the floor. Naked. Completely utterly naked. I had taken off my watch, my crucifix, my wedding ring.

Everything. As naked as the day I was born. I wasn't masturbating; that is I hadn't started, but I couldn't conceal what I had been planning to do.

And Alec simply stood by the door, fully dressed, and made me carry on while he watched. He didn't interrupt me, didn't join me or show any reaction. Only when I was done, he made me crawl across the floor to him on my hands and knees, still naked, and he didn't even bother to undress, but he made me take his penis out of his suit trousers, and lick him until he climaxed in my mouth. And he made me swallow it. And then he made me spend the rest of the evening naked. While I cooked the supper. While I washed up. While he watched television. He made me lie on the floor in front of him with my legs apart. He made me. He made me.

And when we went to bed that night he wasn't careful or attentive or considerate. He was selfish and brutal and magnificent. He called me a slut and a tart and I agreed. He made me lick him again, and lick his anus.

This was all new; this wasn't us; we didn't have sex like that; what we did was make love. We did it properly, romantically and slowly, and we had always been like that. Now suddenly in one evening everything had changed and I wanted to talk about it, to discuss what was happening to us, but Alec didn't give me the chance. The next morning, a Friday, when the cold light of day shone in through our bedroom window, we were both quiet, perhaps even ashamed.

He rang from the office at lunchtime. 'Have you done the weekend shopping yet?'

'Yes.' He knew I always did it on Friday morning.

'Good. Are you dressed?'

'Yes! Of course!' Only it wasn't really 'of course', because when he'd come home yesterday, I hadn't been.

'Right. Take your clothes off. Ring me back when you have.' He hung up.

I hesitated and considered and worried and finally undressed. I folded the clothes neatly on the seat of the chair and then phoned him, certain that his secretary knew I was naked: you could hear the scorn in her voice.

'Alec? I've done that.'

'Everything?'

'Yes.'

'Right. You'll be staying like that until Monday morning. I may be home at the usual time. I may be late. I may be there in half an hour, but I'll expect to find you naked.' He hung up again.

He arrived at the usual time, perhaps just a little early. Enthusiasm or suspicion? I wondered which.

When I heard his key in the lock, I huddled deeper into the armchair. He found me there. Naked, as he had instructed.

'Good girl. Have you been masturbating?'

'No!' I was horrified at the question, at the lack of sensitivity.

'I bet you're lying. Get down on the floor and show me your cunt.' Alec didn't use words like that. Never. And he didn't make demands like that. Ever. Yet I did what he asked, stretched myself out, open and available, spread my legs wide so he could see the undeniable evidence for himself.

He sniffed and smirked. 'As I thought. So!' He settled down on the arm of the other chair. 'You like being kept naked, do you?'

I made no response but there was no point in attempting a denial. In the silence he considered me a moment.

'What would you do if someone else had come to the door?'

Again I made no answer.

'Would you answer it? I mean you could hardly leave it unanswered.' Still I stayed silent. 'I asked you a question, Naomi. Would you answer it?'

I considered what options there would have been if that had happened. 'Yes.'

'Yes! Yes? You would have answered the door? Naked?'

'Yes.' Was I telling the truth? Would I really have done that? Certainly a week ago I wouldn't, but now? 'Yes, I would.'

'You like that idea, do you? Showing yourself off to someone else?'

'Yes.' The single word simply burst out of my subconscious with too much eagerness ever to be taken back or denied.

He smiled: a thoughtful, self-engrossed smile. 'Right then. I'd better see who else might like to come and have a look at you flaunting yourself like this.'

For the whole of the rest of the weekend, I wasn't allowed to wear a single scrap of clothing, and he kept talking about who he might get to come and see me. He kept making me expose myself to him, and play with myself and lick him. By Monday I was exhausted and sore and more fulfilled than I have ever been.

During the week, things returned to normal. Neither of us mentioned what had happened during that strange weekend; we behaved like any normal couple, living normal lives. We made love several times and Alec was his old self: a careful, attentive and considerate lover.

And then it was Thursday again, and night time. We were lying tucked together in bed, both naked, and his erection was poking into the crease of my bottom. He had his arms round me, his fingers stroking gently and insistently at my nipples. I was hoping for something more but then he stopped and ran his hand right down the front of my body.

'Have you shown all this to anyone else yet this week?' He put only the slightest emphasis on the word 'yet'.

'No.'

He was casual, relaxed, and his voice was soft, but mocking. 'Didn't you enjoy showing off last weekend, then?'

I didn't reply because he knew what the answer would be. He waited a few minutes then leaned over and kissed me goodnight. 'I've asked a couple of friends round for dinner tomorrow.'

My stomach churned and I felt sick. I wasn't ready for this. 'Who?' I could barely speak.

'You'll see.'

'Alec! Who are they?'

'Goodnight.'

He left the next day still refusing to tell me who was coming; just 'a couple of friends'. Did that mean friends of ours, or friends of his? Would I know them? He hadn't specifically said he wanted me to expose myself to them, but that was the implication.

He rang at lunchtime again. 'Do you know what I expect you to be wearing when I get home?'

I considered all the possible answers, but really there was only one. 'Nothing?'

The line went dead straight away. He surely could not be expecting me to greet them naked, whether or not they were friends who knew me.

When Alec came home, I was in the kitchen. As he had instructed, I was naked again. He came up behind me, put his arms round me and ran his hands across my taut nipples and down to my stomach. He dug between my lips and slid his fingers along the ridge, already slippery and expectant. His lips nibbled at my ear.

'Have you been a naughty girl today, then?'

'No!'

'I don't believe you. I'm going up to change. I told them about seven o'clock.'

It was almost quarter to seven before he came down again. 'I've put your dress out on the bed,' he said and wandered through into the lounge.

When the doorbell rang I was still upstairs, trying to decide if I had the courage to go on. The dress he had laid out was the one I had intended for my harem girl costume. Then I would have worn a cropped top bra; now there was no bra, and my breasts are much too big for me ever to go out without one. And it was very sheer; if my nipples erected, they would be plainly visible. They were erect already.

For the party, I would have worn some long harem trousers. Now there were none, and the dress was ridiculously short; the hem would barely come below my bottom. Thankfully he had put out some knickers, white, and not much more than a G-string, but then with that dress I would have had to wear something. If he hadn't allowed me knickers, I wouldn't have carried on because I definitely was not going to allow anyone to see that much.

I heard voices downstairs, not ones I immediately recognised, but as they went through into the living room, Alec called up to me. 'Naomi? Bring us some beers, love.'

I brushed my hair for one last time, pulled the hem of my dress down as much as I could and went down.

Clutching the tray firmly I kicked open the door and slipped into the lounge. They were all sitting at the far end of the room and the three faces looked round at me with broad grins as I approached. Alec waved vaguely towards me.

'Now then, this is Naomi, and I think you know Chris and Paul, don't you, love? You must have met them at one of the office Christmas do's. Oh well of course you do, because you know Wendy, Chris's fiancée, don't you?'

I ran away to the kitchen as soon as I could. Yes, I did know them and they knew me; I had met them frequently at Alec's office or at social events: occasions when I had been fully clothed, nicely made up and elegant. Then I had been dressed to look attractive; now I was undressed to look alluring. Their expressions left no doubt which they preferred. Chris was a couple of years younger than me, and I knew Wendy, his fiancée, well; we used the same gym, and often stayed for a drink together afterwards. I had been to their house and met Chris there. We were definitely more than acquaintances: we were friends. Paul was older than any of us: unfit, overweight, and with lank thinning hair. I had always thought Alec didn't like him much, calling him lazy and arrogant.

Could Alec have chosen the guests this carefully? I could think of no one he could have invited who would have made the evening more humiliating. If it had been a couple whom we both knew, even Chris and Wendy, her presence would have stopped things going too far. If it had been two men whom Alec knew, I could have endured that. Even if he had made me undress completely (and I was still not entirely sure that he wouldn't), I could have tolerated it if I was sure that I would never see them again. But this? This was as bad as it could be. I trembled and felt my sex contract in a sudden spasm.

When I brought the meal in and when I served it and when I passed them dishes and when I sat at the table eating, I kept catching eyes staring at me. I had no idea what Alec had told them, but they could hardly think that I normally dressed like this; they must have known that the whole thing was being laid on so that I could flaunt myself in front of them. All the while my nipples were so tight they were aching, pushing against the fabric of the dress quite blatantly and the harder they grew, the more the men stared and the more they stared the more erect they grew. I was also getting increasingly wet, and when I cleared the main course out to the kitchen, I couldn't help reaching down inside my knickers to caress myself a moment. I stopped when Alec came out with the rest of the plates, and asked him how long the guests would stay because I wanted them gone so we could continue by ourselves. He just smiled and told me not to be impatient.

By the time I returned with the coffee, they had moved to the end of the room and fell quiet when I came in. As before, I felt so naked knowing they were watching intently as I moved and stretched and bent while I distributed the cups; knowing the outline of my knickers was quite visible, the shape of my breasts, even the profile of my nipples. I was pouring the last cup when Alec spoke, still completely calm.

'Before you sit down, Naomi, please take your dress off.'

I tried to stop my hand shaking as I finished pouring the coffee and replaced the pot carefully on the table.

'Alec, I don't want . . .' I stopped. I could not quite work out what it was I didn't want; the dress was hiding nothing and it would have been pointless and unconvincing to protest too much at a small step when I had already gone so far with the big steps. 'I don't want them to . . .'

Alec interrupted me, speaking very slowly. 'Naomi, I know what I want. I think I know what they want. Nobody cares what you want. Take your dress off.'

I gripped the hem in my fists, not knowing at first whether I was holding it down or preparing to lift it up. The faces turned towards me. Two of them showed surprise, grinning and excited. The third was calm and confident. All three were watching me, waiting for me and I was the centre of their world. I inched the hem up a fraction then took a deep breath and pulled the whole thing over my head in one go. Immediately I turned away to hide the state of my nipples and lay the dress over a chair, but quickly realised that I was merely displaying my bottom, totally revealed by the skimpy thong. Instead I faced them again, and picked up my coffee, the cup rattling in the saucer as I carefully lowered myself into a chair. All the eyes still watched me as I crossed my legs and hunched forward. It's not that I am ashamed of my breasts, but sometimes I do wish they weren't quite so generous and prominent. I held the cup low in my lap where it could cover the small dark stain that had already appeared on the pure white front of my knickers.

Nobody spoke. There was an occasional clatter of cups and saucers but I kept my eyes down to my lap and sipped at my coffee. When I did look up, the two visitors were still gazing at me, glancing over at Alec from time to time, waiting for him to indicate what would happen next. Finally he put his cup down and leaned back in his chair.

'What do you think about the knickers, Naomi?'

I stared at him, my throat dry and trembling. Chris and Paul grinned more widely still.

'Well?' Alec was so calm he could have been talking about the colour of the wallpaper, but he didn't say anything else, didn't tell me what he wanted or what I was supposed to do. The silence dragged on while they waited and I sat there stupidly, trying to find words.

I swallowed. 'Do you mean you want me to take them off?'

He shrugged. 'If you like.'

The eager anticipation on the faces of the other two was unmistakable, but making this my decision was so cruel of Alec: so arrogant.

The eyes silently followed my movements as I put the cup and saucer down beside my chair. I set both feet flat on the floor and lay my hands along the top of my thighs. My palms, my chest, my armpits were sweating in the stillness. I glanced round the faces again. Alec pretended not to be watching at all. Paul's leg quivered nervously. Chris tried to look relaxed, but it was not convincing.

I didn't stand up. I just peeled the thin waistband down from my waist and then lifted my bottom enough to allow the elastic to slide underneath and slipped the little garment over my feet. For a moment nobody moved, then Chris glanced across at the other two before he held out his cup towards me.

'Could I have some more coffee please, Naomi?'

A smug childish smirk was painted across his face; I saw Alec grinning too, but Paul had settled into a frightening stillness.

I shuffled across the floor, fetched the coffee and turned back to them. They glanced briefly at my breasts but mostly focused on the full wide triangle of neat brown hair which they hadn't seen before. The eyes followed me as I padded across the carpet, as I poured the coffee for each of them and as I turned to replace the pot. When I came back to rejoin the group, Alec stopped me.

'Just a minute. Before you sit down, Naomi, I told Chris and Paul that you would undress this evening and that they could be here if they liked. However, I didn't tell them why; shall we explain that now?'

139

When I didn't answer Alec continued as if I wasn't even there. 'Naomi is naked because she likes it; she likes nothing better than parading herself around for all to see. Isn't that right?'

Again I said nothing. What point was there in trying to deny it when I was already standing in front of them naked? When I had asked to take my knickers off; when my nipples were achingly erect and my pussy was already damp; when I was beginning to detect an aroma in the air that could only be coming from one source.

'In fact,' Alec continued, 'when I came home the other week, she was lying on this floor, just about where she is standing now, stark naked and masturbating.'

This wasn't even true, but I said nothing and I'm not sure that words would have come out if even I'd tried. Instead I stood and listened as Alec described what a tart I'd been, how I had exposed myself, how I had spent the whole day and night naked, opening my vulva to him whenever he asked, licking him, and serving him. The words broke over me, as the image of each event returned and Alec described my uninhibited acceptance of everything he demanded. The pictures and the words and the insults seeped into me, so that I felt myself growing more aroused as every bedroom secret I had ever had was spread out before these two men. Even the coarse language lifted me, the words he used to describe me, crude, insulting and offensive, emphasised my powerlessness and added a moral nakedness to my physical nakedness. Finally he even told them how he had made me masturbate for him while he watched.

In the following silence, as they all stared at me, Chris spoke. 'You know I've always wanted to watch Wendy masturbate, but she won't. She says it's undignified, not ladylike.'

140

Alec smiled. 'Well, she's right. It isn't ladylike. I expect that's why Naomi is so good at it. Would you like to watch her instead?'

My stomach turned cold. Of course they would want that and I would have to do it. But how could I? I was ashamed when I masturbated alone. I had been humiliated when Alec had made me do it in front of him. How could I bring myself now, in front of three of them, to do something so private? So why did I feel like this? Why was my heart pounding? Why were my nipples as hard as stone? Why was my vagina oozing, a thick sticky trail that would soon start to trickle down my legs? Why was the prospect so unbearably and undeniably delectable and intoxicating? I shivered as I stood waiting for them to decide my fate.

Chris repeated his enthusiasm for the idea but Paul was strangely silent. Alec turned to him.

'Well, Paul? What do you think?'

He stretched out his legs straight in front of him. 'Perhaps.' He was unconvinced as he unashamedly stared me up and down before, finally, addressing me. 'Come here.'

I turned to Alec for support but he just lounged back, watching quietly.

'Alec, I don't want ...' Alec simply raised his eyebrows: we had been down that road before. 'I mean, are you going to let them do anything they want?'

He smiled and shook his head. 'Oh no, darling, no. You're my wife. I won't let them do anything they want. I'll let them do anything I want. For now, I want you to do as you are told.' When I still didn't move, he continued. 'Paul's waiting.'

I shuffled over towards Paul but he beckoned me ever closer until our legs were actually touching. Only then did he reach out his hand and, with an insulting carelessness, slid it slowly up inside my leg. The progress was tantalisingly slow and I could have stepped back before he reached the obvious destination. I didn't move and the hand climbed steadily higher up my thigh until it was pressing hard against the lips of my sex. His mocking eyes fixed on me as he spoke to Alec.

'The little tart's absolutely soaking! I don't think she deserves to be allowed to come.' His hand was still sawing back and forth gently between my legs, milking me of my desire. Finally he pulled it away and proudly held up his palm to show everybody the evidence smeared across it. He raised his eyebrows to me. 'Get down on the floor, on all fours.'

I obeyed. The position would have been exquisitely humiliating at any time; my being naked while everyone else was fully dressed made it even better. I knelt there, waiting, feeling the obscene bestial way my heavy breasts hung down, the nipples long and hard like a cow's udder. My bottom would be presented to them all, possibly even allowing a glimpse of my pussy lips. If so, the wetness I could feel pouring from me would also be revealed. Paul reached out his foot and nudged gently at my hanging breast, then pushed less gently in a tap that became practically a kick and continued until I cried out. Still I didn't pull away, even when he rubbed the harsh ridges of his shoe across my tender nipple, I stayed there. I almost begged him to do the same to my pussy, it would have been all I needed to take me over the top. Instead he leaned over me and, laying one hand on the nearest cheek of my bottom, pulled it towards him, exposing my anus. He sniffed thoughtfully and then told me to crawl round the room, first across to Chris then to Alec and back to him. I could feel myself seeping with every movement, the growing tightness in my vagina squeezing and pushing out the thick juice that my body was producing in response to the humiliations Paul kept piling on me.

When I returned to his chair, and looked up at him, appealing to be allowed to get up, he simply squinted down at me dismissively and told me to turn away from him again and push my bottom right up into the air. I did as I was told, although I was now even more exposed, even more humiliated and my wet and open sex was even more revealed.

'Now then,' he grunted, 'don't move.' Immediately his open hand lashed down on to me and I yelped, a stupid cry of surprise and outrage more than pain, but the second time was harder, and the third harder still. This wasn't play. He intended to hurt me and didn't pretend otherwise. I cried out with every extra stroke that landed on me and in the silence between them, heard my own weeping echoing through the room.

Finally he stopped, and again pulled at my cheeks, pulling me further open and sliding his hands through the wetness he displayed. He turned me round again, squeezed roughly at my hanging swollen breast and turned my face from side to side as he calmly considered the effect his treatment had produced. Again he stared at me but spoke to Alec.

'You know what I'd do, Alec? A great round arse like that? I'd take a cane to it; whip her till she bleeds.'

I shuddered, almost climaxed on the spot. I had never dared imagine such total subjugation. I had never dared hope for so much. He held my chin in his podgy hand, lifting my face, and although I tried not to look, I glanced up just once and met his eyes.

He knew me.

After that, Chris was allowed to have his way. He called me over to where he was sitting and made me lie down on the carpet in front of him with my legs spread wide apart and then he told me he wanted to watch me make myself come. When he had proposed this earlier, the suggestion had horrified me. Now I was so desperate to be allowed the release that I was ready to welcome any hand on my sex, even my own.

I had to open my lips for them all to see inside me, see the pools of excitement gathered at the mouth of my vagina. I had to pull back the hood of my clitoris so they could even see that and push my fingers deep inside myself. Only then was I allowed to settle back and with one hand squeezing my nipples and the other one pinching and circling round and round my clitoris, bring myself to the climax that had been hovering just out of reach from the moment I had seen the dress that Alec had put out for me; that had been building through the whole evening of being stripped, being watched, being humiliated.

I wasn't allowed to dress again afterwards, so when Paul and Chris were leaving, I tried to hide away out of sight, but Paul called me to crawl over to him again. I waited meekly as he leaned down to inspect me once more, examining the marks on my buttocks and the wetness on my labia and commenting to the others on what he found. Then he reached out and slapped me again straight across my bottom and laughed when I cried out.

'That's what she needs, Alec. She enjoys the spanking too much; she needs a cane.'

For the remainder of that weekend, Alec made me stay naked. He regularly made me turn round and bend right over so that he could inspect my bottom, and check the progress of the red prints left by Paul's hand.

The following week was quiet again, and our lives returned to something nearer normal, the way we had been before all this started. Nothing was said and he didn't even ring me on Friday. Even so, I was waiting for him naked when he arrived home; I assumed he would expect it. Instead he barely glanced at me, made some snide remark about my eagerness to expose myself and then told me to get dressed because we had been invited out. He wouldn't tell me where.

Half an hour later we pulled up outside a small modern house on a large modern estate. 'Here we are,' Alec told me as he parked the car. 'Paul's house.' My heart sank as he gaily rattled on. 'You knew that he and Carrie are getting married next month, didn't you? Well, tonight's his stag-night. Bit early, but it was the only night we could get everyone together. In we go!'

Around half a dozen people were already assembled in the living room, including Chris and one or two others that I recognised, but many I had never met before. Paul was faultlessly polite, offering me a drink and behaving in every respect as if this were a perfectly normal social evening.

Except I was the only woman.

'Everybody got a drink?' Paul asked and then led me out into the middle of the room and called for quiet.

'For those who don't know her, this is Naomi. For those who don't know her well, she's a tart who likes nothing better than parading around naked and having her arse spanked. So tonight, she'll have the time of her life.' He turned to me. 'First of all, take your clothes off.'

They were all silent. Some were sitting, some standing, but I counted seven men lounging round that room watching me, waiting for me. I felt frozen, completely unprepared and with nowhere to hide, I turned to Alec for help. He smiled at me, settled back in his chair and crossed his legs. They all waited for me, patient but determined to see me undress and I was not so naive as to think undressing would be the end of it.

They didn't even try to make it easy. If there had been some music, I could have done some kind of dance, made something of it. If Alec had warned me ahead, I could have worn clothes that were better suited. But there was no music and he hadn't warned me; he had just said we were going out. It could have been anywhere, so I had worn ordinary clothes. My bra didn't match my knickers; I was wearing ordinary cheap supermarket tights. Even as I undressed for them, I could have no pride in the unveiling; even that would shame me.

They all just sat round me, sipping their beers so calmly and so unquestioningly that finally I obeyed; somehow obedience was becoming easier. The whole room was tensely silent and expectant when I was standing in front of them but as soon as I started, I could feel a communal sigh of smug satisfaction when they realised that I really would do this, that the treat they had been promised really was about to be delivered. Item by item, I took off my clothes and placed them on a low round leather footstool beside me. No one spoke or commented or encouraged me; no one gave any indication that it was worth watching what I was being made to display. I was isolated, practically ignored as more of me was steadily exposed: as my bra was revealed: as my breasts were uncovered: as my skirt came off and then finally my knickers and I was there for them all to see.

When I was finally naked, and had been made to turn round so they could all see me from all sides,

Alec continued. 'Now then, Naomi, it's time for the high point of the evening. You're going to kneel down here, across this footstool and then Paul and I are both going to cane you.' He swept my neat pile of clothes on to the floor and pushed the stool out into the middle of the room.

I suppose I had known from the moment Alec told me whose house we were in that something like this would happen, but the shock of hearing the sentence pronounced was none the less for that. I could protest, and demand to be taken home; I could refuse to allow it. I could do and say whatever I liked, but no one would take any notice. I was there because I wanted to be. I was naked because I wanted to be. I would soon allow myself to be caned for the same reason. I didn't know if I could withstand the pain, let alone the humiliation of being made to kneel in such a subservient posture, exposed and degraded. While everyone watched me.

But staring round I could see them watching already, the same amused and mocking conceit on their faces, and I was transported back to that night at the Student Union. Amid the calls, the forest of gloating eyes, the smug victory as they witnessed my exposure, my submission, in the midst of all that I had first experienced the enveloping powerlessness; crushing uncertainty; indescribable elation.

I stepped up to my place and knelt in front of the stool as they again gathered around, leaving space for Alec. I glanced round at the circle of hungry faces, their hands clutching at beer cans or else stuffed deep – too deep – into trouser pockets as they clustered round. How would I ever look any of them in the face again after this? True there were some I might never see again, but many I would meet regularly. Chris even smiled at me; I would probably meet him on

Monday, and now he would know so much. Whenever he saw me, whether I was standing in his kitchen or sitting in his lounge, he would remember and he would see me kneeling naked on Paul's floor.

I rested my head on my hands and waited.

Alec was turning a long pale cane in his fingers but he seemed to be looking to Paul for instructions and it was Paul who came up behind me and whose great flabby hands I felt running over my skin, squeezing and pinching at my bottom. He even pulled my cheeks apart, just as he had done before, just to expose me even further and humiliate me even more. He went further than that. He even reached right down to my pussy and pulled my lips apart, running his finger right down the length of my crease.

'There! What did I tell you? Soaking wet!' and he released me at last, with a sudden slap across my bottom that made me start up, and caused a ripple of laughter from the waiting circle. 'Now, head down, bottom up and keep your knees nice and wide apart. We want to see your puss gushing as your arse turns red.' Then he turned to Alec.

'A dozen each should be enough for her, Alec. Maybe two dozen, if you like, but lay them on good and hard. Hold the cane right at the end, and give it plenty of follow-through. She'll scream a bit, but she'll take it.'

I turned my face down towards the leather stool: I would not scream: I would not let them see me cry: I would not give them any reward.

Time stopped before the cane came whistling through the air. Then it hit me and I screamed. I have never felt, imagined, dreamed, such complete irresistible power as that first stroke wiping straight across my skin. It hurt indescribably. There was pain but more than that and less than that. It was so strong, so absolute and inescapable that my gasp was from awe almost as much as from agony. I tried to leap up but my legs were jelly and anyway Alec was pushing me down. My whole brain focused on the agonising fire in my bottom and yet through it all I was aware of a few shocked gasps from some of the men standing round, and above them all, Paul's clear voice calling out 'One!'

Then the second stroke came down, as hard, as horrible, as excruciating as the first, and I screamed again. This time they all called together: 'Two!' and 'Three!'

After four, I managed to sit up and turn to Alec. My grand resolutions were forgotten and I no longer cared if they all saw the tears pouring down my cheeks. I clutched at his legs, begging him to stop, but he just pushed me away and made me go back down again and turn my bottom up for the rest of the punishment.

After six, Alec said I could have a short break. Several of them came up and reached out gingerly to touch me. They laughed at me, felt down between my legs and jeered at the flood they found there. Even Chris came up again, touched my skin, pinched me so that I yelped and he laughed again.

'You know what, Naomi? Your arse is like a beetroot! The whole thing is just one ball of brilliant red. It's magic! And down here,' he went on, running his hand down between my thighs until his fingertips were pressing against the lips of my sex and quivering lightly against the very tip of my clitoris, 'down here you're sopping wet! You're loving every minute of it, aren't you? Admit it! Just wait till I tell Wendy!'

I turned away from him, and collapsed into tears again.

Then Alec returned. 'Time to continue!' he called cheerily. 'Ready?'

I begged him again. Pleaded to be allowed to get up, promised I would do anything that he wanted for him or to him if he would just let me off the rest. The others only laughed, and Alec refused.

'You'll do anything I want anyway, my girl. Now come along! Turn round and let's have a look at you again.' I shuffled back into position and waited for Paul to start again, but before he did, Alec called out that they couldn't see and made me open my legs further.

The next six were just a blur, as the cane repeatedly whipped down on me to the delighted chanting of the voices gathered behind me. The rhythmic lance of total pain was somehow hypnotising so that I totally lost count of how many I had received and was surprised when Alec stopped and, after another short break, Paul took over.

I had thought Alec was harsh, but Paul was a thousand times worse. He was much slower, tapping my bottom with the tip of the cane between each stroke and lining each one just where he wanted it. I could hear myself crying and pleading but he completely ignored me. A couple of the men were even willing to forgo watching the strokes land on my bottom to come and stare at my face as every agonising stroke fell.

He gave me twelve, and the sound of the voices singing out each stroke will be burned into my memory for ever. Thankfully they stopped after that although there were many calls to 'give her another twelve'. For some reason, the pain didn't go on getting worse. It reached a plateau after the first few from Paul and I just felt completely numb right through my bottom.

Yet it was only my bottom that felt numb. Every stroke pressed me against the coarse leather of the footstool, and compressed against my clitoris. It also thrust me across the top of the stool, rubbing my tender nipples over the rough surface. I was utterly on fire and the moment the last stroke was done, I could feel the flow of juice within me ready to boil. I was crying and panting and groaning and I could not have said what I wanted most.

I stayed there, too weak and exhausted to move. Paul came and squatted in front of me, speaking over me to the others, as they gathered to examine the state of my bottom and, at Alec's invitation, to reach in and feel the seeping flow between my lips.

'Now then,' said Paul. 'Before Naomi runs off, I think we might each just give her four with the hand for good measure. You first, Rob?'

After the heavy sting of the cane, their hands were light and quite bearable. Even so, they bruised and each one made sure that I screamed. Paul stayed beside me always: calling up each guest in turn, counting each spank I received, mocking the desire that I could not conceal. I was glad when it came to Chris's turn, sure he would be gentle. I was wrong. He beat me harder than any of the others, harder even than Alec.

Finally, after all the others were done, Paul claimed his turn. He moved round and lifted me off the stool. Then he turned me over and lay me down on my back before pressing my thighs as wide apart as they would go so that, amid the calls and taunts, my dripping sex was openly displayed to everyone there. Then he lay his hand down across the top of my cleft and pressed his fingers inside me, pressing his palm in slow gentle circles around my clitoris. It took only a few seconds before I was begging him to press harder, to squeeze me, to give me more of everything. And just as the orgasm started to break over me, as I reached up with my own hands to cradle my breasts, he slapped me ferociously, his open palm straight across the inside of my swollen lips in a final glorious agony of disdain and I screamed again with the pain, the relief and the pleasure.

Naomi's Second Tale – Hens

Wendy shuffled uneasily, rattling the ice cubes in her glass and avoiding my eye until she could finally come out with it. 'Is this true what I've heard about Paul's last Friday?'

'I don't know. What have you heard?'

Her eyes opened wide. 'You want me to go into details?'

'No.'

'Well then? Is it true?'

'Probably.' I knew I was sounding childishly sulky and Wendy's silence was eloquent criticism. 'Yes.'

'For heaven's sake, Naomi! Why?'

'They made me!'

'Oh, come on! You're an adult. You could have refused.'

'They made me.' Repetition of the pathetic excuse only confirmed its inadequacy, but I carried on talking to hide the weakness. 'How did you find out?'

'Chris told me.' Wendy said. After a short pause, she continued. 'It's not the end, you know. Carrie's going to invite you to her hen-night.'

I frowned. 'She already has.'

'Yes, but now you're going to be the entertainment.'

* * *

Alec drove me there, to the wine bar where they had all gathered. We could hear voices and laughter from far down the street and found the door propped open with a chair to let in some cool air and the crowd of them clustered round a table at the far end. Alec pushed me inside, said he would collect me from Carrie's flat later, and then walked out. I turned back, utterly alone, towards the table of eager, grinning faces.

I only knew three of them: Wendy, Carrie of course and Natalie, her flat-mate. That was it; the rest I had never met before. It was only just seven o'clock, but the party had obviously been going for some time and they had effectively taken over the whole bar.

Carrie was full of herself, but she could afford to be: she would soon be off out of it all. She jumped up when she saw me and called me over. 'Right now, this is Naomi, who you all know about, and for tonight, she's all ours!'

Then she went round the table, introducing everyone I didn't know and ending with the one sitting in the corner, a pretty girl who was by far the youngest of the group and looked barely old enough to be there at all.

'This is Anna. She's Natalie's baby sister and only turned eighteen last week. She's down staying with us for the weekend and we've got to look after her, because she's very innocent.'

The little face wrinkled briefly before turning back to inspect me again. She had looked intrigued at Carrie's comments about me and in spite of the frequent giggles, there was an unsettling hardness about the girl. 'So what do we get to do with her?'

'Anything!' Carrie answered. 'Anything we like! From what I have heard about what happened at Paul's last week, she is game for anything.'

'What shall we do first?' one of them asked.

Almost immediately Anna piped up, 'Let's make her take her clothes off!'

'Anna! We can't do that here!'

'In the ladies' we could!' The girl's enthusiasm was childish, but there was no doubting her determination. Clearly she was not the least intimidated by being the baby of the group and a good eight years younger than me and it was her simplicity, her directness that really worried me. Whereas with most people lack of experience means they do not know how to start, with her it meant she did not know when to stop. I turned to Carrie.

'Look, I don't know what you have in mind or what Paul may have said, but I am certainly not doing anything like that.'

Anna carried on as if I hadn't spoken a word. 'I did it once to a girl at school; I took her clothes away and she had to stay there for hours!'

'Carrie!' I protested again. 'I mean it!' but it was as if I wasn't there. Anna's cheery excitement was frighteningly infectious, and when nobody else objected, I looked round the circle of faces and realised no one would. To suggest anything less would now just seem cowardly.

Anna turned to her sister. 'Nat, have you got those handcuffs?'

'They're in Wendy's car.'

'There you are, then!' Anna was far too pleased with herself. 'We can put her in them! Come on!' She leapt up, caught hold of my arm and started dragging me towards the back of the wine bar. Her sister, Natalie, and Carrie both followed, and also another girl, whom I didn't know.

Anna didn't let go until we were all crammed into the tiny toilets. Then she turned to me. 'Right then. Take your clothes off.'

I again looked to Carrie for help. She and I were roughly the same age, easily the oldest ones there, and I felt that made, or at least ought to have made, a bond between us. She seemed to feel nothing, indeed while Anna bubbled in eager excitement, treating the whole affair as little more than an entertaining schoolgirl prank, Carrie stayed menacingly silent. Anna was playing a game; she intended to win, but it was a game none the less. Carrie was in earnest; her eyes brooded with rigid expectation, displaying an explicit understanding of the situation and of the erotic implications which their plans held for me.

In contrast to both of them the third girl leaned calmly against the door as if bored; so far she had said nothing but when our eyes met she spoke. 'You might as well do it, you know, because if you don't, we'll only tear them off you anyway. Besides, my husband was at Paul's last weekend, so I know you're an exhibitionist little tart: you needn't come over all coy and innocent.' The calm frankness of her tone made the words all the more menacing.

When I still didn't move, Anna grew impatient. 'Right, you two hold her and I'll do it.'

'No!' I said quickly. 'It's all right. I'll do it.' I reached up to the buttons of my shirt and froze. I suppose I could have refused, I could have resisted and struggled but what would that have achieved? There were plenty more of them outside and if they needed more people to hold me, they would get them. Besides, if they already knew what I had permitted last weekend, on what basis could I pretend outrage now?

I trembled, looked round the waiting faces and was lost. When both Alec and Paul had beaten me last Friday, it had been glorious. I had felt so totally alive, so fulfilled, but it had been the presence of the other

156

people that made it so. If no one had been there, had seen me being humiliated, and seen how aroused it made me, and how much that increased my humiliation in a magnificent accelerating spiral, the pleasure would not have been comparable. But they had all been men, and now my captors were all women. The evil of so perverted a persecution raised me higher than ever; I was even less a friend, even more a victim, surrounded here by my own sex than I had ever been before. It was that discordant stretching which held me in its grip. Shame and degradation, even the anticipation of appalling pain, pulled me back. Exhilaration, desire and pride pushed me forward.

So I unbuttoned the shirt, feeling their eyes scrutinising me as my skin and the neat white bra were revealed. The instant I took the shirt off, Natalie grabbed it out of my hand. My bra came next, though I held the cups over my breasts a moment allowing the briefest, lightest caress across my nipples before she snatched that away too, tearing the thin straps over my skin.

I unzipped the skirt next, slid it down my legs, stepped out of it and handed this to Natalie as well. This left only my knickers, modest enough at the front, but cut high and very revealing across my bottom. Knowing what they would see when I took that last item off, I stepped back until I met the unforgiving cold rim of the basin. Every day I had been checking in the mirror and I knew full well that the evidence of last Friday's caning was still clearly visible in thick red lines across both cheeks of my bottom. They were a less brilliant scarlet than they had been at first, but they were still undeniably there, clear irrefutable proof of what had been done to me. It could only make me the object of yet further derision.

Anna was impatient. 'Come on, take your knickers off. I want to look at you entirely naked.'

I pushed my knickers down and off, then just stood there clutching them. I didn't want Natalie to add this final trophy to her bundle, because there was no mistaking their condition. They felt sticky to my touch, and I would not have been surprised if she opened them out to inspect them thoroughly. Nor could I step forward, because although it was bad enough having them all standing in front of me, all unashamedly staring at my breasts and my pubis, it would be worse once they saw my bottom.

Anna, inevitably, insisted on more. 'Turn round. Let's see what the lads did to your bum.'

I turned slowly and it was Carrie, standing by my side, who immediately gasped.

'God, look at this! Look at the state of her! Here, turn right round and show them.'

Anna was equally enthusiastic. 'Wow! That's brilliant!'

I don't know how long they would have spent admiring the fading stripes if Wendy had not come in with the handcuffs. Natalie pulled the knickers out of my hands, but when she remarked how disgusting they were, Anna immediately wanted to see. She carefully peeled them open to peer in at the incriminating gusset and was enraptured and intrigued at the wet stain now revealed.

Meanwhile, Carrie and Wendy pulled my hands round behind my back before clicking the handcuffs tightly round my wrists. They closed with a firm solid click; obviously real ones, not some flimsy plastic toy.

Then Natalie went to the door, taking my clothes with her, and called out to the rest of the girls who all trooped in, laughing and jeering to see me standing there. I was made to turn round so that they could all inspect the marks across my bottom and several reached out to feel them, running their fingers along the raised lines that still crossed both cheeks. Some of them circled right round me, prodding and tickling and several pinched me: my thighs, my bottom and even my breasts, but they all kept coming back to the cane marks on my bottom.

Eventually Carrie led them back to the bar to eat, leaving me standing alone in the small tiled room, listening to the high voices and low music from the other room. Over the next half hour several came back and they all taunted me. Once another girl, not one of our party, came in. She stopped in shocked surprise to see me standing there, handcuffed and naked, and even asked if I was all right. A few seconds later she returned and held the door open while a man put his head round, grinning at the sight I presented.

Eventually, inevitably, when the door opened, it was Anna who sidled in. She didn't go into either of the cubicles, but stood at the basin studiously washing her hands and watching me continuously in the mirror.

Finally she turned round and tossed away the paper towel. 'Sit down on the floor.'

'Why?'

'Just do it.'

She tried to sound strong and decisive and if the nervous tremble in her voice betrayed her, it didn't defeat her. Her evident determination to overcome her own nervousness gave her an authority that I could not oppose. Unable to use my hands to support myself, I knelt down with difficulty then dropped on to my bottom on the cold tiles and sat with my knees together in front of me.

She squatted down in front of me. 'Open your legs. I want to see your fanny.' For all her nervousness, it was still just a game to her, and perhaps that was what gave her the assurance and confidence to press on. I slid my legs open as she stared down at everything now revealed between my thighs.

'More!'

I pushed my legs further apart still and she settled down right between my feet, leaning forward to peer at me closely. 'Have you peed yourself?'

'No!'

'You're very wet, you know.'

I said nothing.

'Is it true that you're an exhibitionist?'

'No.' Yet we both knew I was lying.

'Then why do you get so wet when you are naked in front of everyone?'

'I just do. I can't help it.'

'I think you're an exhibitionist.' She was considering, like a curious, precocious child as she stretched out the tips of her fingers to push my outer lips further to one side. 'Your fanny's ever so big. Has it always been like that?'

'I don't know. I suppose so.'

She now carefully eased the inner lips open. 'And all ragged,' she mused. 'How many men have you slept with?'

'I don't know.'

'Well, guess.' Her head tipped to one side as she continued her examination.

'I suppose about ten.'

'That's not very many for someone as old as you. How many times altogether have you shagged someone?'

'I don't know. I mean I've been married for nearly five years, so quite a few.'

'I've never done it at all; I'm a virgin. Maybe that's why your fanny looks so battered and used compared to mine.' She was still casually opening and closing my lips with the very tips of her fingers as she contemplated my answers. 'Five years? That's about, what? Two thousand nights? I suppose in all that time you must have done it, well, at least a thousand times. That's a lot. A thousand times. A man's cock going in there.' And as she spoke she slowly pushed her finger inside me, right up until her hand was squashed against me and she could push no further. Then she slowly pulled it back out, gazed at its new sheen and even raised it to her nose and sniffed.

She stood up and stared down at me. 'I'm glad I came tonight. You can get up now if you like.' The door banged as she left me.

It was about twenty minutes later that Wendy and Carrie returned carrying a long khaki mac and announced that I was being taken down to a pub. They didn't unfasten my handcuffs, simply draped the mac round my shoulders and buttoned it down the front.

The pub was already crowded, but we found a semi-enclosed corner where we settled round a table. I was pushed right inside with Carrie on one side and Wendy on the other. A huge mirror emblazoned with an advertisement for some whisky or other hung directly opposite me so that every time I looked up, I caught the reflection of our little group. Eight girls were dressed up for an evening out; one sat nervously in the middle, the empty sleeves of an incongruous and rather grubby mac waving about her like flags. I looked ridiculous, wearing a huge mac on such a hot summer evening, but at least I was covered.

Two men up on stools at the bar kept glancing over at us and as soon as Natalie went up to get our drinks, they tried to pick her up. They were quite scruffy, as if they had just stepped off a building site,

161

and looked entirely out of place in what was mainly a young persons' pub. Their matching thinning hair, huge beer guts, and sagging jeans were so similar they might easily have been brothers: Tweedle-dum and Tweedle-dee.

I was given a pint of lager, but as I couldn't pick it up, one of the others periodically held the glass to my lips. Then Anna reached across from the far side of the table and tipped it so far that much of it spilt round my mouth and ran on to the mac. They found this very funny, and would deliberately tip it further and further. Wendy then held up the glass with one hand, pulled out the collar of the mac with the other, and tipped up all the rest so that it ran, ice cold, down my face, my chin, my neck and chest and trickled all the way down my stomach to form a pool on the bench between my thighs.

As one of the men returned from the toilets, he paused by our table; he knew something was going on, but couldn't tell what it was. 'Your friend must be bloody hot in that mac!'

All the eyes turned on me as Natalie answered. 'Well, yes, but that's all she's wearing. I've got all her other clothes in here.' She held up a carrier bag. 'See?' And she took them all out, dropping them on the table one by one. 'Skirt. Blouse. Bra. And here are her knickers. Would you like to keep them? They're pretty well creamed.' They dangled from her fingertips for a second before being snatched away and engulfed in his huge fist.

I could hardly hold my head up, could feel my face blazing red as he stared down at me, mesmerised, licking his great red lips. 'She's a cracker, she is!'

He returned to his friend at the bar, and I saw them pawing over my knickers, but still continually looking over in our direction. Once, when Carrie knew they were watching, she turned and unbuttoned my mac, all the way. She didn't pull it open, but lay it loose across me, threatening at any moment to fall away. The mirror opposite now showed a thin strip of white skin down the middle of my body, which widened fractionally with every movement. With my hands still held behind me, my movements were restricted, but when I lifted my shoulders, the mac slipped more until the gap between my breasts was almost a hand's width across. Beneath the table, I swung my knees apart briefly and, above the table, the whiteness was visible down to my waist. When I looked down, my pubis was exposed.

The other man climbed down off his stool, and strolled down towards the toilets. As he approached us, Wendy started to replace the mac properly over me, but just as he passed, Carrie, on my other side, turned to help, and made sure that in doing so she had to pull it right open briefly so that for a few seconds one of my breasts was fully on display. All the girls burst out laughing and everyone else in the pub turned round to glare at us, and stare suspiciously at me.

When the pub closed, we set off to walk back to the flat that Carrie and Natalie rented. The night was warm and fine, and as we crossed the open car park behind the new shopping centre, we found a figure hovering furtively in the corner of the stairwell. It was one of the men from the pub who had obviously stopped to relieve himself.

Carrie called to him. 'Hey, mister! Do you want a blow-job?' All the others immediately screamed with laughter, while the man tried to squeeze even further into the darkness. Carrie grabbed hold of my arm, dragging me across to where he was now hurriedly refastening his trousers.

'Here! You've been eyeing her up all night. Have a proper look!' and she lifted the mac right off my shoulders and away, leaving me entirely exposed in the middle of the open square, unable even to use my hands to cover myself. The man finished fiddling with his trousers and turned suspiciously. Slowly he crossed the short space towards us, his eyes never leaving me, and stopped, a little unsteadily, a couple of feet away. A broad grin developed, spreading stupidly from ear to ear.

'Very nice! Very nice indeed. Nice big round titties. I like that.'

Carrie turned and looked appraisingly at me, then reached up and pinched my nipple. 'Yes, they are rather nice. Would you like her to suck you off? She will if you want.' Her smirk betrayed that the deliberate crudeness wasn't for his benefit, but just to cheapen me.

His grin widened even further, and then suddenly switched off. ''Ere, you 'aving me on? You the law, or something?'

'No! Not at all. It's a genuine offer. We're just playing a game and my friend Naomi would like to suck your cock. If you don't believe me, you feel her. I bet you'll find she's sopping wet. You feel her cunt.'

The man's piggy eyes narrowed and he took a step forward as his huge grimy hand landed on my stomach and crawled down. He dug his way between my thighs, roughly pushing his fingers along my tender lips before one thick stubby finger was suddenly thrust right up inside me. He laughed stale smoke and beer fumes into my face.

'Well, you're right about that, darlin'. She's fuckin' drippin', she is!' He continued rummaging his fingers through my pussy as I tried to pull away. 'Well, I gotta admit it's been quite a while since I've had anythin' but my own fist round my cock, so if she wants to give me a little suck, I ain't gonna stop 'er.'

Without removing his right hand from between my legs, he started to fumble at his zip with the other. The girls circled eagerly round us and young Anna pushed in so close she could have reached out and touched me. The man finished undoing his filthy trousers and finally pulled his hand away from my sex and held it out.

'Bloody hell! Soppin' wet, she is!'

'Where? Let me see!' Anna grabbed his wrist and inspected the evidence shining across the man's filthy fingers. 'God, so she is! Look! Gross!'

When she let go, the man laid his hand on top of my head as if blessing me. 'Down yer go, then, darlin'. Down yer go!'

I allowed myself to be pushed down until I was squatting in front of him, glad to be away from his groping hands, glad to be able to open my inflamed pussy to some cooler air, but sickened at the sight and smell of what was dangling there waiting for me. Like the man himself, his penis was short, stubby and pasty, and he held it in one hand, waving it at me as I tried to bring myself to put the revolting object in my mouth. Anna was leaning down, watching intently, fascinated revulsion on her childish face. She glanced eagerly from me to the man's cock and then back to me again.

'Come on, Naomi. I want to see you actually do it.' When I didn't move immediately, she put her hand on the back of my head and pushed me forward until the man's cock was brushing against my cheeks and lips.

I opened my mouth and let the foul thing plop in.

'God, she's doing it! She's actually doing it!' Anna was ecstatic, beaming round at the others, but suddenly she stood up and addressed the man. 'You mustn't, you know, actually come right in her mouth. I want to be able to see all your stuff coming out.'

The man smiled and chucked her under the chin. 'If that's what you wanna see, little girl, then you shall.'

She squatted down again beside me to be on a level to see better exactly what I was doing, utterly enthralled and utterly repulsed.

At first I couldn't move. I could feel his cock, only half warm as if it were only half alive, lying like a slug across my tongue. His sour smell filled my nostrils and a rancid unwashed taste filled my mouth. But although I hadn't moved, it was stiffening of its own accord and lengthening steadily in my mouth. I ran my tongue once round the thing and it twitched and swelled. His foul wiry pubic hair was no longer tickling my lips and nose, because I could no longer get the whole of his cock in my mouth. It was fatter now, too, and as I finally made myself work my tongue round beneath the slimy ridge it inflated rapidly. The head was so large that it was difficult to breathe and finally I released him and pulled away. Anna looked aghast as the thing waved glistening wetly in the twilight.

'God! It's huge!' The comment was mostly to herself, but she reached out to grab hold of it in her little fist, her fingers barely reaching round it, and pushed it back into my mouth. From the corner of my eye, I saw her hands disappear under her skirt.

The man reached down himself and gripped his cock round the base as I worked my lips over the head. He was starting to grunt now and his free hand gripped my hair, pulling and twisting painfully.

'That's the way, darlin'. Fuckin' magic.'

The ring of girls sniggered and pressed closer.

His breathing was becoming noticeably laboured and his grunting and encouragement more continuous. Suddenly he grunted even louder, a single strangled 'yes!' and pulled away. I quickly shut my eyes and my mouth as the fountain of cold slimy semen splashed down all over my face.

Anna was absolutely fascinated. 'Ugh! Gross! Look at her. It's all over her face! God! Let's find someone else and make her do it again!'

The mac was draped round me again and we moved off, the others laughing and singing as they danced their way through the empty shuttered streets while I stumbled after them with the man's sperm drying on my face and the sour taste of him still in my mouth. At a Chinese takeaway, Anna found two more men and got her wish.

We waited in the garish lights, peering in at the two customers inside, while Natalie went in to speak to them. We couldn't hear the words, but the meaning was all too sickeningly clear so that when they all turned towards us at one point, Anna knew immediately what was required and calmly pulled my mac wide open. I watched the expressions flow over their faces as I was displayed again, and as I saw the desire in their eyes, I felt the need reciprocated through my own body; utter uncontrollable lust that shook me and a feverish longing to be displayed completely and not just displayed but abused.

It was obvious that they took little persuading as they followed Natalie out and I was directed down an alley at the side of the building where we stopped beneath a security light. The girls gathered round again as one man unzipped his trousers and reached in to pull out his cock, already semi-erect, and wave it right in front of my face. He quickly fed the tip between my lips and was soon fully erect and grunting as he clutched my head and forced himself deeper and deeper into my mouth. When he shoved his hand down inside my mac to maul at my breasts, Anna, who had again pushed up close beside me, immediately pulled the mac away entirely so that everyone could watch his huge hands clutching at my breasts and squeezing my nipple as he pulled and clawed at me.

Anna again asked him to pull out before he climaxed so that she could watch, and he pulled back almost immediately as thick jets of semen erupted right in front of me and spattered over my eyes, down my cheeks and even in my hair.

Anna was jubilant. 'Ugh! It's just so gross! Look at all that stuff!' She was brazenly clutching at her own sex with both hands and almost jumping up and down with excitement. 'Now the other man! Now the other man!'

He slowly, nervously, unfastened his jeans and pulled out his cock. It was quite long but entirely soft, and although I licked him, sucked him and tried everything I could, his cock just didn't erect. Soon it was clear to everyone, including him, that he had had too much to drink to be able to get an erection. Carrie started to scoff, but Anna pushed her way to the front again.

'I know! Slap her with it! Slap her across the face!'

The man seemed a little bemused at first, but he stepped back and swung his long penis from side to side, slapping me across my mouth and cheeks, still wet with his friend's ejaculation. Five or six times he spattered against me before the first man called out from the mouth of the alley and this one rezipped his trousers and hurried away.

They wouldn't give me back the mac as we continued on our way. The other girls ran on ahead,

laughing and singing, waving the mac in the air as if
determined to wake people up and encourage them to
peer timidly from behind their lace curtains at the
spectacle I presented as I hobbled after them,
handcuffed, naked and defenceless through the empty
street. My face was covered with the drying sperm of
two strangers; my legs were smeared with dirt and
mud. But, as we came in sight of the flats where
Carrie lived, my pussy was running with the juice of
utter, unbelievable, arousal.

Her flat was on the second floor, and I could see
everyone hanging over the balcony watching for me.
They cheered raucously as I appeared at the front
entrance and began to climb warily up the open
concrete stairway through the centre of the block to
where they waited for me at the top, crowded on to
the little balcony.

'Look at her! She's filthy! Look at her face!'

I was led through the little hallway and straight
into the living room where they finally took off the
handcuffs and let me rub the angry red weals round
my wrists. Music was already blaring out, several
wine bottles had been opened, and glasses were
scattered around. Carrie came right up close to me,
slopping wine from her glass with every step, and
reached up to pinch my nipple, pinch it hard.

'You're disgusting, Naomi. Look at you! You'd
better have a shower, while we prepare for your
party.'

I was grateful for the chance of a shower, but the
implication of her other comment was less reassuring,
and I walked through to the bathroom trying to work
out what she could mean. I had assumed that I would
be allowed to shower alone, but Natalie, Anna and
one of the others decided they wanted to come with
me.

They didn't even let me draw the shower curtain across, insisting that they wanted to keep an eye on me all the time, so I stepped into the bath, took down the shower head and turned the water on. The cascade running down my skin was wonderful. At last I could wash off the ejaculation of the two men and all the dirt that I had collected during the evening and I played the jet all over me, rinsing my hair as well as my body and getting rid of the sticky beer that had been poured all over my breasts. But standing under the running water made me discover that I desperately needed to pee, and although I put it off for as long as possible, the drinks that had been forced on me during the night were becoming too much. I finally admitted my need to the three girls.

'Well, go on then,' said Natalie, taking the shower head out of my hand. 'You might as well do it there. Sit on the end so we can see.'

'No!' I protested. 'Come on, Natalie, please at least let me use the toilet.'

'No,' Anna interrupted. 'You can do it in the bath; I always do.' Her directness, her total lack of shame still took me aback but, with no choice, I sat down as I was told, but even this was not enough.

'Hold your fanny open. I want to see the piss coming out.'

How could anyone be so callous? How could a girl so young and, by her own admission, so inexperienced, be so completely shameless and depraved? I couldn't act like that now and at her age had been painfully shy and thoroughly naive. Yet it was her look of innocence that enhanced the humiliation of debasing myself at her command. I pulled my lips open while she leaned over to watch intently as I urinated down into the bath.

After I was done, Natalie kept hold of the shower head and as I continued sitting there with my legs wide apart and my lips held open, she played the spray of water over my sex and down as far as my bottom. The intense silence as they watched was broken by Anna. 'Nat? Stick it up her bum.'

'Don't be daft! It wouldn't fit!'

'Take the handle off. It unscrews.'

I am sure the others were wondering, as I was, how this young girl knew so much, but she was right. When Natalie had got the handle off and the weak spray had been reduced to a pathetic dribble, I was made to kneel down on all fours on the bottom of the bath.

I felt Natalie's thin fingers and sharp nails pulling and tugging at me as she pressed the metal ring against my anus. I had never in my life had anything pushed into me there and the muscles naturally closed to prevent any entry. It was Anna, again Anna, who had the solution.

'Squirt some shampoo in first. That should lubricate it.'

The small sharp round nozzle of the bottle was pressed against me and then a sudden squirt of it shot inside. The shampoo bottle was removed and this time when the shower hose pressed, it slipped through the ring of muscle and suddenly the hard alien shape was crawling up inside me, a cruel invasive presence that lacked any sympathy with my own warm and yielding body. The flood of water emphasised the foreignness and maliciousness of this encroachment, and I shuddered, pushing her hand away as I felt myself being bloated and filled.

Once she withdrew the tube, the need to expel the water was paramount. I needed to get up, somehow to stagger over to the toilet and relieve the unbearable pressure, but I couldn't do it. I couldn't risk stepping out of the bath and had only got up into a squatting position when the need became too strong and, despite the gloating audience, despite the shame, despite the ridicule of the baying girls watching me, I let myself go where I was.

Their howls of laughter brought all the others running in from the living room to see what they were missing. They arrived just as Natalie was rinsing round the bath.

'You should have called us!'

'Yes, do it again!'

So a second time I was made to kneel down in the bath and they all watched avidly while a little shampoo was squirted into my bottom and then the long hard end of the shower tube slithered deep inside and a second slow jet of warm water filled my guts.

The bathroom was too small to fit everybody so this time they insisted that I go out on to the balcony. I stumbled out, doubled over but so desperate to release the churning contents that when Carrie set down a small plastic bucket in the middle of the balcony, I no longer had the stamina to protest. They all stood round in gales of laughter as I was led up and allowed to squat over it and could finally release all the water from inside me. So public a display of so intimate a process was alone almost enough to flood me to orgasm.

When I was led back into the lounge, dry again, the chairs had all been pushed out to the edges of the room, making space in the centre where a large towel was spread out.

Carrie giggled when she saw my reaction. 'Don't be shy, Naomi. Come and lie down here, on your back, right in the middle where we can all see you.'

The girls all filled their glasses, perched on chairs or took up positions on the floor, and settled back to watch although, after I was arranged to Carrie's satisfaction, I noticed that several changed their positions, shuffling down to somewhere they would get a better view between my legs. Even little Anna, who had been given pride of place in the centre, edged up closer.

Carrie returned to her seat and called to one of the others to begin. She came out, knelt down beside me and made me part my legs and raise my knees so that I was completely revealed to everyone, as if I were at a doctor's surgery. She remarked at how wet I was, and then the others laughed because I was blushing, but every sneer, every humiliation heaped on me only made it worse. My clitoris was swollen; my lips were swollen and now I was lying spread-legged in front of all these people, most of them strangers, while they probed and toyed with me as they wanted.

The girl started applying some sort of roll-on gel all over my pubis, but when I asked what she was doing, she wouldn't tell me precisely. 'Just making you pretty.'

She smeared it all over my triangle of pubic hair at the front, and even between my legs, right on to the lips themselves. For this she had to pull them open, and the continual pressing, pulling and squeezing inevitably made them swell and moisten even further than they already were. Even this, an entirely automatic reaction, led them to mock and jeer, so she continued for some while, deliberately prodding and teasing just to disgrace me.

Next the girl had a cloth and a bowl of water and she started to wash me. It was the cheers that met this which caused me to look down again, trying to find out exactly what was being done to me. It was then that I discovered that what she had been putting on was a depilatory cream and as she wiped away the cream, all my pubic hair was coming away with it. I was being left as bare as a newborn child.

When she was done, all the others crowded round to see, to touch, to feel the smooth delicate skin. Even Wendy came over and peered down at me, before reaching out to run gentle fingers across the smooth hairless surface of my swollen sensitive lips.

Carrie was delighted. 'That's much better. Now we can see what you've got and now it's play time. In a minute I want to watch you frig yourself, but first, we're going to blindfold you so you won't know who's doing what and spank you. Four from each of us, I think. Turn over on your hands and knees.'

I pleaded with them then to let me go. I really begged and pleaded, literally on my knees, to be excused that. Last week I had received twenty-four strokes with a cane and the pain had been unbearable. Yet I would have preferred to receive that again, even double that, to the utter humiliation of being their toy, to be spanked like a naughty child, to suffer every indignity they could dream up and finally to have to masturbate in front of all of them, in front of friends, work colleagues, strangers and even little Anna. In truth, I knew even before I started that they would not listen to me. And maybe I was not convincing enough, because even as I knelt there, I could feel the growing arousal that belied my tears and that was welling up deep in my pussy. I knew that when they spanked me I would scream and sob and make an exhibition of myself just as I had done the week before, and I began to suspect that they wanted to show that they could better the men in what they put me through.

I was made to kneel on the floor while they all gathered in a semicircle behind me but as the blindfold was placed over my eyes, I was lost. I could feel my sex, newly exposed and vulnerable, throbbing in anticipation of the pain to come and the blindfold was soaking wet with my tears even before I was kneeling in position, my forehead resting on the floor, my bottom straight up in the air.

The first four slaps landed in quick succession straight across my cheeks. They were not nearly as hard as the cane and as I waited for the second four, I began to think that I might survive this. Then the second girl started, much harder and her blows were more accurately placed together in one spot on one cheek of my bottom. I heard my own crying as I waited for the shuffling that told me the next girl was ready. I leapt up the instant the first landed, for she had deliberately aimed much lower, right across the tops of my thighs. The rest of hers were the same, a band just below my bottom that stung worse than anything that Alec or Paul had ever done.

I thought at first this was probably Anna; such a cruel variation seemed characteristic of her, but I was wrong because Anna was next. I heard her innocent voice (she didn't care if I knew which one she was) telling me to kneel up straight and I knew she had something evil in mind. Even so, when her first vicious slap landed not on my bottom but across the side of my left breast, I screamed and my hands flew up to protect myself at the same time as I tore off the blindfold. She just told me that if I didn't take my hands down, she would put the handcuffs back on me. I hesitated before dragging my hands away, and then knelt there, my hands at my sides as I waited to receive the remainder of the child's cruelty. My degradation now seemed complete, and I bore the remainder of her slaps, a second on my left breast then two across my right, with few tears. Someone I didn't know followed Anna and she hit me on the front of my thighs. After that came Wendy, my friend, but she avoided my eyes as she smacked me at least as hard as any of the others, aiming one stroke at each cheek of my bottom and one to each breast. The last girls followed Wendy's pattern as well and as the final stinging slap burnt across my nipple, I collapsed on the floor in tears, my thighs twisting and quivering with a longing I was given no opportunity to satisfy.

They did not replace the blindfold after that but made me kneel back on all fours again as they all crowded round me. Immediately their hands were swarming all over me; nipping and squeezing, nails scraping across the tenderest areas, scratching at the hand prints, pinching at the bruises. My swollen and tender breasts hung beneath me, aching for some tenderness and Anna again focused on my breasts. I remember wondering whether it was jealousy because of the minuscule swellings beneath her own sweat shirt, for she was blatantly bra-less and if it hadn't been for her tiny nipples poking out, she could have passed for a boy. She was carefully examining my face as her fingers pulled and tugged at my breasts, dragging out my nipples as far as she could stretch them, and always watching avidly to gauge my reaction. Suddenly one of my nipples was clamped viciously tight and I looked down to find she had attached a wooden clothes peg to the delicate nipple. The instant shock as the peg closed completely winded me, so that I couldn't cry, couldn't speak, couldn't breathe. She smiled when she saw my agony and calmly took a second peg, stretched out my other nipple and then for a few racking minutes held the jaws open around the nipple and then smiled even wider as she slowly let the spring close on to me.

Within seconds, my nipples had gone so numb that the pain was surprisingly bearable, but it returned the instant she took the pegs off again and Carrie told me that they now wanted to watch me masturbate.

I tried refusing and I tried pleading again, but they ignored all my pleas and settled down to watch again, a comfortable and respectable audience waiting to be amused by the naked entertainer who was spread out before them. Yet I was wet, visibly and undeniably wet and lying on the floor as I was with all of them gathered round me, they could all see the evidence. It was so shameful and the worst part was that I knew what effect their presence would have. I was already aroused from everything that had already been done to me and, as my fingers slid down between my lips, to have them there witnessing my own self-abasement was the final glorious straw that destroyed all my self-respect.

Still, they all watched me closely, and each time I was nearly there, when I was tantalisingly close to coming, they made me stop and only allowed me to play with my nipples until some of the urgency had died down. Then I was permitted to touch my clitoris again, until I was once more nearly ready to come.

Ultimately it was Carrie who fetched a carrot from their kitchen and ordered me to use that to bring myself off with, but they all giggled at the obvious ease with which the thing slid inside me and the way it immediately triggered my complete loss of self-control as I climaxed so loudly.

And it was Natalie who then fetched a plate of butter and a second carrot and insisted that I push this one into my bottom. The utter humiliation of being made to masturbate seemed insignificant compared with what they now demanded. The thing looked huge, although in truth it was not much thicker than a man's cock, but I pushed it deep into the yellow butter, and it looked even more disgusting and threatening once it was shining ready for its sickening purpose. Yet it was also more alluring, and the prospect of being publicly stretched in so intimate a place by so huge and obscene a phallus made me tremble. I did finally succeed as they all sat watching in rapt attention.

And it was finally Anna who demanded that I pull it back out again and put it in my mouth and lick it clean.

And at the end, they carefully replaced the blindfold and settled me down on my back again. And as I lay there, still naked, each of them came in turn and squatted over my face while I licked them. I could see nothing, just felt each of them come to take up her position; the feet either side of my head and then the person squatting and a vulva was lowered down and pushed on to me. I had never in my life kissed a girl like this, and had never considered how different they might be. Some had masses of thick hair; some had none, although whether these were completely shaved or just underneath, I don't know. Some had huge lips, thick fleshy curtains that filled my mouth; some lips were so small I could hardly find anything there at all. Some held themselves above my mouth; others pressed down and rubbed themselves against me. Some were wet and flowing the instant my tongue reached up to them; others were relatively dry. Some climaxed almost at once; some were slow and demanding but they all stayed until they were satisfied. Some were sweet and fragrant; some were bitter and sweaty and I am certain that one of them had only just been to the toilet and hadn't wiped herself at all, not in either place.

And every one of them came to me, all eight presenting themselves in a steady succession. Each aroma that filled my nostrils was subtly different but all unmistakably feminine and all pungently aroused.

I had no idea which was which, and I was sorry for that. I would like to know which was Anna: one of them had seemed not only small and closed, but also clean and sweet, and I could imagine that as being Anna, barely eighteen and, as she had confessed, a virgin. But had she meant just with men or was I the first person of either sex who had tasted her vulva and brought her to orgasm? Equally, Anna could as easily have been the one who came to me straight from the toilet, dirty and sour. In many ways that seemed more likely.

And I would like to know which was Wendy. We had been friends for many years and she had taken my side several times earlier in the evening. Yet when the opportunity had arisen, when I was lying there on the floor, naked and helpless, when she had the chance, she too followed the lead of all the others, coming to squat over my face, compelling me to lick her sex, to push my tongue into her vagina, to nibble at her clitoris and accept her juice smeared across my mouth, added to the juices of the others. Whichever position she had taken in the queue, even if, out of some last vestige of loyalty or sympathy, she had hesitated as long as she could, she had ultimately taken her place above me and forced me to lick her to orgasm. Someone, and maybe this was Wendy, had also presented the tight bitter ring of her anus and required me to lick her there as well. Just because we were friends, it hadn't stopped her adding to my humiliation, but I would have liked to know how far she had gone. I needed to know how to react the next time we met as friends; whether I should say nothing about it, whether I could ask for an apology, or whether she would order me to take my clothes off again, lie down on the floor and lick between her legs until she climaxed.

And which of them was last in the line? Who had lowered herself over me when she was already so wet that I almost drowned in the river of her arousal? Who was it who then leaned down and pulled my legs so wide apart and slapped me? Who had known that after the first vicious stinging blow across that most tender part of my body that I would lift up my hips in a wordless appeal for another? And a third and then a fourth landed straight across my open sex, until I again made so shameful a spectacle of myself by losing control as I was convulsed in another racking screaming climax.

Kate's Tale – Baby Chloe

I'm not gay; I don't 'do' girls and never have done, at least nothing beyond an exploratory pubescent kiss; our mouths closed as firmly as our eyes (I had read in a magazine that you were meant to shut your eyes) and it had been uninformative, reassuringly unrewarding and never repeated.

Nor am I cruel. There was just something about Chloe from the moment of our first encounter that annoyed and riled me, so that the longer it continued, the more Chloe deserved everything she got.

Nor am I promiscuous; I mean I've sometimes enjoyed a little variety when it could be arranged without complications, but I was as near married to Barry as it is possible to be without actually putting on the silly white dress and all that stuff.

But Chloe was so pathetic and wimpish that when she was there available and I was already annoyed with her, I suppose I simply took the opportunities as each one was presented. Something in Chloe's timid acquiesence seemed to invite ever greater lengths so that the more meekly each demand was accepted, the more I was encouraged to persist. It's not something that I'd ever do again, and I'm certainly not proud of myself, but I've done worse.

I had worked at Walton Matthews for four years, and I like to think that they were pleased with me. I got a first at Bristol, came top in my year of the Walton Matthews' graduate intake and I was the first woman in all their eighty-six-year history to have made the grade of Senior Account Executive below the age of thirty. I don't mean to boast, but I work hard and expect that to be recognised and supported. Now I had just three days within which to compile a full financial report for Fletchers Engineering, which was planning a reverse takeover of one of the last big Sheffield steel companies, and the last thing I needed was to be foisted with some silly student fresh from university and still wet behind the ears. I know someone has to train the new ones, and I suppose I wasn't welcomed by the first Senior I was placed under, but this could hardly have happened at a worse time. Fletchers, based in Lancaster, was one of the newest and most promising clients we had (one that I had been nurturing personally for nearly two years) and although I would have welcomed an offer of help with the work, what I needed was a competent, skilled assistant, not a trainee.

Chloe appeared nervously in my doorway one Monday morning, looking about ten years old. Her training seemed to have taught her how to work the door handles and not much else and I had only that one week, during much of which I was already committed to meetings, before going to Lancaster to wrap it all up. The trip had been arranged almost a month previously, leaving London on the Tuesday morning, spending all day Wednesday and Thursday there and returning late on Thursday evening. I had been looking forward to this because overnight trips didn't happen more than two or three times a year and were all the more welcome when they did. Apart from being pampered in a hotel at someone else's expense, I enjoyed being away from home and independent; it didn't hurt to get a break from Barry. New city: new partner. Well, sometimes, anyway.

I drove; I expect Chloe had a licence, but I didn't ask. I'd made the trip so often over the last year or two that I could have done it blindfold. But the journey up would be the first chance we would have to talk, and although I resented her presence and had been quite unimpressed with her performance so far, I was trying to keep an open mind. We set off in plenty of time but the M25 was practically solid and we were only just at Luton by eleven o'clock when I stopped for petrol and coffee.

I didn't intend to stop again until we reached Lancaster, but it was less than an hour before Chloe was squirming uncomfortably in her seat and then, trying to sound offhand, asking how long the journey would take.

'Depends.' I was equally off-hand in my reply. 'Three hours, I would guess. Possibly four; depends on the traffic. If we get past Birmingham OK it should be all right, but half the M6 is coned off so the whole of that could be one long car park.'

She was silent but, after squirming for a few minutes more, brought the subject up again. 'Are we going to stop on the way?'

'No, I don't think so. If we get on, we should be able to get a good two hours work in tonight at least. Simon Fletcher is taking us out to a concert this evening so we can't work too late.'

She perked up at this. 'Ah. Did he say who was playing?'

'No. But it's Mahler, so I hope it'll be good.'

'Oh. I don't know them.'

I let it drop; there was little hope that any further conversation on these lines would be productive.

Chloe was still squirming, more and more obviously, and although I could guess what her problem was, I ignored her; if the girl wasn't willing to ask for what she wanted, she would have to learn to do without. Perhaps I was just being obstinate, but it had become a matter of pride until, as we crawled along the elevated section of the M6 north of Birmingham, I started to question the wisdom of my stance. If Chloe had a real need, my upholstery might be the first thing to suffer.

'Are you all right? Are you having your period?'

'Oh no!' Her answer was immediate. 'No, I'm fine.'

'Good.'

Chloe immediately realised what she had said, and at last conceded. 'I just do rather need the toilet. Do you think we could stop at the next services?'

I was victorious. 'The next one would be Birmingham North. Could we at least wait until Keele? Then a nice cup of coffee will set us up for the last bit.'

She said nothing in reply, and stayed silent for the next twenty minutes, even after the traffic cleared at junction 10A and was quickly followed by the sign announcing services in one mile or fifteen. She bit her lip, staring longingly up the slip road as we zipped past. Then she leant over to look at the speedometer, and I guessed she was calculating how long fifteen miles would take if we continued at 85 miles per hour. I let her complete the sum and grit her teeth before breaking it to her.

'The next services are at Stafford, and then Keele is right after that. Half an hour at most.' And then added, 'Unless the traffic gets bad again.'

She almost sobbed. 'I'm sorry, Kate, but I don't think I can wait that long. Couldn't we please stop at the first one?'

'Oh, for heaven's sake, Chloe! You went when we stopped at Newport Pagnell. You can't need to go again this soon.'

I knew I was being harsh, and that it was largely anger at our slow progress which was making me look for ways to blame Chloe for the heavy traffic. I knew too that a good manager would have been trying to cultivate a better long-term working relationship, but I won't tolerate weakness and I've never had much time for all that networking stuff, not with other women anyway.

Chloe collapsed under my onslaught. 'I'm sorry, but I do.'

'I'll have to put you in nappies at this rate!' It was a cruel sneer.

'What?' She sounded appalled at the suggestion. 'You can't do that. I mean I'm sure I can wait a bit longer if I have to.' Her answer came out in a rush, the words tumbling from the heart, not the brain.

I snorted and glanced over at her. 'It's all right, Chloe. I was only joking.'

'Well, yes,' she answered, blushing scarlet. 'I know.'

It could have been just a flash of intuition, or maybe there was actually something in her tone, but she sounded unconvinced and unconvincing. When I turned to face her, she refused to look up, just peered down at her fingers, twisting in her lap.

'Yes,' I repeated, 'I was joking.' The girl turned to look out of her window at the lines of holiday traffic as we sped past. 'But you weren't, were you?'

Chloe swallowed, and then turned to look straight at me, the defiant excess of innocence that broadcasts a lie. 'Yes, I was. Of course I was.'

I didn't argue with her, but I certainly didn't believe her either, and we lapsed into silence until I turned off the engine at Stafford Services.

'Well, we certainly don't want to risk any accidents, so off you go. I'll be in the restaurant.'

I watched her disappear off to the ladies' and went to get a cup of overpriced and overstewed coffee. I also bought a drink for Chloe, so that when she came to join me she found it standing on the table, unmistakably intended for her: a fizzy orange; in a plastic beaker; with a straw.

The implication was so obvious that I thought at first she was going to protest. The struggle was visible on her face, but she held her tongue; maybe she thought that objection would have been even more babyish. She drank it all down, eventually, and I managed to get her all the way to Lancaster without having to stop again.

It was gone three o'clock by the time we arrived at our hotel, whereas I had been hoping to have arrived, checked in and out again before two. Then the fun started. I honestly believe the cretin of a hotel receptionist must have been measuring his experience in hours. He smiled obsequiously.

'I'm sorry, Miss Skye. Your fax clearly states one single room, en suite, for two nights; continental breakfast.'

'All right. Well, I'm sure my secretary faxed you again last week to make it two. Anyway, never mind what was booked. Just give us two rooms.'

'I'm sorry, I can't. We're completely full. It's graduation week at the university you see.'

'Are you telling me that you don't have a free room anywhere in the hotel for a regular guest?'

'Sorry!' He smiled, but he wasn't.

'Fine.' I spat my response at him. 'We'll go somewhere else. This time and all future trips.'

'I think you'll find everywhere is full. All the students' families have come up for graduation week, you see.'

'Yes. You told me that already.' I trembled in an icy silence trying to decide who to blame: the spotty boy waiting so smugly for my decision or the irritating girl for whom I now needed another room. The horrible truth was that I knew in my heart which of the three people standing there was really to blame for failing to change the booking, and that realisation only made me angrier. Finally the boy spoke again, and the smile was back.

'I can change you to a double, if that would help. I mean I know it's not ideal, but as you are both young ladies . . .' He let the words hang in the air. I didn't jump at it immediately so he carried on.

'Twin beds, of course.' The thought that it might have been anything else had never occurred to me.

'So I should bloody well hope,' I snapped back at him.

'Yes, of course.' He glanced up from under his neanderthal eyebrows and we both knew that I had accepted his offer of the double room whatever further protests I put up now.

Actually the room wasn't bad. It had a good bathroom and two double beds, so although I wasn't going to be able to invite anybody back, I probably couldn't have done that anyway with Chloe somewhere else in the same hotel; not without it being all over the office within minutes of our return.

We didn't unpack, just dumped our stuff. Chloe disappeared into the bathroom (again) and we were round at Fletchers' offices by four. I've always found Simon Fletcher difficult to deal with; I can never gauge what is going on in his head, which is something that normally I'm good at. He has a personal assistant, emphatically not a secretary, called Jody Wallace and I can't work out the relationship. Neither of them is married and they don't live together, but I don't know if they sleep together or if he's gay or what the score is. They certainly have a great rapport and trust each other implicitly. Sometimes Simon looks as if he wants to jump me, but he's never followed up any encouragement. I can't figure it out.

The meeting went well and we had covered a good deal of ground by the time we broke off just after six o'clock, arranging to meet at our hotel at seven when Simon and Jody would take us to the concert. Simon had seemed very taken with Chloe, in fact they both did, but that didn't please me entirely: I was the one who had put in all the work.

To be fair, Chloe had been right on the ball during our discussions, raising a couple of good points; however, she ruined everything, just as we were getting down to the detail of the funding arrangements, by interrupting it all to disappear off to the lavatory again.

She was really starting to annoy me by now. If she'd been a man, I wouldn't have felt so strongly that her failings reflected on me, but as we were both girls, it was too easy to lump us together.

In the car afterwards, I confronted her. 'Is there something wrong with you, Chloe?'

'How do you mean? No! No, there isn't.'

'So why do you keep having to run off to the lavatory every ten minutes?'

'It's not every ten minutes.'

'Twice on the way up here. Then at the hotel before we came out, then you interrupt the negotiations to go running off again. It's ridiculous!'

'I didn't know you were counting.' She was mumbling with all the grace of a sulky schoolgirl.

'Well? Are you sure there's nothing wrong? Were you telling the truth about having your period?'

'Yes, of course I was! I just have to go a lot, that's all.'

'Well, it can't go on. I'm sorry but it looks bad. Bad for you, bad for me, bad for Walton Matthews. I was only joking about putting you in nappies, but if this goes on, we'll have to do something.'

'All right then.' Her voice was so low, almost inaudible over the engine, the air-conditioner and the outside traffic, that I had to ask her to repeat herself.

'All right. I said all right. If you are so keen for me not to embarrass you and that will help, well all right. Do it.'

I was struck dumb. I was still not entirely sure how serious I was in my proposal. It all seemed highly bizarre, although since my grandmother was incontinent, and I had sometimes had to help her, I was less disconcerted by the idea of an adult wearing nappies than many people might have been. It was really Chloe's attitude that annoyed me. She seemed so unconcerned, so unwilling to consider the effect her actions had on others.

On the way back into the city, there was a new hypermarket off the roundabout at the motorway exit and as we waited for the traffic lights, I turned to her again.

'Look, Chloe, I don't want to be difficult about this, and it is firmly understood in Walton Matthews that what happens during off-duty time on these out-of-London trips is never carried back to the office. That means if you want to get yourself laid by every waiter in the hotel, I won't go telling tales back at the office. The same goes for what I do. But we need to make a good impression here. It is important and if it would be easier for you this way, then I think you should take the easy option. After all, nobody else need know.'

'All right. I've said all right. I don't mind!' She seemed annoyed that I had raised it again instead of acting on her earlier offhand acceptance.

So I pulled into the hypermarket car park and went in to try to get some nappies. They didn't have any for adults, but had some small towels which would do perfectly well and they did stock plastic incontinence pants in an adult size. That success moderated my temper a little, and I suppose recollections of my poor Nan's embarrassment over the subject helped too. I tossed the package into the back of the car and tried to rebuild some bridges with Chloe until we got back to the hotel. It wasn't entirely successful.

We went up to our room and after I had freshened up, I left Chloe getting changed while I went down to the bar to meet our guests.

The concert was excellent and, by the interval, even Chloe seemed to be enjoying it, but then I can't imagine anyone failing to be stirred by Mahler's second.

The second half was, if anything, even better until Chloe started fidgeting. Finally she asked to be let out, meaning we all had to stand up, as well as half a dozen other people down our row. Jody Wallace was all concern and attention and that only annoyed me all the more. As soon as we were alone again after the concert, I admit I lost my temper entirely.

'What the bloody hell are you playing at? Are you doing this on purpose? The whole idea of you wearing those bloody things was so that this wouldn't happen.'

'I'm not wearing them.'

'What? Why on earth not?'

'I've changed my mind.'

'What?'

'I've changed my mind; you can't treat me like that. It isn't fair. And anyway, I don't know how to put them on.'

190

'Oh for God's sake! You've put nappies on a baby before, haven't you?'

'No.'

'What? Don't you have any babies in your family? Have you never babysat anyone else's children?'

'They've always used disposable ones.'

It was so pathetic an excuse that I drove for several minutes in silence. 'Well, if you weren't even wearing them, why the hell did you have an orange juice in the interval?'

'I thought I'd be all right.'

'Oh for heaven's sake!'

I was still livid when we arrived back at the hotel.

'Well, I'm sorry, Chloe, but you are going to wear one of those things from now on. I'm not having you running back and forth all day tomorrow, interrupting every meeting. Nor do I want you waking me up every half hour tonight, for that matter. Get ready for bed and then I'm bloody well putting one on you myself.'

I let Chloe go into the bathroom first, and sat seething until she finally emerged in a pretty, but quite long and demure nightdress.

'Right. You'd better get up on the bed then.'

'I'll get my mat.'

'What?'

'My mat. I brought a mat with me. I put it under the sheet at night in case I have an accident.'

'I see. So you do have a pr – accidents sometimes. Why the bloody hell didn't you say so?'

'I was embarrassed!' She spoke so softly that I believed her. Perhaps the whole sullen act was only there to hide her shame; certainly I could see that I might have behaved similarly in her position. I even began to feel slightly embarrassed myself, that perhaps I had been rather too hard on the poor girl if she really did have a problem.

But no. If she had a problem she should deal with it, not let it mess up everybody else's arrangements and certainly not leave it for me to sort out.

I discreetly turned my back only to be confronted by her reflection in the dressing table mirror as she fetched a wide square of pale blue plastic from her case and unfolded it on her bed. Then she lifted the hem of her nightdress and carefully lay down on the bed in the middle of the mat.

She looked over to me, and our eyes met in the mirror. She could see that I had been watching her, in spite of my grand gesture and pretence.

'OK, I'm ready,' she said.

I hadn't really thought through how I would set about this. For all my bravado, I had never actually put a nappy on anyone except small babies, and that had been quite a time ago. I unwrapped the packet of towels, shook one out and approached the bed and the little half-naked figure waiting for me there.

She appeared quite calm and acquiescent: the nightdress was pulled up her legs to reveal no more than the tip of a tiny curl of pale brown hair in the deep valley between her tightly closed thighs. Yet as I approached, her eyes blinked nervously and she turned away, then reached down and pulled the hem higher up her body. I concentrated on folding the nappy in half diagonally and lying it down neatly beside her on the bed. That way I didn't have to watch. When I turned back, the nightdress was up as far as her waist, but my eyes were immediately drawn to her pubic hair, a huge lush carpet that spread luxuriantly up Chloe's stomach almost as far as her neatly dimpled belly button. It was so rich and extravagant an expanse that although it covered and concealed her sex completely, it had a sensuality all of its own. It was too evident, too prominent to be disregarded or to be considered as secondary to the vulva that it veiled, and I longed to have an excuse to touch it, somehow to experience that shamelessly provocative spread and to pull my fingers through her curls.

I realised that I had been staring, but tore my eyes away, up to Chloe's face where I found her own eyes set on me. They glistened, as if tears would come at any provocation, and her lips trembled. If she was ashamed of her accidents, I had done nothing to help by staring at her so blatantly. Yet it gave me the chance I wanted and, without thinking, I grabbed it.

I smiled at her and put on my best jolly gym-mistress voice.

'That's a splendid little bush!' and I ruffled my fingers through the curly growth as if this was just an objective comment, one woman to another. The contact was fleeting and I immediately turned to pick up the nappy from beside her and carried on in a brisk business-like way, but I had done it. I glowed. I had done it. I had touched the curls, felt the soft expanse in my fingers and it was hypnotic. I could barely contain myself as I continued with the job I was there for.

'Now then, lift up your bottom so I can slide this underneath.'

She pressed down with her feet and arched up her hips so I could push the end of the nappy under, reach round, grab the far end with only the very lightest contact with her skin, and pull it through. Now the next part. The short end must come up between her legs. She should have known that and yet she was lying back on the bed again with her legs straight down and tight together so that I would have to ask her to move. I wanted to be strong, dynamic and powerful, but I have never asked a girl to open her legs before, and I didn't know how to do it now.

'Could you, er . . . I need to get the other part between your legs.'

She blushed, and I felt myself doing the same, but she slid her legs apart so that I could reach through to the small white triangle hidden beneath her. I snatched it up and quickly folded the other corners in, but when I started to put the first safety pin through the layers of thick towelling, I pushed my fingers back down inside the nappy, but only to protect her from being pricked by the pin. Not to feel the soft curls brushing against my fingertips again; not that at all. The second pin followed the same pattern.

'There!' I said. 'That's done.'

I turned away, snatched up my own nightdress and left her stretched out across her bed, as I hurried into the bathroom, shut the door firmly behind me and leaned against it for a few moments while I composed myself again. I was able to calm my breathing and was back in control when I sat down on the loo. But the noise of my own pee splashing down into the bowl echoed deafeningly round the cold tiled room and I was sure that Chloe would be able to hear me. But there was nothing I could do now, and so I sat and listened to the flow and deliberately turned my mind back to Barry; a safe reliable image of a safe reliable partner who never had – and never would – upset my equilibrium.

As soon as I was changed, I scuttled back into the bedroom, turned off the light and resolutely turned my back towards Chloe's bed. But I couldn't stop her whispering goodnight to me across the darkness.

In the morning, I opened my eyes to find myself staring into another pair of eyes just a few feet away. Chloe was obviously wide awake, and looked as if she had been for some time.

'Good morning, Kate.' She smiled across at me with a cheerful honesty that I had never seen on her face before. She was almost another person entirely. 'Did you sleep well? I did! Better than I have for ages!'

I checked the clock before I mumbled an appropriate greeting and pulled the blankets up over my face.

'The thing is,' she carried on blithely, 'I rather need you to take the nappy off. I'm afraid it's quite wet.'

I didn't move. I just lay with my face safely hidden under the covers and allowed the previous night's memories to wash back in. Chloe disturbing everyone during the concert. Those huge moist eyes when I was angry with her. Her obedient acquiesence to wearing a nappy. Putting it on. Her body spread out on the bed. Her vast field of brown pubic curls. Warm damp curls that my fingers had touched. Her docile tolerance when I asked her to open her legs.

But something more. I could believe, just, that she hadn't known previously how to put a nappy on. But now she knew; now she could have no real need for me to do it for her again. More than that, she certainly didn't need me, and never would have needed me, to help her take one off. She was just playing pathetic for its own sake, as if this was some game, a sort of doctors and nurses, that I would want to play. Well, she could manage on her own.

The words were forming in my mouth when I paused and allowed the thoughts to stretch forward another move or two. She had put the ball in my court. Did I want to keep it in play, or did I want the game to be over? I ought to tell her she should do it herself, but she had given me a choice.

If I spoke those words, she would accept and agree; she could scarcely do otherwise. She would get out of bed and go through into the bathroom and close the door; that would be the end of the affair. If she had wanted to take the thing off, she could have done it by now without waiting for me to wake up. So why was she asking me, her boss, to be bothered with her embarrassing personal problems?

But supposing I accepted her request for help, then what would happen? I would go over to her bed, unpin the thing, open it out, and there she would be again. Presented for me. There would almost certainly be another opportunity to touch her, to feel those soft curls, maybe even to see better what was hidden deep within them. Perhaps not when taking the old nappy off, but certainly when it came time for the clean one to go on.

No, that wasn't me. I wasn't going to get caught up in the whims of this pathetic adolescent. I was ashamed enough already of what I had done last night and frightened of what I had nearly done: what I couldn't trust myself to refuse if the opportunity arose. Worse still, Chloe's request strongly suggested that my response had been thoroughly transparent. I turned my mind back to Barry: his big firm body; his strong arms; his deep masculine chest. A chest, I suddenly realised, covered in short brown curls almost identical to those curls of Chloe's that I was trying to forget.

'I think you can manage that much on your own,' I said and turned over. For a while there was silence from the other bed, but then I heard her moving about, the springs squeaking and I desperately wanted to turn over and watch. If I couldn't touch her, surely I could at least look.

The noises stopped and then the voice drifted across again, so small, so in need of comforting and the image of that rich triangle of brown curls washed back into my mind.

'Please? Kate? I'm just not sure that I can get the new one on properly, you know, so that it'll stay. And I don't . . .' her voice wavered, almost broke, 'I don't want you to be angry with me again.' I gave in.

'Just a minute.' I threw back my sheets and blankets, quickly pulling down my own nightdress from where it seemed to have ridden right up to my hips during the night. I put on my dressing gown and tied it firmly. I didn't want the sheerness of my own nightdress to betray any secrets that I would prefer to keep to myself. That realisation made me start to feel tricked; I had been manoeuvred into something that I knew I should have avoided, had decided once already that I would avoid. I turned back to her bed, determined to be as brief as possible.

But then as I stepped up to where she was lying, her eyes stared up from that pale round face with such pain and pleading, like a puppy on a saccharine Christmas card, that I was a little melted. And below the face? Below that her clothing came down as far as her waist and there it stopped. Her legs were together again, but the same entrancing field of chestnut curls was spread like a feast across her belly, beckoning me, tempting me again to touch her, to feel, to enjoy.

There was one nappy screwed up on the corner of the mat, and Chloe was holding out a fresh one to me. I carefully spread out the clean white square, folded it neatly across and turned away for the pins, refusing to be drawn to her, refusing to acknowledge what was being offered and what I was steadily getting more curious to explore.

When she obediently slid her legs apart and lifted up her bottom, I found I could see more of her than had been possible in the dim artificial light the evening before. It was hypnotic: so intimate, so close that all I needed to do was reach out and I could have touched her. Not just the brown curls this time, not just the hair covering her sex, but the girl herself. The soft warm skin that I could now see so clearly. And she was quite different from me: her lips thin and tightly closed together like a young girl. The hair spread all over them and disappeared down beyond her sex. Evidently she didn't trim her hair, and I found myself wondering if those firmly sealed lips had ever been opened by another hand, or whether she was as virginal as her shyness suggested. Although she could present herself as openly as this, it was almost as if in her innocence she didn't understand what she offered.

I reached between her thighs to the doubled-over corner of the nappy and pulled it up. My fingers grazed against her thigh, brushed lightly through the thinner hairs on her lips and I was no longer fully in control. My hand pressed against the soft damp folds of her vulva. I touched her. I touched her skin, and I shivered, felt her shiver too as I quickly pulled away.

But almost immediately she started to sit up. 'Could I get up a moment, Kate?'

'No, just wait a moment. I haven't finished.' It was too dangerous and I couldn't risk anything more and I needed to get her properly covered up and safely dressed. I needed to get away among other people, away from temptation.

'Oh, but please!'

'Stay still!' I know I was angry, but I was frightened too, and I pushed her back down flat. But as I turned back to pick up the long side corners of the nappy, a dribble of pee emerged from somewhere within those thick curls, at first just a little trickle that ran down on to the nappy but then it strengthened, pushed out a short distance until it was no longer running through the dampened hairs but now landing in a little pool between her thighs, a couple of inches below her crotch. As Chloe cried out suddenly, a single strangled sob of despair, the flow stopped briefly, and then emerged again, powerfully now, a thin jet that rose up in a gentle arc curving through the air in a glorious golden rainbow landing down between her feet. Chloe had turned away, but I was hypnotised, disgusted and bewitched. The jet continued, swaying from side to side and splattering onto the mat before finally the curve subsided and the last trickle joined the first small pool soaking into the already saturated nappy. Finally it stopped.

Chloe turned to me, biting her lip, the tears still welling in her eyes.

'I'm sorry, Kate, I'm terribly sorry. Sometimes it just comes on me so quickly I can't help it.'

Her utter shame was so evident that I couldn't bring myself to be angry. My own feelings were so confused that I could barely bring myself to reply. I carefully pulled the ruined nappy out from underneath her, muttered something about rinsing it out and hurried through into the bathroom. I was balancing the magic bundle on my palm while I started to fill the basin when I felt the wetness starting to soak through the thick towelling and then it trickled through my fingers. I turned the tap off and simply watched, relishing the feel of the girl's pee, still warm, running between my fingers.

It was all too much for me, too new, too magical, too overwhelming. I carefully peeled the nappy open again to reveal the sodden centre and I leant forward and pressed my face into it. The warmth, the wetness, the obscene wickedness of what I was doing was just too much and I wiped it over my face, inhaling the sour smell as I ran it over my eyes, my cheeks and my lips. When I lifted it away, I licked my lips and tasted her. It was disgusting and glorious.

I carefully reparcelled the cloth to keep in the warmth, and balanced it on the edge of the basin while I shrugged off my dressing gown and nightdress.

Then I took up the exquisite bundle again, stepped into the bath and finally spread it over me, wiped it all over my face, across my breasts, my hungry nipples, down my stomach to my own neat tuft of ginger hair and ran it briefly between my legs. But there was so little of the nappy. And it was cooling so quickly and the precious contents were dripping away even as I pressed it to my breasts again and squeezed it like a sponge. I watched the little rivulets run down and drip off my nipples. My other hand had already felt its way between my legs and through my own hair, where I dug into my own wetness, slurped my fingers round the deep soft cavern, and that was all I needed. I threw my head back and, remembering the girl just outside, picturing that image of her spread open on the bed while she was powerless to prevent her own body shaming her, I tried to control my cries as I drowned in wave after wave of euphoria at the glorious lush decadence of such total depravity.

Our relationship was strained for the rest of the day. Chloe was clearly mortified by what she had done. I was equally ashamed of what I had done. Thankfully it was a busy day, and we were almost never alone together.

The dinner for our clients that evening was a success and Chloe's work during the day had impressed me again; she hadn't interrupted any of the meetings and she came across well during the evening. Then, as we were halfway through the dessert course, she started shuffling awkwardly. I decided to ignore it; she could easily hold on for another half hour or so, but she turned to me and asked in a loud whisper if she could have the room key.

I think she realised immediately the stupidity of what she had said and could see that I was annoyed that she had revealed we were sharing a room. At best it betrayed that there had been a mess-up in the booking arrangements, and Walton Matthews doesn't make mistakes, or possibly that we were trying to save money on our expenses. It could be even worse: they might have thought we were trying to cheat.

I put her off, partly I suppose out of spite because of what she had said, but mainly because I was angry enough to let her suffer a little longer. It wasn't long before she started on me again.

'Please, Kate? Could we go upstairs?'

Simon Fletcher was studiously ignoring this. Jody Wallace was less well mannered.

'Are you all right, dear? Is anything wrong?'

'No, she's fine,' I interrupted quickly before Chloe had a chance to make anything worse. And then just as I turned to her, there was one of those sudden silences across the room and her voice, intended as a discreet whisper, sounded clearly enough for everyone at the table to hear.

'Please Kate, I'm ever so wet.'

The other two looked up in horror, and I suddenly realised that they had completely misunderstood the meaning. Coupled with the revelation about our sharing a room, I couldn't blame them, but I can't remember ever having been so embarrassed.

Well, I suppose it was wrong of me, but I had just had enough of being shamed by Chloe and of the entire trip being ruled, and possibly ruined, by the requirements of the bloody girl's bladder. I turned to

Jody, and spoke in the soft matter of fact voice fitting for women sharing an intimate medical confidence of this sort. However, I made sure it was loud enough for Simon to hear.

'Well actually, Jody, I may as well tell you. Chloe does have a bit of a bladder problem and I have had to put her in nappies. It is all rather embarrassing for her, and quite unpleasant. However, I'm sure she can wait a little longer.'

Simon shot up like a jack-in-the-box at my explanation. Even Jody seemed more amused than disgusted.

'Oh, I see, Kate. Well, I mean do take her up if you think you should. Can we help at all? I mean if there's anything we can do, please say.'

I smiled her away and told her that Chloe could certainly wait until after the meal, but Chloe interrupted me.

'Actually, Kate, I would like to go soon if we could.'

I made her wait until after the desserts. And the coffee. And the mints. I was watching her squirming as each minute ticked by, now utterly silent and clearly in great discomfort, but frankly, I didn't care. When Simon Fletcher finally put down his coffee cup, Chloe almost jumped up out of her seat. I ignored her and turned to the others.

'Would you like a night-cap? A brandy perhaps?' Chloe's groan was audible to all of us.

'Thank you, Kate, but I think we should call it a night. I believe Chloe is rather keen to get back to her room, and we have much to do tomorrow.'

After we had said our goodnights, I stormed back through the foyer to the lifts. Chloe was dragging along behind, and although we didn't have long to wait in the lift lobby, I was glad when the lift arrived, because the lobby smelt rather unpleasant.

When we got in the lift, the smell was worse, and as we rose higher, I glanced round to see Chloe standing in the corner, staring at the floor, her face a brilliant scarlet. The lift was empty, but my whisper wasn't nearly as restrained as it should have been.

'Chloe, I certainly hope that isn't what I think.'

'I'm sorry, Kate. Really I am. I did ask over an hour ago if I could come back. I just couldn't wait.'

I bit my tongue as she waddled down the corridor ahead of me and waited pathetically outside our door for me to arrive with the key. Once inside I turned on her, finally letting loose my anger at the way she had embarrassed me; interrupted the concert; disrupted our meetings; prevented my clients from enjoying a nightcap, and seemed entirely incapable of controlling her own body.

If the girl had possessed the slightest spirit or courage, she would have objected. But she just stood there, meekly accepting my tirade and waiting patiently for me to finish, her face turned to the floor, her hands clasped in front of her, the fingers turning and twisting together. She didn't put up the slightest objection or defence and even as I was speaking I realised that she never would. Whatever I said or did to her, she would accept it with that same placid humility.

I paused to let her respond.

'Well, Chloe? If you want to behave like a spoiled baby then I'm bloody well going to treat you like one. First, I'd better get you out of that nappy.'

Chloe said nothing but meekly pulled the ridiculous blue mat from under her bed again and spread it out. Then she pushed off her shoes, hitched her skirt up and lay down carefully so that her bottom was right in the middle of the mat. She put her hands over her eyes and turned her head away, but not before I saw the first tears starting to well up.

I took hold of the hem of her skirt and drew it up once again, right up to her waist, and picked carefully at the elastic of her plastic pants to pull them off her legs before I turned my attention to the nappy that was now revealed. It wasn't just wet, it was visibly sopping, completely saturated with Chloe's pee. More than that, as I carefully removed the pins on each side and peeled back the soggy corners, it was filthy; stained dark and ugly. Her face still turned away, Chloe lifted up her bottom and I carefully pulled the foul mess out from under her, wrapping the cloth over on top of itself.

Her pubic hair was matted flat and shining and around the whole area, the skin was visibly damp and flushed red where it had chafed all day in the tight binding. She was going to need a bath.

I didn't say anything, simply reached out to the buttons of her blouse and started to unfasten them. Still there was no reaction. She lay there quietly as I steadily undid her blouse and pulled it down her arms. Then I unzipped the skirt, and since it was already rolled up to her waist, I briefly sat her up and pulled it off over her head. Finally, I rolled her over, unclipped her bra, pulled the straps away from the girl's shoulders, then rolled her back face up again and peeled away the flimsy little white scrap.

At last the little breasts appeared and she was naked. I sat down on the bed to examine the figure stretched out in front of me.

There was a gorgeous virginal innocence to such tiny swellings, barely noticeable at all when she lay on her back. The nipples were pale, soft and puffy; small rounded cones in the centre of perfect little rings that were scarcely any darker than the rest of her breast. So clean; so new. And not erect. Not like mine. Beneath them, a thin angry red line encircled her chest, where the tight elastic of the bra had dug into her soft skin. Briefly, I traced my finger tip along the narrow ridges.

She didn't move, although she knew that she was now fully exposed to me and that I was now examining her for my own pleasure. She still had her hands over her face, hiding her feelings away so that I've no idea what she could have been thinking, or hoping, or dreading. Yet she presented such a bizarre contrast; from the pure and innocent little breasts at one end of her body to the thick, almost matronly, growth of pubic hair on the disgustingly fouled belly at the other end. Eventually I realised that she had spread her fingers a fraction and was staring out at me between them.

'Go and run yourself a bath.'

She scrambled to her feet and padded through into the bathroom. Watching her neat little round bottom as she walked, I was consumed by the compelling vulnerability of the girl; a defencelessness which fascinated me so that I was powerless to resist. I wanted to discover, I needed to discover, just how far she could be pushed. I stayed for a few moments sitting on the bed, squeezing at my own painfully tight breasts as I listened to the water cascading into the bath in the other room. Then I took off my jacket, no longer caring that the engorged state of my nipples was now clearly visible through my blouse. I had made up my mind to indulge myself and I followed into the bathroom.

Chloe was standing with a bunch of toilet paper in her hand, unsuccessfully wiping at the filthy marks across her skin. She stopped the instant I came in, guilt written right across her face, and hastily tossed the paper into the toilet bowl. The bath was only a few inches deep, but it would do. I turned off the taps.

'That'll do. You only need enough to get you clean; you're not here to pamper yourself. Get in.'

She quickly stepped in and sat down. There wasn't even enough to cover her thighs and she sat there shivering with her arms crossed in front of her chest, her forearms squashing the little nipples flat. I took the face flannel and dipped it in the water. No wonder the girl was shivering; the water was barely luke warm, but at least she was learning not to complain.

'Stand up, girl! I can't wash you like that.'

Her eyes widened as she heard me. 'Please, Kate, I can do it.'

'I doubt that; you don't seem able to do anything much.'

'Please?' She was begging now and reached out her hand for the flannel.

'I told you to stand up; please do as I say.'

She reluctantly got to her feet and stood facing me. Her arms were still covering her breasts, so I snatched away one wrist and scraped the cloth briskly up and down the length of her arm before moving, as quickly as I decently could, across to her body. The miserable protests had stopped and she waited meekly while I wiped the flannel over her shoulders and then down across her front. Beneath the flannel, I could feel the tiny tips of her nipples so I rubbed more harshly across them and she would have pulled away if I hadn't been so tightly gripping her arm.

Then I moved further down her body, across her pale flat stomach and at last down to the wide triangle of dishevelled hair covering that part of her which had been seducing me from the outset. I rinsed the flannel out again, resoaped it and ran it straight down across her soft tummy, before I made her turn round and face the wall. I was getting too impatient to spend much time on her back and quickly concentrated on the smooth round bottom. It was so perfect, so pure and pale that I had an immediate desire to mark the unblemished skin. I made her lean forward further and bend her legs so that I could run my hand down the neat crease between her cheeks and right between her legs. I pressed hard against her, so that she protested and tried again to pull away. It was all I needed. I reached out with finger and thumb and caught a thick nugget of her soft flesh from the fullest part, pinching hard so that she cried out.

'For heaven's sake, girl! Do keep still! You really are disgustingly dirty here, you know. I think it would be best if you move your legs apart and bend right down.'

Inch by inch, she slowly bent forward and slid her legs apart until her bottom was fully revealed, then her anus, the thick lips of her sex and eventually even the thinner inside ones, barely peeping out of the plump crease. I wrapped the flannel tightly round my hand and concentrated on the ridges again, rubbing vigorously and harshly against her skin, pressing heavily with my fingers and digging right in between the sensitive folds. When she tried to stand up, I slapped her across one full cheek of her bottom and pressed her back down again.

It wasn't until she sniffed that I realised she was actually crying, so I slapped her again.

'For heaven's sake, Chloe, now you're even crying like a baby!'

'But it hurts!'

'You should have thought of that before. Now turn round and let me do the front.'

Cautiously she turned back towards me again, her frightened little face still tear-streaked as she waited to be told how I wanted her next. Again I made her move her legs wide apart so that I could wash right

207

inside the crease of her sex. Again I rubbed harshly at her delicate lips with the coarse flannel as she continued to snivel.

I pulled at a tuft of her long pubic hair. 'Don't you ever cut this, Chloe?'

'No.'

'Why on earth not?'

'I didn't know I was meant to.'

'What? You attend to the hair on your head, don't you? And under your arms? Why do you just ignore this? Look at it! It's just a straggly mess.'

Then a thought occurred to me as I yanked at a small tuft of the soft bush. She was just so timid standing there in the cold bathroom, far too easy an offering. Whether Chloe would like the idea or not, I no longer cared. After all she had put me through, she had forgone all rights to be consulted.

'I'll never be able to get it all properly clean in this state. I don't know if there are any scissors around here.' I turned to the drawers of the basin vanity unit and started hunting through. But I knew there would be no scissors; I had stayed in this hotel many times before. But I also knew there would be a little complimentary toilet case, containing all the disposable necessities that a forgetful traveller of either sex might need: a toothbrush, shampoo and, of course, a disposable razor and a tube of shaving cream. Before long I found them and held them up.

'Ah! Now look at this! This would be much better. If we get rid of all that straggly hair completely, it will make it much easier to clean you up if it should happen again.'

'No! Please not that!'

'Nonsense. Come along, rinse yourself off.'

'Please, Kate, I really don't want you to shave me. I'll look so silly.'

'Frankly, I don't care if you do. Besides. I'm not going to shave you. You are.'

Initially she looked terrified, but there was something besides that. As she sat so demurely in the bath, I realised that there was more than fear and humiliation; there was an earnest excitement shining in her face. She was longing for the chance to be further toyed with, to suffer a still deeper humiliation. She didn't speak, didn't argue any more, but her own hands came down and joined mine ruffling through the long hairs. I was disappointed not to be doing this myself, but there was an even deeper satisfaction in making her do it to herself, forcing her to be the instrument of her own disgrace.

'Here,' I said, and handed her the razor and tube of shaving cream, 'off you go. Call me when you are done.' I left her sitting there.

I poured myself a drink from the mini-bar and for a time I lay on my bed while I waited for her, and tried to decide how far I wanted to push this, whether I could ever reach the limit of Chloe's submission. So far she had put up no more than the merest token resistance with the result, and probably to the intent, that at every chance she could crawl ever more deeply into the role of victim. We were away from our homes, our work, our friends; that code, those ethics, no longer applied. There was nobody else in the building who knew who we were or what we were. We were liberated.

I refilled my glass but still hesitated. This was the final choice; everything that had happened so far I could explain, if I had to, as having been necessary, but we had reached the limit of that. From here on, there could be no excuses; I was going out on a very long limb, and Chloe could cut it off whenever she chose. I took a deep breath, put down my glass, and stood up. Then I took off all my clothes.

Back in the bathroom, Chloe was sitting on the end of the tub, one foot in the water, the other propped up on the side of the bath. She looked up as she heard me push open the door, gasped as she stared at my face, at my breasts, at my sex and then hurriedly turned away and returned to her work.

She was nearly finished, and after watching her nervous movements a while, I took down the shower head, adjusted the temperature and started playing the warm spray over her hands and her thighs as she sat there.

She put down the razor and waited meekly, making no attempt to cover herself, while I rinsed off the last scattered flecks of shaving foam. Somehow her vulva looked smaller now that it was bare: both more available and also more delicate. The inner lips were so much more prominently visible: thin, pinkly scrubbed ridges that joined modestly at the top and then curved down through the open cleft of her sex. She shivered when I reached out to run my fingertip down the shining wet surfaces; the outer lips plump and fleshy; the inner lips so soft and smooth and separated, only just separated but all the more inviting for that, by the glimpse of a slender narrow entrance. My fingernail was lured automatically to slither down the inner surfaces of the valley.

I managed to pull myself together, and made her stand up in front of me, made her turn and made her bend, so that I could see all of her, examine and devour all of her and play the gentle spray across every inch of her trembling little body. My fingers roamed in complete freedom over each part of her skin as I directed the spray, so that through the whole process, she was aware at every stage exactly which part of her I was contemplating. Even when I made her lift her arms up over her head, I ran my thumb across the light stubble of her armpit, letting her realise that now I knew another of her secrets. I wanted to leave her nothing: no coverings, no intimacy that was not exposed and at my disposal. Her eyes were shining anxiously under the bedraggled short fringe; her skinny little arms hung weakly back down at her sides; and on and on; the tiny swellings of her pale breasts; her chubby little nipples; her dimpled navel; her prim round bottom; and that neat naked cleft. Her skin was unblemished; no scars, no moles, no marks at all: entirely clear and clean and new as a virgin. And it tempted me, seduced me, and corrupted me. Such purity cried out to be defiled. A bottom so flawless demanded stripes. Breasts so unsullied deserved to be scratched with nails. A vulva so innocent needed to be desecrated.

I finished with her bent double, her own hands pulling open the cheeks of her bottom so that I could direct the water, the stream twisted now from a gentle spray to a single thin bruising jet, beating hard and impatiently against her closed and terrified anus. For this last act, I had stepped into the bath myself and stood close behind her, appraising the view that she presented. For the first time in my life, I longed for a penis. I wanted something huge, something hard and angry that I could have thrust into her with vicious disregard for her pain. Something to bring on the tears; to pierce the innocence of her freshly revealed vagina; more even than that, something to break the chastity of the pale little puckered bottom that was struggling to resist the pressure I kept directed against it.

I moved the jet away and played long sweeps across her buttocks. 'You know you'll have to be punished for what you've done, don't you?'

The only answer was a soft strangled sob, so I stepped back and slapped her as hard as I could

211

across the fullest part of her bottom. She screamed, a cry so loud it shocked me, and tried to stand up.

'It is very rude not to answer when you are spoken to, Chloe. And if you are rude, you will be punished. Do you understand?'

This time her words broke through her sobs, although they were still barely intelligible. 'Yes, Kate. I'm sorry.'

'Right, and you must realise you will be punished for it.' I slapped her a second time, as hard as I could again, across the other cheek. Her cry this time was a little strangled, but still pleasingly sorrowful, and I smiled to myself as I turned off the water and replaced the shower head.

When I turned back to her, I found her bottom was already glowing with a satisfyingly red handprint on each cheek. That was good, but I wanted more than that, more than pain, because my victim could so easily tolerate that and welcomed it so readily. This needed to be a total humiliation that would stay with her long after the pain had faded. I made her lie down in the bottom of the bath.

She realised straightaway what I was going to do, and she lay there with her palms flattened against the sides of the bath, staring up at me, the terrified little face expectant, almost eager, as I towered over her, but I let her suffer for a while. From where she lay, she would see my legs rising above her and my own lush pubic bush pushed forward and I gazed down between my breasts, real breasts, full, round and sensual breasts that ached with the pressure of so many hours' stimulation, whose strong hard nipples I squeezed and milked. Then I moved my hands down my body, across my stomach; slender but now slightly rounded from the effect of a gratifyingly full bladder, and on down to my own sex, where my thick dark hair contrasted so totally with her smoothly shaved skin. I twisted the strands in my fingertips, pulling open the lips to expose the full wetness of the ripe folds within. She stared up with renewed horror at the steady slurping revelations. When I continued, even pulling open the top of the inner lips, the greedy tip of my clitoris would have been exposed to her, but below that, almost invisible, but opening nonetheless as I tickled the tip of my long fingernail across the mouth, the little dark opening which she knew was going to release the supreme humiliation she would have to endure. I let my lips fall back closed, and when she thought I had changed my mind and spared her, I moved my feet up either side of her head and squatted down.

There was no doubt now what was coming. I was poised only a few inches above her; if I had relaxed, my buttocks would have touched her face. Instead I hung there, tensed and ready. Looking down between my thighs, her tear-stained face was working fearfully. The red-rimmed eyes stared up at me, glistening still in the corners; her mouth fluttered and trembled as she tried to find words.

'Please, Kate. Please don't do that.'

So I did. Her pathetically inadequate appeal was enough to persuade me and I let myself go. As soon as the first few drops spattered on to her chin, Chloe turned her face away but I gripped her head in my hands and turned her back so that the full force of the spray that followed washed across her, splashing over her nose and tightly shut mouth, across her eyes and filling the hollows beneath them, running through her hair and drenching her entirely. When her face was completely covered, I stood up and directed the stream across her chest, over her laughable little breasts, filled the indentation of her navel and down as far as the clean scrubbed crease of her sex. Only when I was completely empty did I reluctantly step out of the bath, but I wished even then that I could have found something more to do, could have opened my bowels and fouled her immaculate innocence utterly.

She used her hands to wipe the worst of the pee off her face, and asked to be allowed to turn the shower on again, but I refused. Instead I let her lie there and watch while I took a few sheets of toilet tissue and wiped myself clean before tossing the damp twist of paper down into the bath on top of her. I walked out and left her lying there.

I had no experience of beating anybody; had never spanked anyone or caned them but I knew what I wanted. One of my dresses had a thin leather belt which I took out and laid across the bed before I called Chloe through into the bedroom.

She stumbled through, her face still wet and shining, the hair matted down and streaks across her breasts and stomach, and hovered just inside the door, her hands pathetically trying to cover her nakedness as she tried to see what I had planned for her next. Then she saw the belt lying across the bed and her eyes widened and turned miserably towards me again: the silly child had really believed her punishment was over. Rich rolling tears began welling up again and her mouth opened and shut several times before any sound came out.

'Please, Kate. I've said I'm sorry. I really am.'

I made her climb up on to her bed and kneel there, her knees spread wide, her head and elbows resting on the bed so that she could turn and look down between her thighs and in the mirror behind her, could see the reflection of her own bottom, presented entirely open and undefended to whatever I chose for her.

I stood behind her and to one side. I hadn't actually told her to look through at her reflection but how could she resist? How else could she know what would happen to her and when? Her wide shining gaze followed every movement of my hands as they traced across the smooth tight surface of her bottom. It was damp and slightly sticky, and the centre of each round cheek still carried the red stain of my earlier slaps. Her knees were so far apart that her anus was entirely revealed to me, the little pleats stretched taut, and I let my hand run down the central crease and press against the little crinkled rose, the sharpened tip of my fingernail working its way irresistibly painfully through the delicately gathered folds. She whimpered and tried to twist away, but I pressed my other hand down on to her back and held her firmly in place. When she still twisted, I reached round underneath her to where the little curve of her baby breast hung down, and I gripped that in my hand and squeezed hard until she cried out again.

'Stay still until I tell you to move.'

When I released her she did stay still, but the sniffles still sobbed out with each breath. They were cut off instantly as she held her breath when she saw me pick up the belt, double it over and bring it straight down on the bed right beside her. As it pounded into the mattress, the noise alone made her tremble and I'm sure that in that instant she understood as clearly as I did how effective this was going to be against her bare skin. She turned her head and stared up at me a moment, then carefully clamped a roll of blanket between her teeth, pressed her face down into the bedding, clenched her pretty fists and waited.

I wanted the moment to last for ever. She was kneeling there, pink, scrubbed, shaved and gloriously naked waiting for me to hurt her. I was standing erect over her, proud and powerful. Where she was naked as a sacrifice, I was naked as a warrior, an amazon queen whom no one dared disobey. I felt myself seeping and for a moment was tempted to turn her over and have her lick me, but I wanted this first, this demonstration of authority, of power, of majesty.

I took a single step backwards, lifted the belt high above my shoulder and then lashed it straight down across her bottom. Her pale slender body immediately jarred, leapt as if it had been shocked and then relapsed into a protracted shudder while the jumble of tangled blonde hair shook and rolled and her skinny legs kicked wildly and ineffectively behind her. The long scream was almost, but not entirely, muffled by the bedding and before she had time to draw breath again, before the first wheal had even formed, I whipped the belt down again on to the same expanse of creamy pure skin. And then again. And again.

I paused then, and she immediately twisted her head round to me and moaned a single 'enough!'. I put down the belt and sank down on to the end of the bed. Now at last I ran my own hands across my body, across my achingly hard breasts and pulsing soft vulva. At last treating myself to some of the pleasure that I so desperately craved as I cherished the damaged beauty of the little figure in front of me.

Her whole body was shaking now and a trickle of tears pushed out from behind her tight shut eyelids. Her bottom was stretched open before me and at last the clear thin red stripes were starting to appear, marking right from one side of her cheeks to the other, in a livid angry scar of scarlet. It was hypnotic to watch each line emerge from out of the quivering white skin like some sacred snake of pain. Each magnificent wheal swelled and darkened across her smooth flesh and rose into a glorious livid mottled red ridge. I ran my fingertip along the lines, each one broken in the middle where the central valley between her buttocks had curved away from the flailing belt. And down in that valley, down where my hand was automatically starting to descend, in an area that still shone in clean whiteness, nestled the enticing dimpled recess of her bottom. It was disappointing to discover that the belt tip hadn't once curled round to lick right across that delicate, secret little brown centre.

She cautiously brought her thighs back together, and they rolled and writhed in slow circles, squeezing the thick swollen lips against each other, milking an increasingly rich flow from somewhere deep within her. Her own hand reached back and slithered across her swelling lips while her long middle finger shamelessly dug up into the crease, curling back and probing deep inside. As she pushed open the puffy lips, the clear aroma and glistening dew on the folds within revealed her reaction to the ordeal she had suffered. Her sobs had turned to groans, to desperate pants of longing for release, and her other hand ground hard against her own sex, the fingers pressing at her lips, grating down the folds, crushing the tiny soft bud of her clit. Her groans were building steadily in volume and ferocity, becoming almost brutal animal grunts that matched the increasingly merciless rasping of her fingers across her own tender skin until she simply froze. There was a single agonised wail as her entire frame was shaken by a sudden trembling and then she collapsed down on to the bed.

She lay quivering on her side with her hands still clamped between her thighs. Once she opened her eyes, eyes still red-rimmed and tear-stained but with a satisfied glow for all that, but she blushed a deep scarlet and turned her face away when she saw me sitting there, watching, a witness to her complete abandonment. But I went over, tugged the bedclothes out from underneath her and then spread them down over her little naked body and tucked them in. I even leant down to place a light kiss on the damp pink cheek before I returned and climbed, also still naked, into my own bed.

'I do hope you have learned your lesson, Chloe, and that you will behave rather better tomorrow.'

I turned off the light and turned away from her, barely grunting an acknowledgement of her whispered 'goodnight', but I couldn't sleep. For over an hour, I listened to her turning and fidgeting; I think we were each waiting for the other to go to sleep, but neither of us could relax. Finally I forced myself to stay still and had actually started to drift off when I was disturbed by unmistakable rhythmic sounds and inadequately suppressed squeals from the other side of the room.

Followed by Chloe's soft voice.

'Kate? Are you awake? I'm afraid I've wet the bed.'

Tina's Tale – Maid in America

I know we should have objected. Everything they did
to us was so repulsive and monstrous and degrading
that to this day I simply cannot understand why and
how we allowed it all to happen. Why didn't we
protest all the time it was going on? Why didn't we
complain immediately afterwards? We were abused,
both of us; humiliated and treated like dirt.

Yet for both of us it was the most exhilarating and
powerful night of our lives and hour by hour, while
the nightmare unfolded all round us, we relished, in
guilt and shame, every second of our ordeal. How can
we complain about that?

Matt and I met during our first year at Uni
although it wasn't until the third term that we were
properly a couple. Still, when the long summer
holiday was looming and we both wanted to see
something of America, it seemed natural that we
should do it together even though we were still only
just getting to know each other well. We were
nineteen and for both of us it was our first big love.
I'm not saying we were virgins, but neither did we
have loads of notches on the bedpost.

We decided to start in the south and travel round,
seeing as many different places as we could manage
in the time: the Mississippi, Baton Rouge, Dallas and,

if we could, El Paso, Los Angeles. All the glorious names of Hollywood and television beckoned; places with glamour, with fire and spirit; places utterly different from our own homes in sensible suburban England. We hired a camper-van and on this particular evening were on the way from Memphis (which was a disappointment) to New Orleans (which was not) when we stopped in a small town just off Route 51. It looked like something straight off a 1950s film set. There was only a single street, and the biggest building on it was the library. Otherwise a post office, a drug store and a scattering of small shops pretty well made up the whole town. Right at the end of the street, almost out of town altogether, was a bar cum diner where we could eat. We parked in its own little parking lot and made our way inside.

It was another swelteringly hot day in a succession of swelteringly hot days and a Saturday, so I suppose more people than usual had gathered in the town. The bar was cramped, unattractive and smelly, much like several others that we had visited, but it offered a mechanical rodeo steer which customers could ride on; the hand-written sign offered a prize of ten dollars to anyone who stayed on for a full three minutes. After a few drinks Matt suggested we both have a go, and although I was reluctant to make such an exhibition of ourselves, he was keen. Matt paid his quarter, climbed up as the music started and lasted less than twenty seconds. As soon as he hit the mats, there was a roar from all the other drinkers and then they started goading me to follow. At first I refused, and they jeered. So I hesitated, and they taunted. Finally I surrendered, and they cheered. Surrounded by so much enthusiasm, for our quaint accents as much as our youth and eagerness, I suppose it was hot enough, they were persuasive enough and I was just drunk enough to try.

I was magnificent. I had ridden often when I was younger and I held on, gripping with my legs this wild iron and leather beast as I was thrown up and down but I still had the grip to stay and the louder they cheered the better it got and I waved my free arm and clamped tight with my knees and lasted the full three minutes. The exhilaration was magnificent. The barman gave me the ten dollars plus a 'Joe's Roadhouse' T-shirt, that I immediately slipped out to the ladies' room to put on. The applause and appreciation was all so inspiring and intoxicating and irresistible that I was about to have another go, was already sitting up on the thing, lapping up the cheers and admiration from the crowd around me, when suddenly the whole room fell quiet and in the stillness I looked round to see a policeman standing just inside the door.

He was a huge ox of a man, not just broad although he was that, but also simply fat, with a vast belly pushing out over his belt. In spite of the oppressive heat, he stood there in full uniform, jacket buttoned up, cap on his head and the inevitable dark glasses that seem to be issued to all American policemen practically at birth. He stood with his thumbs tucked into his belt, chewing gum and staring round the bar in the silence. Not complete silence, because the juke box was still playing some wailing Country and Western song, but no one spoke; no one moved. Everyone in the bar stared and waited for the man to act. I felt as if the headmistress had caught me misbehaving, even though I had nothing to feel guilty about. I didn't get down from the top of the steer, but I pulled the little waistcoat over my breasts, just for the extra protection.

He moved the gum to the side of his mouth and addressed one of the young men standing nearest to him. 'Turn that thing off.'

'But, Sheriff, I . . .'

'OFF!' The interruption came out in a roar that left no space for argument.

As soon as the music was killed, he turned his attention to the barman but his voice was now much softer, with a quiet menace that somehow scared me even more than his shouting had done.

'What time is it, Joe Bullen, by your watch?'

'Well, Sheriff, it's about five after ten, but . . .'

'Five after ten. Uh-huh. That's what I have. And what time is your licence until?'

'Ten o'clock, but you see . . .'

'Uh-huh. That's what I thought: ten o'clock.' He paused, turning his head in a wide silent circle that swallowed all the rest of the bar, even Matt and me. 'Well, I suggest that you all get the hell outa here because if any of you's left by the time I count to five, I'm gonna take you in, and it will be the back end of next week before I get around to even thinking about any bail. And you'd better believe it.'

All the customers clearly did believe it and made an immediate rush towards the door. I called to Matt to help me down, but that only drew the sheriff's attention to me. He strolled up, still chewing slowly at the gum, sniffed, looked me up and down with undisguised disgust and then grabbed my arm and simply pulled me bodily over the side of the wooden animal so that I fell to the floor, and would have landed flat on my back if he hadn't been still clutching my arm.

Matt, gallant as ever, ran up and tried to help and pull me away.

'Hey, watch out! You're hurting her!'

The sheriff didn't say anything, but he practically threw me across the room at Matt and we both hurried out to our camper and joined the crowd scattering in all directions from the car park. We hadn't fixed on anywhere to camp but soon after the lights of the town had dwindled into blackness behind us, a quiet country road opened up where we pulled off into the trees and settled down for the night.

It must have been at least an hour later and we were both fast asleep when I was jerked wide awake by the crunch on gravel of another car pulling off the road beside us. I grabbed Matt and as he turned over we heard a car door open, and quietly clicked shut.

I immediately feared the worst. I had seen the films and read the reports and knew this would be the end. However calm and rational I tried to be, I could think of no one who would have cause to come creeping up with no lights on his car in this deserted corner of the countryside. Steps were approaching us across the gravel; there seemed to be only one man and he moved softly round to the back of the van. He stopped.

The back door of the camper was yanked wide open and we were both blinded by a huge torch. The beam bounced around the inside of our little home; the tiny gas stove, the sink, the pile of clothes and then on to Matt and me staring out of our sleeping bag. At first I could see nothing behind the beam, but when the light swivelled round to the side I could at last see the uniform, the cap, the badge and knew it was a police patrolman. I breathed again, even giggled with relief.

He was a younger man than the one at the bar, and although he didn't look a great deal friendlier, at least he wasn't some wild axe murderer. For a while he said nothing, just shone the steady white beam across where we lay, side by side. Finally a similar affected slow drawl commanded us.

'OK, you kids. Out you get.'

Matt answered him. 'Just a moment. Give us a minute to get dressed.'

The reply snapped straight back. 'I said out and I mean NOW.'

I didn't know what to do. On one hand I had been warned that you should never try to argue with American policemen but on the other hand I was only wearing the T-shirt from the bar and a pair of knickers, and Matt had just the T-shirt that he always sleeps in. I felt horribly exposed and vulnerable and the prospect of getting out of the sleeping bag just as we were was quite unthinkable.

So we both stayed there. I think Matt was as unwilling as me but we were both completely dazed by being so suddenly woken and by the demand now being put on us. But the patrolman abruptly raised the stakes. He didn't say anything, but we both saw him quite clearly as he carefully transferred the torch to his left hand, then reached down to the ugly black shape of the gun hanging from his belt. He raised it until the horrible little round eye of the barrel was staring straight at me and then he pulled back the hammer. In the still night, the click was paralysingly loud and I suddenly realised that it would mean nothing to him if he simply shot us both where we were.

'OK, OK,' I practically shouted at him, 'we're coming.' I scrambled out of the sleeping bag and saw I was being followed by Matt. In a few seconds, we were both standing at the back of the van as he cautiously shone his torch round the inside again and, satisfied at last, turned to us. Quite swiftly, but taking long enough for him to see all he wanted to, he played the beam up and down each of us as we stood trembling half naked in front of him. Finally he snapped it off.

'Right. Into the car.'

'Can we at least get some clothes? Please?' I put all my feminine pleading into my voice.

He considered me for a few seconds, snapping the torch on again and playing the beam briefly up and down my bare legs. 'You got thirty seconds.'

There was no doubting him. Matt snatched up his jeans while I grabbed the denim skirt I had just taken off.

The man watched as we struggled into our clothes and checked his watch again. 'OK, time's up. In the car.'

Matt turned back to the van. 'I'll just get our passports.'

Then it was all like some movie again. The policeman, who until then had been as languid as a cat in the midday sun, reacted with the speed of a snake. As Matt reached over to the bag just inside the door, the policeman grabbed him by the collar, spun him round until he was slammed up against the side of the camper and before I could really see what was happening, he had caught both Matt's hands behind his back in handcuffs. Within seconds we were both thrown into the back of the huge black and white police car that was lurking on the edge of the road.

We were separated from the driver by a wire cage, and through the thick squares the little shiny hairs on the back of his round bullet head glistened as he radioed through to the police station. Once he had reported in and flamboyantly replaced the handset in its holder, he turned briefly to survey us with smug satisfaction etched across his broad smile. Finally he started the car and I watched the back of his thick spotty neck as we bounced back down the dirt track towards the town.

We stopped outside the police station, opposite the huge stone-columned library, and with no words beyond an occasional terse command, we were herded inside. The reception desk gaped empty and after the briefest glance, the proud protector of public morals knocked on the glass panel of a door leading through to a small office at the back. The single word 'SHERIFF' was splashed across it in thick black capital letters.

He didn't wait for a response but pushed open the door. The last dregs of that cool mean dignity he had been struggling to present at last dissolved, to be replaced by a glee and pride that could no longer be restrained as he dragged us after him into the office.

'Sheriff, I caught these two camping out down the reservoir woods. Caught them clean, yessir. Practically naked they was!'

The sheriff must have been expecting us, forewarned I suppose by the patrolman's radio message, because he was standing, almost posing, against the broad plastic blinds that covered the window. He said nothing, but nodded us both down on to a narrow bench against the opposite wall and, in case we didn't understand, the patrolman steered us both down before taking up his position against the door: arms folded, legs apart, on guard. The sheriff flopped down behind his huge scruffy desk, laid his cap and sunglasses neatly down in front of him and, for a long while, simply sat scrutinising each of us in turn as he methodically chewed his gum; I found myself wondering if this was still the same piece. Somewhere out in the darkness beyond the window blinds was the sound, familiar from so many films, of crickets clicking in the night while inside the air-conditioner hummed and whined but did nothing to cool the tensely crowded room. Finally the sheriff sniffed.

'I seen you two kids earlier tonight. Down in Joe's Roadhouse, didn't I?' The tone was strangely flat so that neither of us answered, unsure whether it was an accusation or a comment. 'You sounded like foreigners, to me. That right, is it?' He spoke slowly, with an affected nonchalance as if he were merely making polite conversation.

Matt answered him quickly. 'Well, no, we're English.'

The sheriff sucked noisily at his gum. 'English, huh? Well now, that's foreign so far as I'm concerned.' He considered me for a moment, staring blatantly at the front of my new prize T-shirt, proudly emblazoned with the Roadhouse logo.

'Well, foreign or not, I guess you know that it's a felony in this state to engage in sexual intercourse on State property? And them forest woods is State property. Oh yes indeed. So.' He watched the ceiling fan circling for a few moments. 'You got anything to say for yourselves, have you?'

It didn't sound too serious and really there was little we could say, but Matt suddenly piped up. 'Well yes, Sheriff. We weren't engaging in sexual intercourse.'

The sheriff looked down at us, chewed slowly a couple of times. 'You weren't, huh? Officer Jackson finds you naked as jay-birds in a camper-van and you want me to believe that you were not engaging in sexual intercourse.'

I suddenly realised that we might have a way out. Because Matt was right; we weren't. We had only fairly recently in our relationship discovered the pleasures of oral sex, and although we had certainly done that in the sheriff's precious State-owned forest, we had not actually had sexual intercourse.

'That's right, Sheriff,' I joined in with a fervour that I could never have managed to affect had I not known myself that I was telling the truth.

'Uh-huh.' He clearly didn't believe me, but he levered himself carefully out of the small creaking chair and stepped round the desk to drop down on the little bench beside me; it groaned as he settled his weight. Still chewing his gum, he stared at me, past me at Matt, and back to me again. His podgy fingertip was almost delicate as it traced round the outline of the proudly bucking Bronco and the Roadhouse lettering spread across my chest.

'You, er, you givin' the boys a free show, were you?'

'No!' I protested. 'We were just having some fun!'

He nodded silently as his forefinger continued to trace the pattern, even where it crossed straight across the middle of my breast, even where the attention and the gentle pressure of that circling fingertip was causing my nipple to rise slowly from its warm sleep.

'So this T-shirt,' and he plucked at it, careless that his fingertips were gripping right through to pinch my skin inside it, 'this T-shirt belongs to the bar, then, does it? I mean it has their name all over here.'

His fingers traced round again and I mumbled an admission that he was right, but that I had been given it, had won it. I didn't want him to think I had stolen it, nor that I was working at the bar without a visa.

'Uh huh.' He sat back again and surveyed us both, slowly, carefully from me to Matt to me again. 'Well, I'll have to check that out, honey. Take it off.'

And that was how it started. He told me to take off my T-shirt and because I was always brought up to believe that the police are good and they're on our side, and you should do what they tell you, I obeyed. I mean not at first, because it did seem a bizarre thing to expect me to do, there, in that room, with all those people around me.

But he didn't look as if he was going to take advantage of me or anything, and the patrolman who had brought us in was still leaning against the door. Even the sudden silence through the room seemed more like peace than tension. And I looked at Matt, who was still handcuffed and he was staring wide-eyed at the sheriff, who was leaning back against the wall now, his narrow eyes almost shut in his big round red face and barely looking at us, but nobody said anything. I wanted someone to seem to be on my side and no one was, but it was all so calm that I felt maybe it wasn't such a big thing to do and I reached down and pulled the T-shirt up over my head and then handed it to the sheriff, who reached out one huge hand and swallowed it up in his fingers.

He didn't look at it, and the patrolman didn't look at it. They both looked at me and of course, because they could see them now, they looked at my breasts. I've always been proud of my breasts; they are round and full and I always thought they were attractive; it was only since coming to America, where it seemed all the women have huge breasts, that I was unsure. Still, I was not ashamed, and the men were looking at me and seemed quite pleased with what they could see, so that I remember feeling really quite proud of the attention. I had been proud in the Roadhouse, when all those people watched me on the bronco. And I was proud now. I even pushed my chest out a little further.

The sheriff laughed. 'There, you see, child. Wasn't so hard, was it? I mean,' and here he reached forward and flicked with his fingertips at the underside of my nipple, 'I mean it ain't as if you've got a whole lot there to be modest about, is it?'

He turned away and just as he was shaking the T-shirt out in front of him, examining the bright red logo, we heard someone come into the outer office and then a shadow fell on the glass and a knock sounded at our door. I expected the sheriff to turn the visitor away.

'Keech?' he called through the closed door. 'Come on in, you might as well see this as well.'

The door was pushed open and another man appeared around it, his face immediately breaking into a wide grin as he saw me slouched there, exposed. I brought my hands up to cover my breasts.

The sheriff wagged his finger, as if I was no more than a naughty little child. 'Oh no, girl. You don't got the right to cover yourself up. Not yet, you don't.'

There was a quiet certainty in his way of speaking and acting that made me obey, so I let my hands slip down to my sides again, but somehow it didn't seem quite so innocent any more. I could feel my nipples, sticky from the sweat drying on them, hardening under the gaze of the three policemen. And Matt, too, of course, because I could see that he was glancing across at me from time to time, with a look strangely mixing fear and hunger.

The sheriff sniffed again, and said nothing, but he held up his finger in the same warning gesture once more, poked it into my chest right between my breasts and pushed until I was half lying against the back of the bench. Then he simply reached down, and pulled the hem of my skirt up to my waist. I was so dumbfounded I really didn't know how to respond, but beyond where my skirt was bunched up at my waist, I could see the white of my knickers suddenly revealed. He just smiled as he stared down at me and for a moment nothing else happened. He looked at me; the other two men watched and moved in closer as the sheriff rested his hand on my stomach for a minute. But then he simply slid his hands up my legs to the elastic waistband and pulled down my knickers. I was still looking down the length of my body, somehow hypnotised at what was happening. It all seemed so remote, seemed to be happening to someone else, to some other girl who was lying there being stripped naked by a bunch of grinning leering strangers, but not to me. Not the girl I was. The girl who lived in my house, went to my classes, wore my clothes. This was all someone else. This was the white skin of someone else's stomach, it was some other girl's bikini tan line, and finally someone else's bush of pale pubic hair which was now visible above the elastic of her knickers.

But it wasn't. It was me, and deep inside, there was someone relishing every minute, someone whose heart was beating double time at the experience and who was moistening fast at the way the whole situation was developing way outside her control.

At first the clothes caught under my bottom where I was half lying back on this silly bench but for some reason, I just don't know why, I lifted my bottom up a little so that the knickers came free and he was able to pull them right down to below my knees. Still without speaking he placed his huge cool hands on my naked thighs and eased them apart so that he could look in. Except I don't think it was so much for his benefit as for the other men, because he pushed me round so that they could all see better.

Then he peered down further, nearer, his narrow eyes tightening as he glowered closer at me. 'What the hell is this, huh? What you got hanging outa your pussy?'

I felt the hot prickling blush shoot all over me. 'It's my tampon.'

'Your tampon? Well, get rid of it, girl. I sure don't want to look at a thing like that on a pretty girl.'

He recoiled, clearly quite appalled at what he had found and for a moment I felt a flash of triumph. I had found a way to better him; I had some weapons still. But I was wrong. He was still the one giving the orders, and he would not let himself be put off by something so trivial and feminine.

'Just get rid of it, girl. We don't need nothing like that round here.'

I slowly struggled to my feet. Matt was staring over at me and if anything he was even more ashamed than I was. I looked round the group and finally found my voice. 'Could you tell me where the toilet, er, the bathroom, is?'

The two patrolmen were leaning on opposite sides of the door like twin columns; one of them snorted at my question and it was again the sheriff who answered.

'Straight across the hall.'

I quickly stood up, anxious to smooth down my skirt, to cover the humiliation of this cruelly intimate revelation, but was immediately hobbled by my knickers, now gathered round my ankles. I leaned down, about to pull them back up, when the sheriff stretched out his huge open palm again in a gesture so unmistakable there seemed no purpose in trying to disobey. I slid them off and dropped them into his hand then scurried out, suddenly reminded that even though I had managed to pull my skirt back into place, my breasts were still naked. I darted across the empty hallway to the tiny squalid cubicle, carefully pulled out the tampon and flushed it away. Actually it was clean because my period hadn't really started but I didn't yet know Matt well enough to risk any accident during the night.

Back in the little office, nobody had moved. The two patrolmen waited silently either side of the door as I slid between them and hurried back to my seat, sinking down carefully into the little space that was left for me between the sheriff, lounging back comfortably into the corner, and Matt, held awkwardly erect by the handcuffs behind him.

I settled between the two of them, my fiancé on one side, my enemy on the other. One I loved; I would do anything for and he could melt me with a kiss. The other I despised; he scared me and he could strip me naked for his pleasure. I pulled my arms over in front of my breasts, but the sheriff leaned over me again and quite gently but very firmly moved my arms aside.

'Now then, honey, let's us see if that's better, huh. Why don't you just slip this little bitty skirt off and let me see.'

I looked round me for support, but I was alone. Matt was half slumped down, his head hanging as he stared down into his lap. The two patrolmen were simply watching, waiting, patient, not even visibly excited by the scene unfolding. The sheriff too was patient. He idly ran one finger down the slope of my breast and across my nipple as he waited for me to obey him but he could see he wasn't going to have any trouble. I reached round to the back, unzipped the skirt and shuffled it off, awkwardly to avoid having to stand up. This time he didn't reach out for it, so I held on to it myself, clutched it in my lap as the sheriff repeated his slow trail down my breast and the nipple rose up to meet his fingertip. Finally he took the skirt out of my hands and tossed it over on to the end of his desk.

For a moment nobody moved or spoke. Everything was exactly as it had been before, except that now I had to sit there naked in the stifling room with four men, all of them fully clothed. Eventually the sheriff levered himself up off the bench, and repositioned himself on the edge of his desk, absolutely straight in front of me, staring wordlessly as we sat there. He casually picked up his huge night-baton off the desk and reached forward to tap it gently on the side of my knee before he started another trail. This began by twisting in between my knees before running along the top of my thigh and pausing at the crease where my thigh joined my belly.

I waited for him to move.

He waited for me to move.

The other three watched and finally I gave in. I shuffled my thighs apart and his thick black wooden truncheon continued its path across the skin of my stomach, down through the tuft of my pubic hair and lightly over the crease of my sex. I shivered, and pulled away, but he only chuckled again and ran it up and down my lips. He was deliberately twisting and pushing gently, not forcing it inside me but demonstrating to the eager spectators that as it slid to and fro past the entrance to my sex, there was little resistance, that I was almost sucking the huge heavy baton right up inside me.

He was still lazily chewing at the gum as he sneered down at me, periodically letting his mouth fall open to reveal the mess of saliva and dirty teeth churning endlessly. Then the stick stopped its circling and paused for a moment before rising slowly, steadily up my body, straight up the valley of my ribcage but deviating briefly to grind hard and painfully across my nipple before it reached my throat. He lifted it then and waved it in the narrow space between us, right in front of my face. It was a menacing if not exactly threatening gesture, that wafted an unmistakable scent through the room.

'What's this then, huh? What's this all over my nightstick?'

The two men by the door sniggered at his question as they watched the glistening stick circling slowly like some hideous vulture. Finally it stopped right in front of my eyes, but still I said nothing. There was nothing I could say, no excuse for so undeniable an arousal when subjected to such humiliation.

'Huh, honey? Looks like pussy juice to me. Yes, sir, pussy juice is what I reckon.'

I still said nothing and he gently lowered the baton until the cold wet tip was resting right on my mouth. Again he twisted and drilled it against my lips until I finally relented and let it in a fraction. He gloated even at this small victory and ran it over my teeth until the rasping bruising was so painful that I turned and tried to spit it out again. He snorted again, loving every minute of his power, glanced across to see what effect all this was having on Matt and a more devious smile spread slowly across his shining face. He glanced over at the two by the door and I'm sure he winked at them, before he turned back to us.

'Better see how the boy's cooking. Stand up, son.'

When Matt stood up, with some difficulty because of the handcuffs, the sheriff calmly smiled into his face but at the same time reached down and quite openly grabbed hold of the crotch of Matt's jeans. Matt immediately buckled over, twisting away amid a howl of shouted protests to defend himself against so sudden and so intimate an invasion. The sheriff simply chuckled and finally released him.

'I reckoned so! Yes, sir, I reckoned so! The boy's got a horn on him!' He reached up and patted Matt's cheek; at least, it was heavy for a pat but I suppose too light to be called a slap. 'You got something on your mind, boy? Huh? You never seen this little girl's pussy before, maybe. Is that it, maybe?'

'No, sir. I mean, yes, I have seen her.'

'Is that a fact?' The sheriff nodded, his hand still resting on Matt's shoulder in a gesture that was an ominous cross between friendship and control. 'Is that a fact.' He repeated the remark almost to himself but it was a statement this time. 'You've, er, sampled this little girl's charms before, have you?'

Matt hung his head down. 'Yes.' His voice was little more than a whisper.

'Tonight?' In the silence, the trap was visible.

'No!'

'Well, anyhow, she won't mind if we have a look at what you got in your pants, will she?'

And without another word, as the other two giggled like schoolboys, he started undoing Matt's belt. Matt again tried to twist away but the handcuffs prevented him from fending the sheriff off and when one of the other patrolmen grabbed his arms from behind and held him tight, there was nothing he could do. In a moment, the sheriff had unzipped his jeans and pulled them and his underpants down to his ankles with as little regard as he had done for me.

The shabby T-shirt came only down to Matt's waist so his cock and balls were immediately exposed to all of us and it was clear that the sheriff was right. He did have an erection, at least partially, and we all stared while Matt, his face brilliant red, hung his head in an agony of shame and mortification.

But the sheriff wasn't yet finished. He still had his arm round Matt's shoulder and hugged him tight against his great belly as we all gazed down at Matt's erection waving forlornly in the air, wiltingly visibly. Then the sheriff reached out again and this time he actually took hold of Matt's long thin cock between his stubby fingers and thumb and after a moment started slowly masturbating him. It was a sickeningly hypnotic sight. The thin pale skin of Matt's cock being steadily slipped up and back by the sheriff's stubby red fingers. There was no attempt at intimacy, but the cold mechanical movement made the action all the more alluring. The patrolman behind still held him tight, although Matt struggled to pull away, his efforts becoming ever more desperate as his erection strengthened. I sat agonised and fascinated as the appalling scene was played out just a couple of feet in front of me. He was twisting, squirming, and the tip of his cock was shining now where a tiny tear-drop had already leaked out. His breath was coming in agonised grunts as he tried desperately to get away from the steady pumping hand. The sheriff didn't increase the pace of his movements as his victim's rising excitement became increasingly evident, but when Matt looked over to me with shame on his face, his misery was perfectly clear. The imminent climax was urging him to lose himself in the concentrated sensations that the red podgy hand was provoking. The mortification of being so obscenely masturbated in front of these other people, of being masturbated to orgasm by a grinning, leering man in front of me, was almost equally strong. Almost, but not quite. A wail was torn from Matt's throat and the sheriff immediately released him and pulled back. But for Matt it was too late. Nobody spoke, the hum of the air-conditioner droned, and Matt sobbed out the tortured guilt of his disgust and self-loathing while the rest of us watched the few weak spurts of his ejaculation forced from him. As the last one dribbled pathetically down his bobbing cock, he sank back on to the bench beside me, humiliated beyond bearing. I put my arms around him and hugged his head into my breast.

When I looked up, the sheriff was returning to his place behind his desk. He too looked revolted by the spectacle. He nodded towards the patrolman who had brought us in.

'Get them outa here. Jackson, you call Doc Wallasy. Tell him I need him to come over and examine a suspect, see if there's any evidence for a felony charge. You can tell him it's a girl needs examining. Keech, you take them outside; they can wait in the holding stall until the Doc gets here.'

The newer arrival, Keech, squatted down in front of Matt, pulled his jeans and pants off over his feet then hauled him up on to his feet by his pinioned arms. The other one reached out for my arm, but I shrugged him away and we trooped out in a line, the sheriff's door slamming behind us.

Just beyond the outer office, and divided from the public part by a swing door, the corridor widened out to form a small waiting area where we were left, Matt in just the stupid T-shirt, but me in nothing at all. We sat down on a bench, a foul-looking thing in tan-coloured PVC that stuck to our skin and left the sweat to form in pools around us.

The reception desk was in an L-shape so that the duty officer could attend to anyone who came in through the front door but could also keep an eye on us, waiting in that limbo between freedom and the cells. The second patrolman, Keech, took up his place behind the desk there and frequently glanced back at us, making some joke at our expense to himself or to his colleague.

Our side of the waiting area was filled by the bench and a couple of others like it while along the opposite wall was a heavy wooden table and a dispenser for chilled drinking water. There seemed to be nobody there except the three men we had already seen, and from time to time one or other would come through to help himself to a paper cup of water from the huge gurgling pot. No one offered any to us, but as each went by, he would glance over, grin and leer. Matt's hands were still fastened behind him, so that he had no way of shielding or even hiding his cock, but I kept my legs clamped tight together and clasped my hands in my lap. But then Keech ordered me to keep my hands down by my sides. I did, until he had gone.

The night didn't seem to get any cooler as the time passed and I suppose we must have been there for about half an hour, so it would be around midnight when the sheriff came ambling back. He looked annoyed to see us there, as if he had forgotten about us, and he bellowed out across the hall.

'Jackson! Where the hell's that doctor? Did you even call him?'

'Yes, sir, I did. But his wife said he was out with Mrs McGerry so he could be a while.'

The sheriff snorted.

'She's havin' a baby!' Jackson added smugly, as if privy to a huge secret.

The sheriff snorted again. 'It's about time you were back on patrol, boy. You've been hanging around here long enough.'

With that, he stalked back into his office and, after a last wistful glance towards us, Jackson picked up his cap and disappeared into the darkness outside the front door. The lights of his car washed briefly across the windows opposite us before the sound of the clattering engine faded out into the chirping of the crickets.

I didn't notice that Keech had returned to his place at the desk until I heard his call: 'Hands, sugar,' and I looked up to see him glaring over the desk at me. So I obeyed him again, replacing them by my side, and he gazed briefly at the triangle of hair that he had made me reveal, at Matt sitting beside me, and nodded happily.

Except that later, when I heard someone moving about outside, I automatically moved to cover myself, and I didn't realise that Keech was still watching. The first I noticed was when he lifted up the desk flap and ambled out towards me, shaking his head slowly.

'You don't never learn, do you, sugar? Stand up now, and turn around.' Only then did I see the handcuffs swinging casually from his hand.

He pulled my wrists up behind my back and I felt the horribly unforgiving steel wind round them and click tight and tighter. Then he slapped my bottom, a hard stinging stroke, and walked off chuckling to himself.

I sat back down, and after that I had no way even to try to cover myself and they had all seen everything anyway. There no longer seemed to be much point in trying if all I was doing was betraying my embarrassment. So I just sat on the bench beside Matt and tried to ignore what was going on in the little police station, tried to work out what was happening in the world outside, what the time was and when we might be released. From time to time Keech returned to check on us but I just let him stare; once or twice he lingered, slowly sipping his little cup of chilled water and enjoying my embarrassment as he stood directly in front of me.

The sheriff never came back but one time Keech came through and sat down on the bench beside me. He sipped at his water a moment, glancing from one of us to the other with a cruel sparkle in the narrow eyes that peered over the top of the cup. Finally he screwed up the cup and tossed it across the room into the bin. Then he turned and leaned right across me and carefully picked at Matt's cock with his finger and thumb. Just lifted it and let it fall back on Matt's thigh. Then again. The third time, Keech held on to it, and rolled it neatly and carefully between his fingertips until it started to swell. At this, he began slowly sliding the skin up and down the growing length so that, in spite of everything, it started to stiffen again. Matt looked over at me, pleading for help, but there was nothing I could do. I had done this for him many times and it should have been my hand that was doing it now. The memory of how often, and how recently, I had caressed him this way didn't help me, and I am sure it didn't help Matt. He turned his head away, humiliated and ashamed, but Keech just laughed.

'You don't like to watch that, huh, sonny? Do you like to see this?' Then he released Matt, leaving his cock, now clearly half erect, quivering on his thigh. He turned to me. 'Open your legs again, sugar. Let's us see what you got in your little honey-pot.'

I did as he said. I didn't want to, and I didn't feel the same necessity to obey this man as I did the sheriff, but I was afraid. I knew that his demands were much more sinister, but there was still no doubting his power. I shuffled my feet apart and let my thighs slide open across the sticky plastic seat. As I did so I could see in the corner of my eye Matt's cock stirring again. Not shrinking, not recoiling in disgust at what I was being made to do, but flexing steadily; growing and thickening. Keech had seen it too, and sniggered, mocking and encouraged. Now he lay the palm of his left hand flat on my stomach and used his fingertips to splay my lips apart, holding me there entirely exposed while the other hand, with one finger clearly and unambiguously extended, slid slowly up my thigh until the tip was brushing right in among my pubic hair. I shivered, and automatically clamped my thighs together, but Keech made me open them again, and this time insisted that they be spread even wider.

His hand slid back across my skin to its place right between my legs and he sat smirking into my face and from time to time grinning across at Matt.

'This OK for you, is it, sugar? 'Cos your lover boy seems to like it well enough.' And sure enough, Matt's cock was now fully erect and glistening across its beautiful round pink head.

Keech did not actually penetrate me, but his finger toyed and tickled at my lips, flickering across them, patting at my clitoris sometimes, always threatening to drive straight into me but never doing so. Although he was watching me intently as he played his little game, he was also keeping a close eye on Matt squirming on the bench next to me. Once or twice he even stopped toying with me and transferred the action back to Matt directly, taking up his cock again and twisting and pulling at his erection.

The game was interrupted by the sound of the main door being pushed open as another set of footsteps and another voice, female this time, went into the outer office. Keech pulled away and stood up, almost but not completely guiltily as he peered round to see who it was.

'Hey, Bonnie? Is that you? Guess what? The chief's caught himself another couple of minnows. English, this time. Come and see!'

The swing door was thrown back and a woman police officer came through into our little waiting area. She was short, middle-aged, over made-up and with a vast, tightly buttoned bosom shoved out in front of her; she reminded me of an aunt I have always hated. I immediately pulled my legs back together, but Matt's erection was still fully displayed, and she chuckled, clearly unsurprised to see his condition.

Keech looked up at her and then nodded down at us both. 'You want a run, Bonnie? With this little lady perhaps?'

In the stillness that followed such a casual remark, I felt my head would burst. The words resounded, echoed and repeated in my skull as the horror of their meaning clarified. I would not have been surprised if she had wanted to amuse herself with Matt; sitting there with his erection so blatantly displayed, that seemed almost natural. For Matt, that would also have been preferable, because even though she was probably thirty or forty and quite unattractive, any woman would be preferable to a man if he had to suffer that. But Keech had suggested me, and that prospect was just too appalling to consider. I know some girls, even one or two of my own friends, have admitted they wonder what it would be like with another woman, have said they wanted to try. I never have. The whole idea is just too disgusting to consider. The woman sauntered over and stared down at me.

'Who are they?' We were toys in a store, incapable of understanding or response.

'They was down that lovers' lane by the reservoir. The Chief seen them headin' out that way and sent Bob Jackson out to pick them up.'

She nodded. The indecision was clear on her flushed face, but so was the lust. She was just turning away when we heard the sheriff's voice, roaring out from his office.

'Keech! You get in here, boy!'

As he turned to go, Keech glanced back at us, and at the woman, Bonnie.

'You might as well. I mean Gillespie himself has already been foolin' around; brought the boy right off, all over the floor.' The door swung shut behind him, leaving me and Matt alone with her.

She glanced over her shoulder briefly, but then, assured that there was nobody around, settled down next to me and when I pulled away, she slid up closer. She looked over at Matt, grinning at his exposure and

243

visible arousal, until he turned away in shame and humiliation. But when she spoke, it was me she spoke to. And I felt myself blush crimson as the sweat prickled under my arms and my stomach turned.

'Come here, honey. Stand up in front of me.'

So then it was my turn. She settled herself comfortably on to the bench and waited as I slowly got up and stood in front of her.

As I faced her, my hands shackled behind me, I was completely exposed. She didn't try to touch me, not at first, but she looked me up and down for a few moments and then made me turn round. It was more frightening when I couldn't see what she was doing, particularly because I was being told to turn round for just one reason: so that she could see my bottom. So when I turned, I knew she was staring at me. Even before I felt her fingers tracing over the surface of my cheeks and up and down the groove, I knew she was examining me, and considering. I have caught men staring at my bottom like that a few times, but they have quickly looked away, shame and embarrassment written across their squalid faces. This woman was different; she showed no shame.

She had me turn back again and made me stand right in front of her and for a moment just stared. But then her hand reached out and although I recoiled automatically the moment her skin touched mine, she shook her head and made me step up closer again until her hand touched my leg, wrapped round it and slid, slowly, like a snake climbing a tree, up my thigh. I had been able to tolerate her fingertips on my bottom. Somehow that seemed a less personal, less intimate part of me, but as she climbed steadily higher, I shivered in revulsion. This was much nearer to my heart. Illogical maybe, but the front just is more private than the back. We are used to people jostling our backs in trains and buses. Not the front.

I stared at the steadily climbing hand. I realised that I was holding my breath as she reached the top of my leg, but she just continued, over my hip, up my side and only after she had reached the bottom of my ribs did her hand start to slide inwards until inevitably it reached my breasts. As her thumb reached out to the swollen nipple, she looked up at my face, her eyebrows raised, almost an enquiry. Not a request for permission, because she must have known that wouldn't come, but a casual question, what I would do if, when, she continued her exploration.

I said nothing and looked away, so she said nothing, and continued. Her hand moved on up to cup my breast firmly, the spread fingers covering the round swelling and pressing when the nipple was centred in the middle of her palm. She squeezed briefly, then slid half off the breast so that her thumb could rub over my nipple. The greedy little smile came back to her face.

'Cute little titties you've got, honey. I mean kinda small by US standards, but kinda cute.' Then she squeezed my nipple much harder and this time she meant it to hurt.

She released me, sat back a moment, staring openly as she calmly took a cigarette packet from one of the top pockets of her uniform jacket and then a lighter from the other one. She methodically lit her cigarette and nodded her head towards the table behind me. 'Fetch that ashtray, would you?'

I went across to the other side of the room, but because of the handcuffs, had to turn with my back to the table in order to pick it up, and then when I got back to her, had to turn my back to her again to hold it out to her. I felt awkward, ungainly, and I knew she had only done it to humiliate me.

She took it. 'Thanks.' She placed it carefully on the seat next to her and flicked the ash into it. 'Now stand here in front of me again. Let me have a proper look at you. No, with your legs apart.'

My immediate reaction was to look over to Matt for help, but he was as powerless as me. The twisting, writhing of his hands in their steel clamps sent tremors up his arms, but he could do nothing else, and he turned away in shame. But his cock was again fully displayed, standing proudly erect like a spire from the short tangle of dark hair in his lap. The woman followed my glance and grinned. She made no move to touch him: there was no need, for his humiliation was complete from the reaction she was able to produce without any physical contact being made.

She turned to me again. 'Come along, honey. A little nearer than that. I won't bite, you know.'

I shuffled up closer as she transferred her cigarette to her left hand, and her right came out to push between my legs and rest on the inside of my thigh. I shuddered, and she sneered, sliding her palm steadily upwards until she reached practically to the top, almost repeating her earlier action except that this time it was on the inside of my thigh. Then I felt the tip of her thumb extend and snake across my lips towards the back and then the nail scraped back, just edging in between the lips and over my clitoris at the front. It was very light, almost tickling, but as she continued, repeating this same movement over and over while she sat slowly smoking her cigarette and watching the reaction on my face, it became impossible to resist. I tried not to respond, not to let her see the effect she was having, determined to tolerate whatever she did. I consciously forced my mind to focus on the things we'd seen during the day, our route, our next stop; fervently shutting out the mounting pressure that she was causing.

But she knew. I could feel a small trickle slip out of me and run down on to her fingers. She smirked. Her strokes were stronger on my clitoris now, and I knew that more of it was pushing out to receive her caress. I felt my thighs tremble.

I had sympathised with Matt when he had been in the same position, but had been hurt that he responded so easily to another embrace. Now I understood better what he had endured and, worse than that, could envisage the unendurable disgrace if I were to concede so little loyalty or even constraint, that I let her masturbate me to orgasm in front of him. She seemed determined to do it, and when I heard, in spite of myself, my breath pushed out in a rasping sigh, she settled back further and pressed her hand even more firmly up into my sex.

If it had been Matt's hand, even with this woman watching, I would have felt excused and permitted. But it wasn't. It was this vile red-faced matron, whose gaudy rings scratched at my thighs, whose auburn curls and grey roots shook just in front of me. But a hand is a hand. And when the hand is determined and patient and your body has been stimulated already, it doesn't matter which sex the hand is. I quivered again and my knees trembled, almost gave way, but I managed to pull myself together although I failed to prevent a low squeal escaping.

And she stopped. Just as I was nearly there, on the very brink, but she had timed it to perfection and sat back, watching me sway unsteadily, my breath gasping, my eyes unfocused, my hips circling in a slow frustrated spiral of longing. And she laughed, a nasty coarse throaty laugh, stubbed out her cigarette, and strode out to the front office.

I collapsed back on to the bench and Matt and I leaned against each other. Unable to put our arms round each other as we longed to do, we pressed our bodies together, each wordlessly trying to make amends for the shameless way we had each responded to the uninvited stimulation to which we had been subjected.

It wasn't long after this that another car's headlights played across the windows and another step could be heard coming in from the night, to be greeted by Keech.

'Hi, Doc! The prisoners are through here. I'll tell Sheriff Gillespie that you've arrived.'

The sheriff himself led the group through a few minutes later. Behind him walked a short elderly man on whose round face the concern and exhaustion of too many working nights was clearly drawn. Both Keech and the woman sidled in at the back. The doctor glanced with little interest over at us as the sheriff cleared the floor.

'Keech, you clear that table and bring it out here.' He turned to me. 'Right, girl. Get yourself up on here and let the Doc do his job.'

Dr Wallasy protested that a table in the middle of the police station wasn't a fitting place to carry out such an intimate examination. 'I do normally expect to have a proper examination couch.'

The sheriff scoffed. 'Why, Doc, I don't think you need to worry yourself too much about that. She's just some tramp. She don't normally even have a bed to sleep in. Hell, she was sleeping in some old van when young Jackson brought her in so this is probably the best she's had in quite a while.'

The woman hauled me up by the arm, and dragged me out to the table. I was pushed back against it and then she bodily lifted me up until I was sitting on the end and pushed me down flat. With my hands still fastened behind me, there was nothing I could do to prevent her as I collapsed down with the steel of the handcuffs digging into my spine. She and Keech moved down to the end of the table to position themselves where their view would be unobstructed.

Dr Wallasy opened up his bag, and retrieved a flat wooden stick like ones my own doctor had used on my tongue to examine my tonsils. He came up and stood beside me, staring down at my quivering body spread out before him. He sucked in his teeth for a moment and then, in a bored flat monotone recited his speech.

'Well now, girl, I understand that Sheriff Gillespie has grounds to suspect that you have been engaged in sexual intercourse unlawfully and you have denied this. I am a qualified medical practitioner licensed to practise in this State and I have been instructed to determine the facts. I am therefore going to conduct a physical examination of your genitalia.'

His hands descended to my breasts and started to prod, gripping each nipple in turn and pulling and twisting as he peered at them.

'There's certainly engorgement of the nipples. This would often suggest sexual activity, although it's not in itself proof of sexual intercourse.' He straightened up, sucked his cheeks, stared a moment longer at my breasts and then moved down to the end of the table. My knees were resting on the hard edge and my feet hanging down, but he came up until he was almost touching me as he continued to speak.

'Now then, I gotta ask you to open your legs for this, girl. I'm gonna examine both the external and internal organs.'

There was a hushed expectation in the room as everyone heard these words and the implications they held. The sheriff shuffled closer to his side of the table and the other two craned round from behind the doctor to get a better view. Glancing over, I saw that even Matt was looking up in anguished anticipation; more than that, despite everything else, he was visibly starting to get an erection again.

I lifted my knees, seeing the crowd of eager hungry faces gathered around my feet, the eyes darting between my face and the pink shell of my sex held closed by my thighs. I tried to feel shame, but could only savour the attention of so much impatience, all waiting on me, on my body, as if I was special.

And I let my legs fall open to reveal myself. I have never in my life been so utterly displayed and exposed to so many people, let alone so many strangers. The eyes all stopped darting and focused now, focused intently on the seeping throbbing lips of my pussy as I felt the cold air wafting over me.

'Now then.' The doctor continued his examination and his running commentary. He was the only one maintaining any sort of professionalism.

'There's also clear engorgement of the sexual organs here. You can see that the labia are considerably extended and enlarged. There has also been considerable secretion of vaginal fluids.'

I closed my eyes in shame, imagining how wet I must appear, for I could feel myself flooding, trickling out over my bottom and down on to the table. The hard round edge of his spatula pressed against the delicate skin of my inner lips, quivered for a moment and then twisted its way just inside me. The man bent down to peer at what he had revealed.

'Well, she ain't a virgin. That's for sure.' The doctor turned to the two standing behind him. 'Perhaps it would help if you two could hold her ankles; that would be a little less of a strain for the girl.'

They immediately rushed to this task, and soon had my legs lifted up, pulled wide open, and my knees bent so far back on my chest that my thigh tendons were stretched taut. On his side, Keech in particular clutched my ankle to his cheek and gazed, utterly absorbed, at the vision exposed before him.

Then the doctor returned to his task. The steel probe was pleasantly cool, but he pushed it deeper and deeper inside until I cried out as I felt it reach right to the top of my sex. The doctor peered closely before he stood up, shaking his head and slowly withdrawing the probe.

'No sign of semen, I'm afraid, Sheriff. So it looks as if no felony has been committed.'

The speed of the sheriff's chewing had increased markedly when he faced this disappointment.

'There isn't, huh? You sure of that?'

'Why, certainly. There's no semen deposited within the vagina, and that's the only clear evidence of intercourse having taken place.'

Sheriff Gillespie looked devastated. He had been so convinced that he was right and that this humiliating examination would prove him so that the thought it might prove him wrong seemed not to have crossed his mind.

'But just look at her, for heaven's sake, Doc. There's stuff practically pouring out of her. This girl's got a flood in her pussy as would float the whole damn US navy.'

'I know, Sheriff. I don't deny that. But what I am saying is that there's no sign of semen in her. And that means I cannot prove she has had sexual intercourse.'

Sheriff Gillespie turned away in disgust, his hands pushed down deep into his pockets. 'Huh.'

'Well unless . . .' the doctor started but tailed off. The sheriff was on to him at once.

'Unless? Unless what?'

'Unless they was doing, er, "unnatural" things.'

Gillespie looked round from the doctor to me and back to the doctor again.

'Unnatural things? What the hell is that supposed to mean? Unnatural things?'

'Well, not to put too fine a point on it, Sheriff, I mean sodomy is what I mean. Now that's a felony too.'

The sheriff was not at all mollified. 'I know that. I know what's a felony in this State and what is not, thank you.' He considered me carefully as I lay, still stretched out, and if the two holding my ankles had started to lose some of their enthusiasm when they had heard the doctor's preliminary finding, they could clearly see what was coming next. So could I. So, eventually, did the sheriff.

'Well, just get on with it then, Doc. Turn her over and check her out.'

I could have been a sack of sand for all the care they showed as they pulled me up to my feet, turned me round and then flattened me back on the table again, face down this time. The doctor wasn't satisfied.

'Bring her down aways. You'll need to get her hips bent over the table edge.'

The two officers yanked enthusiastically at my ankles, dragging me down across the hard surface of the table until I was bent over the end. I saw the doctor return to his place, the steel probe still in his hand and then he squatted down out of sight.

'Now. Let's see what we have here. Just try to relax, please, and you will make it a whole lot easier for yourself.'

I don't know how he expected me to relax. No one and nothing had ever penetrated me there, but as I opened my eyes, I found I was directly in front of Matt. All the others had gathered at the far end of the table where the doctor was pulling open the cheeks of my bottom and rubbing some cold jelly right into my bottom hole. I felt the tears beginning to well in my eyes but Matt smiled to me, blew me a kiss and smiled down ruefully at his penis, now unmistakably erect. He had at last abandoned the shame of his arousal at my mistreatment, and finally acknowledged the power of the stimulation.

His cock twitched again as he heard me sucking in my breath as the thick probe at last wormed inside me and pushed unyieldingly deep into my insides. Craning round over my shoulder I could just see the cluster of heads gathered, all staring; all avidly intent on my bottom. Doubtless all able to see, and draw their own conclusions, from the trickle I felt winding out of my sex and running down my thigh.

The fingers that were holding the probe were now pressed right against my skin, that most delicate, sensitive and exquisite spot between my bottom and my sex, and I quivered in yearning at the pressure. Finally the probe was withdrawn and the doctor held it carefully up to the light. The small crowd all gathered round so that they too could examine the evidence and doubtless pronounce their own views on the meaning.

The doctor sighed, long and slow. 'Sorry, Sheriff. Nothing there either. I'm afraid she was telling the truth.'

I could not see clearly what was happening down at that end of the table. I was still held down flat, a hand pressing firmly on my back, but there was a long pause before the sheriff spoke.

'OK. OK. Well, if that's a fact, then there's nothing you can do, Doc. But thank you for sparing us some of your precious time.' I couldn't tell whether this sarcasm was criticism for his failing, or simply the sheriff's natural bleakness. I was released as the doctor collected his bag and shuffled out of the room, although when I stood up, I could still feel the discomfort where the probe had been pushed so far into my bottom, and the grease he had put on it was melting and starting to run down again.

The sheriff stuffed his hands deep into his trouser pockets and glared at us thoughtfully. Finally he made up his mind.

'Well, I guess I can still charge them with camping on State property without a licence; that's a one-hundred-dollar fine if nothing else. I'll go and make out the report. Meantime, you two take the prisoners back and lock them up.' He paused, about to turn away before he added as a sullen afterthought, 'While you got them there, you might teach them not to bring their immoral ways back to this God-fearing county again.' He strode out, leaving us alone in the charge of Keech and Bonnie.

As we were led back to a large square cell right at the back of the building, I tried not to imagine what the sheriff had meant; it could have been anything, but I feared the worst. However, as we were pushed into the cell, at least Matt and I were still together; that was some consolation.

A narrow wooden bunk on iron legs ran round three sides of the cell; the fourth side was entirely plain except for the heavy wooden door in its centre and, in the middle of this, a six-inch square barred opening. A row of small windows high up in the back wall looked out into the night, a line of impenetrable blackness like so many missing teeth. We were pushed down side by side on the bunk while Keech stood over us, his thumbs tucked into his belt.

'Well, Bonnie, I guess I should be a gentleman and say ladies first. I'm sure a little slut like that could suck your pussy for you just fine.'

Bonnie sauntered across and stood over me, considering. I turned away, sickened at the prospect that Keech had raised again. Bonnie, however, didn't seem particularly keen on the suggestion and I took some comfort from that. Perhaps this was something that Keech wanted to watch happen more than something that he had cause to believe might happen. I tried to look superior and discouraging, but they were both dressed in their heavy official uniforms while I was completely naked. My hands were still cuffed behind me and, as if that wasn't enough, they had both just watched while I was spread across a table while probes were pushed into my vagina and up my bottom. They were unlikely to be intimidated by anything I could do.

Bonnie ruffled her fingers in my hair. 'No, I don't think I care for that idea particularly. But I do believe that this young lady needs to learn some better standards of behaviour, both as regards publicly flaunting herself in a roadhouse and cohabiting with a man before she's married. Huh? What do you say, honey?'

I didn't know what to say. I didn't know what on earth she was getting at. Although I was hugely relieved that she didn't fancy me, when she moved across and sat down directly opposite us, I started to worry that she was going to offer me to Keech instead, and that prospect was only marginally less horrifying. He was just an arrogant, selfish slob, who would probably have no finesse or tenderness at all and the more he could hurt me, the better he would enjoy the conquest. It was hard to decide which would be worse: the shame of sex with her or the physical pain of sex with him.

But I was wrong, for the depths of her twisted mind had thrown up something worse, something which combined both pain and shame in a manner I could scarcely consider. She beckoned me.

'Come over here, girl.' She reached up when I was standing in front of her and took hold of my arm; her grip was firm, uncompromising, and yet not overtly aggressive. 'I know what I reckon would be appropriate for you and I'm going to do it: I'm gonna tan your backside. So just you get down here over my lap.' She pulled me down as Keech's exultant gurgle rang round the room.

'Way to go, Bonnie! You tan her hard!' He was almost dancing with glee at the prospect that now opened up before him and positioned himself against the opposite wall where his view would be unimpeded. He folded his arms and prepared to watch the show; the grin practically split his head in half.

I did struggle, did try to pull my wrist free of her, but I admit with little real determination. Firstly I didn't really have any great expectation of getting free and secondly I couldn't think what I would do even if I did. And besides, there was the desire, the need that had been built up by the treatment to which I had already been subjected, by the sheriff, by Keech, by her and, finally, by the doctor. They had all humiliated and abused me. They had all fingered me, molested me and provoked me. None of them had allowed me release. And now, to cap it all, this woman wanted to do something more: to expose me again, and abuse me again and touch me again. The prospect was shamefully exciting and I knew that I would be obscenely aroused by her handling me again, touching me, feeling me.

I allowed myself to be pulled down across her lap, as she reached a matronly arm round my waist to pull me closer over her thighs. On one side of her, my legs were trailing down to the floor, my feet almost up as far as the end bench where Keech was sitting, so that I had to keep them firmly together to try to guard what little modesty I could.

On the other side of her legs, my breasts were hanging down and she reached round once to grasp them, one after the other in turn, squeezing me until I felt bruised.

The woman squirmed her thighs apart, settled me down better on her lap and, with one arm across my back, reached round until her fingertips were just touching the start of the swelling side of my breast. For a moment, she rested her hand on the fullest part of my bottom, straight across the central crease. Then it whipped up and landed back down on me, right down on the left cheek.

And it hurt; it really hurt. I yelped and Keech laughed and jeered and then she hit me again. The same cheek, just as hard and I cried out again and tried to pull away from her, but she was strong, much stronger than I expected for a woman of her age and she gripped me tight, her arm pressing down across my ribs and her fingertips digging into the tender flesh of my breast. And she hit me again, the same side of my bottom, exactly the same place. I kicked out this time, tried to push myself up off her lap but she held me down and when I kicked out again she just hit me again. I know I was crying now, begging her please to stop because my bottom was really stinging, much worse than I had imagined could be possible from just being smacked, but she wouldn't stop. The strokes just came down time and again, I have no idea how many, but always aimed at the same cheek and it was so sore. I was weeping and begging her and kicking up to try to get her to leave me alone but she just went on and on and on.

She stopped when, in spite of all her attempts to hold on to me, I started sliding off her lap and she pulled me back up over her thighs and there she rested for a moment, her hand tracing up and down the crack between the cheeks of my bottom while Keech hooted and chuckled over in the corner.

'Hell, Bonnie, you should see that little girl's legs go! Like a hog at branding time, she was. And the more those legs kick up and around, the more she shows off all her sweet charms.' He leaned forward, and then he too slapped me across the bottom. 'Sticky little thing she is, too. You check her out, Bonnie!'

I knew he was right, even though the tears were still running down my face; I realised that kicking out like that would have caused my thighs to open and would have revealed the lips of my sex and even my bottom hole too. God knows what I must have revealed, with my bottom still greased and juicy from the doctor's examination and my pussy wet and dribbling as a result of the attention I had received from him and all the others. And Bonnie wasn't going to let that kind of opportunity pass. She leaned forward, her elbow digging into my back, and used both hands to pull the cheeks of my bottom right open. They both peered in, sniggering like children as they examined me, pressing their fingertips on the very centre of my bottom, so that I clenched up to keep them out, only making them snigger more and press harder.

Then they moved further down between my legs, pulled me even further agape and peeled my lips open, first the outer ones then even the small inside lips. I think they were both fiddling about with me, pressing and pulling at me, for I felt their fingers slip and scrape across my skin. At one time one of them pushed three fingers right up inside me, and then they both laughed when they were pulled out again, sticky and glistening. They pulled at the little skin over my clitoris, peeled that away to uncover even that delicate, private little part of me and mock what they found, taunting me that my lips were so wet, that my clitoris was so erect, that my vagina was so eager.

When they had finished, Keech returned to his bench and the woman pulled me back into place on her lap again.

'Well, we don't want you to enjoy this too much, honey, and I'm just sorry I don't have the wooden butter-paddle that I used on my kids when they was growing up. Still. My hand's as good as ever it was.'

She made me wait, listening no doubt to my sobs as I lay there, anticipating the next stroke from her great fat palm. For a few seconds, before she lifted her hand away, she let it rest on my skin again, her fingers tickling lightly at the flesh she was about to bruise again.

Then the hand lifted up, paused for a few agonising seconds and came back down. I screamed out again, the pain was worse than ever, still on exactly the same spot, now bruised and tender beyond belief. I begged her again, pleaded, screamed once more when the next stroke landed and kicked wildly to get away, to dilute the agony over a wider area, to press my groin harder against her knee as I writhed and as she spanked me again.

And again.

And again.

Finally she stopped, gently eased me off her lap on to the floor and let me kneel there, weeping and shivering until at last she unfastened the handcuffs and I clamped one hand over my wounded bottom and the other clutched at my overstimulated sex. My bottom was such a burning bruised blistering red where so many handprints had landed that I couldn't stand up. My sex was so wet I was dripping through my fingers.

Keech jeered, mocked me again.

'Bonnie, I reckon you could start a forest fire with that backside!'

She laughed. 'You could put one out with the flood from that pussy.'

I was humiliated by both comments.

Keech stretched his leg out until the toe of his boot was pushing in under my sex again, pressing harshly against me. I pulled away quickly, despite his mockery, because I wanted him to continue, but I knew if he had, that I would disgrace myself even further. He pulled away and turned back to Matt. We had all forgotten him.

'Well now. What do you know? The boy's little dicky's come back up again.'

Of course we all looked across to Matt, and indeed his cock was now half erect, a glistening silver thread running from the tip to the thigh against which it rested.

'And I tell you what,' Keech continued. 'I've got a horn on me myself now.' And with no shame, not a glance either at us or the woman standing beside him, Keech calmly unzipped his dark blue uniform trousers and reached in to pull out his own cock. It was fully erect, the round circumcised head shining a deep dark red. The man held it in his hand, obscenely working himself up and down as he stood no more than three feet in front of me.

'Well, sugar? What do you think, eh? Better size than that dinky little thing of your boyfriend's, huh?' He thrust himself forward until his cock was waving just a few inches from my face and the sour smell wafted across. He turned to Bonnie and sniggered.

'What do you think I should do with this, Bonnie? I mean I feel spoiled for choice: yes I do.'

I squeezed my thighs together, but he noticed the movement, and cackled again. 'Oh no, sugar. I think you'll be all right.'

And with that he stepped across, calmly put his hand on the back of Matt's head, and offered his cock up to Matt's horrified mouth.

Matt recoiled, almost falling off the bench in his determination to get away from the policeman. Keech grabbed his hair again, and pulled him back upright.

'Listen, boy,' he hissed. 'You can have this in your mouth or I can turn you straight over and stick it in your ass. Your choice.'

Matt didn't move. He didn't speak. He seemed to be scarcely breathing, but when Keech pulled his head closer again, and once more held up his cock, Matt's lips slowly opened and I watched in horror as the huge round head of Keech's erection was fed inside. I couldn't bear to watch and tore my eyes away in disgust, only to see, judderingly and unmistakably, Matt's own cock climbing back to a similar erection.

I turned away immediately, but Matt's reaction was perfectly visible to the other two. Keech sneered down at me.

'You see that, sugar? He's not as unwilling as he'd like you to believe. Go on, then. If you want. You go on down and do the same for him. I don't mind.'

The condescending mockery revolted me, but for hours now we had been mocked and toyed with, stimulated and left to suffer. I found my eyes drawn back to the sickening spectacle as Keech continued rhythmically pumping his cock in and out of Matt's lips. Yet Matt was visibly aroused in spite of it all, and as I watched, I saw his eyes searching round for me. And this was Matt's cock I was being offered, now gorgeously, pulsingly erect, and I know how much he likes my mouth. So I crawled over between his stomach and the patrolman's legs and enveloped him in my mouth, hearing the groan of ecstatic agony that escaped from Matt's lips as he felt the contact.

But whether that was the cause or not, the groan was immediately followed by a sudden frenzied juddering from Keech, muffled protests from Matt and I felt spatterings of Keech's semen landing across my shoulders before Matt was again pulled tight up against the man's groin. Simultaneously, before I had even started, my own mouth was filled with an eruption from the cock I was tasting and I struggled to swallow down the gushing flow that threatened to choke me.

As the flow stopped and I felt Matt wilting rapidly beneath me, it was impossible to pull myself back upright with no hands to help me. Instead, I licked softly at the velvety pink skin and tried to pass some message of support and encouragement to him. He had endured so much, much worse than I had done, but at least we had survived and now it was all over and these foul people would soon be gone, finally leaving us alone.

I thought.

Until a slow trail of sharp fingernails came crawling possessively across my shoulder blades and down my spine, tracing the curve as it wound down the length of my back. The nails stopped at the start of my bottom. That was when the voice started.

'Sit up now, honey, 'cos I think it's my turn, and I've changed my mind about you. In fact, I've got a little favour you can do for me.'

She gripped tightly round the top of my arm and dragged me back up but stood directly in front of me:

just as I had been made to stand in front of her earlier; just as Keech had positioned himself for Matt. Her hands were firmly set on her hips; her legs solidly placed on the concrete floor; her eyes fixed on me, the same slightly questioning look from her raised eyebrows.

As I looked up at her, knowing, wondering, dreading, she suddenly grinned and her hand reached out to me, stroked down the length of my cheek in a caress that would in any other circumstances have been affectionate and sympathetic, but here, in this hot sweaty jail cell, was avaricious and condescending.

'She's a cute little thing.' Her words didn't seem to be directed to anybody in particular. 'Cute face,' she continued, her fingers tracing down my jaw. 'Cute mouth.' There was an ominous emphasis on the word as her fingertips trailed along my lips. I said nothing; offered no reaction that she could feed off. 'Very cute. I think I'd like that.' She shifted her weight from one leg to the other, swivelling her hips slightly beneath the heavy uniform skirt.

She nodded. 'Yep. Cute mouth.'

The emphasis had now become unmistakable. To me, to Matt and to Keech. He paused in the middle of refastening his trousers, scanned eagerly round the three other faces in the room and then hurriedly finished buckling his belt before settling back on the side bench.

'Well, help yourself, Bonnie. That's what the Chief said.'

'I think I will.' She was already reaching up under her skirt. 'I think I will do just that.' Her hands reappeared, now tugging at a huge pair of white cotton knickers. She pulled them right off, returned to the bench on which she had spanked me and crooked her finger at me.

'Come on over here, honey. I've got a little job for you.' She slid the hem of her skirt smoothly up her thighs, revealing first a wide stretch of black nylon, followed by the broad band at the top of her stockings and then an expanse of pasty white skin. At the top of that, beyond where the tight elastic of her stockings had dug itself into the flesh of her thighs, just below where the skirt now ended, was a thick unkempt bush of matted black hair.

She shuffled her feet apart and pointed to the floor directly in front of her. I considered the options. What could they do if I flatly refused? Anything. They could do anything that they wanted and I had no doubt they would. We were alone, stuck in this squalid little station house, miles from any major city or consulate; we might as well have been back in the old West where the sheriff's word was law. With a last wordless appeal to Matt, I made my way across to the grinning, beckoning woman who sat smugly, almost serenely, waiting for me to obey her summons. I knelt down at her feet. And froze. I just couldn't bring myself to do something so utterly disgusting, so obscene and degrading, and do it in front of Matt. How would I face him every day for the rest of our lives after he had seen me with my face buried between another woman's thighs? I looked round to him, asking perhaps for him to forgive me if my refusal got us killed there and then. But then I saw the look on his face. He wasn't appalled. He wasn't ashamed. He was offering sympathy to me in this horror that I was facing. In my selfishness, I had forgotten that he had already suffered the humiliation of having to suck the patrolman to orgasm. His reaction to that disgrace had been such a profound arousal that he had become erect himself, had climaxed himself in my mouth. How would he live with himself, let alone live with me, if I resisted and avoided an equal shame?

The policewoman rested her hand on the back of my head; not pressed, just rested, but at the same time she swivelled her thighs further open to expose not just the coarse black hair but now the thick puffy lips which, even while I watched, slowly peeled apart like some obscene monster, until she was finally yawning open, slimy and crimson, right in front of my eyes. The presentation was so utterly enthralling I couldn't move. I was paralysed by the repulsive vision that quivered so close in front of me, prepared for me, waiting for me, beckoning me.

'Come along, honey. I'm waiting for the touch of your sweet tongue.'

And I gave in. I crawled forward between those great fat thighs until I was surrounded by the thick sour smell of her gaping sex, by sweat and grime. The aroma was so strong that I almost gagged. As I leaned in further, the tip of my nose touched her rough wiry hair and still I forced myself on. Finally I knew that by reaching out my tongue, I would touch her. Her skin. Her sex. Her labia. It seemed the most horrifying and disgusting act that I could imagine and so I did it. I licked, as lightly as I possibly could get away with, at her flesh. It tasted foul, bitter and sweaty and I recoiled immediately, wiping my mouth against the back of my hand. The woman just laughed bitterly and reached out to my hair.

'Well, honey, I'm so sorry if this ain't the sweetest meat you've ever tasted, and it may well be that your own cute little pussy is one hell of lot prettier tasting than mine, but frankly I don't care and I don't plan on finding out, because I just don't go for that kind of kinky thing. Besides, I don't suppose you will be quite so fresh and appetising yourself when you get to my age, and you've had three kids, more men than I can remember and you've been working all day. Still, that's beside the point. For now, you just do what I told you. You get your gorgeous little tongue working deep in there and you don't stop till I tell you. Is that clear?'

I swallowed hard, leaned in again and then she grabbed me by my hair and dragged me right into the sodden crease of her sex. My nose was engulfed in her flesh and I could feel the hard nib of her clitoris pressing against me. My mouth was enfolded between her flabby lips so that I could scarcely breathe, my lungs were filled with her scent, her flavour; my ears filled with her command.

I pushed out my tongue and lapped.

She tasted sour; pungent and rancid. She was no sweet young girl, pure and clean and dripping fresh honey. She was a mature woman; someone who had been around a while; whose sex tasted of robust seasoning and experience. Like the gravelled voice of an old jazz singer, it was rough and unrefined and utterly enslaving. As I pressed my tongue in deeper between her ragged lips, and the thick syrup flowed freely from her loose, luscious sex, I found myself thinking that this wasn't a pussy: this was a cunt. This was strong and commanding, this had all its own power and vitality and somehow it felt right that I was kneeling before it, a supplicant at its gate. And I lapped and swallowed down the flow that my own nursing had produced, and the more I lapped the richer the response.

Her lips were so full, so ample and voluptuous that when I drew her all into my mouth, it was a complete mouthful: soft, succulent and exquisite. If I pushed it all out, I could slide my tongue round in wide lapping circles and up through the deep central divide to her loosely covered clitoris. Its hood hung slack and wrinkled so I could slip the tip of my tongue beneath it until she recoiled at its touch on the smooth round head of the clitoris itself. Without stopping my licking, I brought up both hands so that my fingers could join in feeling the slimy surface of her baggy lips and her deep lavish opening. I pushed a finger inside her, tentatively, because I know how aggressive and invasive that can feel, but she barely seemed to notice me at all and I had pushed all four fingers deep into her before there was any long-wailing sigh of acknowledgement.

Her hips were beginning to rotate now, a slow coiling grind like some great beast that would devour all it encountered. Her hands rested lightly on my head to keep me in place, to guide me and ensure I didn't weaken now that her own needs were building. Glancing up, her eyes were shut, her lips parted and the tip of her tongue protruded from her painted mouth. Her breath came grunting out in an even tortured rhythm as I continued digging far into her with the fingers of one hand, pinching and pulling at her hanging folds with the other and all the time lapping my tongue round in great all-covering circles that scooped more of her juice into my own mouth with every loop.

Her grunts started to get lower and her thighs moved steadily further open as the pressure on the back of my head increased and I was pressed tighter and tighter into her open sex. She was so wet that her sex was practically dribbling on to the floor and I could hardly feel the sides of her vagina. Her fingers kept twisting and tangling my hair as she squeezed me in, squeezing as if she would swallow me. Her grunts, like an animal in pain, were torn in slow moans from somewhere deep in her throat and her thighs had spread so far that they were almost in a straight line. Suddenly she stopped, was absolutely still.

And then there was a single racked groan as she clamped her legs back like a spring trap, twisting her hips, grinding herself against my face, squeezing and crying and hugging my mouth to her opening and still the honey was pouring from her like the juice of an overripe fruit and it was running down her lips and down my chin and her thighs were squeezing me so hard I was in pain and could scarcely breathe and she cried, literally cried, great sobs of passion that were jerked from her with every thrust of her hips against me as she called out obscenities and endearments and pulled me to her and shoved me away and yanked me back again and juddered, trembling, collapsing in front of me.

Finally Bonnie released me, and I pulled away, wiping the taste of her on to the back of my hand, although her pungent aroma still clung to my cheeks, lips and chin and filled my throat with every breath. She smiled down at me.

'Well done, honey! I've always said it takes a woman to really know how to eat pussy.'

After all that I had done, her crude dismissal of our tie was painful and humiliating. I turned away from her and crawled silently back to my seat beside Matt.

She stood up, brushed her clothes down and started to follow Keech out, and although we weren't given back our clothes, before she left us in the cell, she did at least release Matt's handcuffs as well.

The second the door pushed shut, Matt threw his arms around me. His erection was still proudly and urgently pressed between our stomachs as his hands gripped at my breasts. He bent down to suckle at my nipples, and as he did so, I saw over his shoulder

Bonnie's flushed and inquisitive face peering through the small square panel in the cell door. I no longer cared. Instead I shuffled further back to the narrow bunk, and stretched myself out.

Now I had my lover to myself and I opened my legs as wide as ever they had been stretched by any of their investigations during that long night. I brought my knees up and let them fall open. Now I would expose my sex one final time to the intense eager gaze of the woman outside. Then Matt sank down on me and at last his magnificent greedy cock was digging down between my lips and into my dripping channel. We were both so deeply stimulated that it was mere seconds before we both exploded in grunting panting ecstasy, me watching over his shoulder the trembling concentration on the face of the woman at the door. Matt was unaware of our audience, but as soon as his climax was done, I pushed him off me, and sprawled across the bunk.

And I stayed stretched out, my legs apart, my entire body open to the doorway, and to the envious narrowed eyes still peering in from out there. Now I could reveal to her not just my quivering sex, my wide slippery lips, but also the river of semen that was now finally there, at last running from me. Matt knelt on the floor kissing me: kissing my mouth, my eyes, my breasts and I just let her watch.

After all, there was now a man, young, virile and eager worshipping my naked body.

No one was worshipping hers.

NEW BOOKS

Coming up from Nexus, Sapphire and Black Lace

Brought to Heel by Arabella Knight
July 2000   Price £5.99   ISBN 0 352 33508 4
Lustful desires provoke these girls to their perverted pleasures, but such wickedness is soon exposed by that most stern mistress, the cane, and then the guilty must come under her cruel kiss to suffer sharp sorrow and sweet pain. The pest, the predator, the pilferer – each with appetites for dark delights. Tempted, they feast upon forbidden fruit, but they cannot escape paying painful penalties. All must submit to discipline as they are sternly brought to heel.

Purity by Aishling Morgan
July 2000   Price £5.99   ISBN 0 352 33510 6
Henry Truscott, dissipated hero of *The Rake*, finds himself faced with the prospect of living on his brother's charity. His efforts to create a new fortune lead him along a path of debauchery and perversion, from stripping girls in Mother Agie's brothel to indulging three ladies at once in a Belgravia drawing room. Nor are his associates idle, with his wife being pursued by the sadistic d'Aignan while the flame-haired Judith Cates becomes embroiled in Sir Joseph Snapes' bizarre sexual experiments.

Serving Time by Sarah Veitch
July 2000   Price £5.99   ISBN 0 352 33509 2
The House of Compulsion is the unofficial name of an experimental reformatory. Fern Terris, a twenty-four year old temptress, finds herself facing ten years in prison – unless she agrees to submit to Compulsion's disciplinary regime. Fern agrees to the apparently easy option, but soon discovers that the chastisements at Compulsion involve a wide variety of belts, canes and tawses, her pert bottom – and unexpected sexual pleasure.

Surrender by Laura Bowen
August 2000   Price £5.99   ISBN 0 352 33524 6
When Melanie joins the staff of The Hotel she enters a world of new sexual experiences and frightening demands, in which there are three kinds of duty she must perform. In this place of luxury and beauty there are many pleasures, serving her deepest desires, but there is also perversity and pain. The Hotel is founded on a strict regime, but Melanie cannot help but break the rules. How can she survive the severe torments that follow?

An Education in the Private House by Esme Ombreux
August 2000   Price £5.99   ISBN 0 352 33525 4
Eloise Highfield is left in charge of the upbringing of Celia Bright's orphaned daughter, Anne. Disturbed and excited by the instructions left by Celia for Anne's education, Eloise invites Michael, a painter of erotic subjects, to assist her. As they read Celia's explicit account of servitude to her own master, they embark on ever more extreme experiments. But Anne is keeping her own diary of events . . . Celia, Eloise, Anne – three women discovering the pleasures of submission; three interwoven accounts of a shared journey into blissful depravity. By the author of the *Private House* series.

The Training Grounds by Sarah Veitch
August 2000   Price £5.99   ISBN 0 352 33526 2
Charlotte was looking forward to her holiday in the sun. Two months on a remote tropical island with her rich, handsome boyfriend: who could ask for more? She is more than a little surprised, then, when she arrives to find that the island is in fact a vast correction centre – the Training Grounds – presided over by a swarthy and handsome figure known only as the Master. But greater shocks are in store, not least Charlotte's discovery that she is there not as a guest, but as a slave . . .

SAPPHIRE · SAPPHIRE

A new imprint of lesbian fiction

I Married Madam by Daphne Adams

June 2000   £8.99   ISBN 0 352 33514 9

Anna has a blast making the rounds of East London dyke pubs with her best friend Joan, but it's no cure for the rut she's fallen into with her girlfriend, Valerie. Still, life gets more exciting when she meets the enigmatic Marlene: a tall dark German who wears silk suits and smokes exotic cigarettes. She's a Dietrich-dream-come-true, even though she's the opposite of Anna's usual type. But, as Anna gingerly extracts herself from her five-year relationship with Valerie, she's not even sure if she knows what her type *is* anymore. Marlene herself is an unknown quantity – after Anna finds out that she moonlights as a lesbian dominatrix.

Ice Queen by Suzanne Blaylock

August 2000   £8.99   ISBN 0 352 33517 3

Drawn together by an accident of time and circumstance, a disparate group of women all hide behind masks of cool deception, but when their paths cross the ice soon melts in a furnace of deception. Magdalen Duhamel, a gorgeous out-of-work actress, is one of these women. *Ice Queen* explores the myth and reality of the cold and calculating female icon – and the frequently discovered truth that all is not often what it seems.

BLACK
lace

Primal Skin by Leona Benkt Rhys
July 2000   Price £5.99   ISBN 0 352 33500 9
Set in the mysterious northern and central Europe of the last Ice Age,
Primal Skin is the story of a female Neanderthal shaman who is on a
quest to find magical talismans for her primal rituals. Her nomadic
journey, accompanied by her friends, is fraught with danger, adventure
and sexual experimentation. The mood is eerie and full of symbolism,
and the book is evocative of the best-selling novel *Clan of the Cave Bear*.

A Sporting Chance by Susie Raymond
July 2000   Price £5.99   ISBN 0 352 33501 7
Maggie is an avid supporter of her local ice hockey team, The
Trojans, and when her manager mentions he has some spare tickets
to their next away game, it doesn't take long to twist him around her
little finger. Once at the match she wastes no time in getting inti-
mately associated with the Trojans – especially Troy, their powerfully
built star player. But their manager is not impressed with Maggie's
antics; he's worried she's distracting them from their game. At first
she finds his threats amusing, but then she realises she's being stalked.

Wicked Words 3 various
August 2000   Price £5.99   ISBN 0 352 33522 X
Wild women. Wicked words. Guaranteed to turn you on! Black Lace
short story collections are a showcase of erotic-writing talent. With
contributions from the UK and the USA, and settings and stories
that are deliciously daring, this is erotica at the cutting edge. Fresh,
cheeky, dazzling and upbeat – only the most arousing fiction makes
it into a Black Lace compilation.

A Scandalous Affair by Holly Graham
August 2000   Price £5.99   ISBN 0 352 33523 8
Young, well groomed and spoilt, Olivia Standish is the epitome of a
trophy wife. Her husband is a successful politician, and Olivia is
confident that she can look forward to a life of luxury and prestige.
Then she finds a video of her husband cavorting with whores and
engaging in some very bizarre behaviour, and suddenly her future
looks uncertain. Realising that her marriage is one of convenience
and not love, she vows to take her revenge. Her goal is to have her
errant husband on his knees and begging for mercy.

NEXUS BACKLIST

All books are priced £5.99 unless another price is given. If a date is supplied, the book in question will not be available until that month in 2000.

CONTEMPORARY EROTICA

THE BLACK MASQUE	Lisette Ashton	
THE BLACK WIDOW	Lisette Ashton	
THE BOND	Lindsay Gordon	
BRAT	Penny Birch	
BROUGHT TO HEEL	Arabella Knight	July
DANCE OF SUBMISSION	Lisette Ashton	
DISCIPLES OF SHAME	Stephanie Calvin	
DISCIPLINE OF THE PRIVATE HOUSE	Esme Ombreux	
DISCIPLINED SKIN	Wendy Swanscombe	Nov
DISPLAYS OF EXPERIENCE	Lucy Golden	
AN EDUCATION IN THE PRIVATE HOUSE	Esme Ombreux	Aug
EMMA'S SECRET DOMINATION	Hilary James	
GISELLE	Jean Aveline	
GROOMING LUCY	Yvonne Marshall	Sept
HEART OF DESIRE	Maria del Rey	
HOUSE RULES	G.C. Scott	
IN FOR A PENNY	Penny Birch	
LESSONS OF OBEDIENCE	Lucy Golden	Dec
ONE WEEK IN THE PRIVATE HOUSE	Esme Ombreux	
THE ORDER	Nadine Somers	
THE PALACE OF EROS	Delver Maddingley	
PEEPING AT PAMELA	Yolanda Celbridge	Oct
PLAYTHING	Penny Birch	

THE PLEASURE CHAMBER	Brigitte Markham		
POLICE LADIES	Yolanda Celbridge		
THE RELUCTANT VIRGIN	Kendal Grahame		
SANDRA'S NEW SCHOOL	Yolanda Celbridge		
SKIN SLAVE	Yolanda Celbridge		June
THE SLAVE AUCTION	Lisette Ashton		
SLAVE EXODUS	Jennifer Jane Pope		Dec
SLAVE GENESIS	Jennifer Jane Pope		
SLAVE SENTENCE	Lisette Ashton		
THE SUBMISSION GALLERY	Lindsay Gordon		
SURRENDER	Laura Bowen		Aug
TAKING PAINS TO PLEASE	Arabella Knight		
TIGHT WHITE COTTON	Penny Birch		Oct
THE TORTURE CHAMBER	Lisette Ashton		Sept
THE TRAINING OF FALLEN ANGELS	Kendal Grahame		
THE YOUNG WIFE	Stephanie Calvin		May

ANCIENT & FANTASY SETTINGS

THE CASTLE OF MALDONA	Yolanda Celbridge		
NYMPHS OF DIONYSUS	Susan Tinoff	£4.99	
MAIDEN	Aishling Morgan		
TIGER, TIGER	Aishling Morgan		
THE WARRIOR QUEEN	Kendal Grahame		

EDWARDIAN, VICTORIAN & OLDER EROTICA

BEATRICE	Anonymous		
CONFESSION OF AN ENGLISH SLAVE	Yolanda Celbridge		
DEVON CREAM	Aishling Morgan		
THE GOVERNESS AT ST AGATHA'S	Yolanda Celbridge		
PURITY	Aishling Morgan		July
THE RAKE	Aishling Morgan		
THE TRAINING OF AN ENGLISH GENTLEMAN	Yolanda Celbridge		

SAMPLERS & COLLECTIONS

NEW EROTICA 3	
NEW EROTICA 5	Nov
A DOZEN STROKES	Various

NEXUS CLASSICS

A new imprint dedicated to putting the finest works of erotic fiction back in print

AGONY AUNT	G. C. Scott	
THE HANDMAIDENS	Aran Ashe	
OBSESSION	Maria del Rey	
HIS MISTRESS'S VOICE	G.C. Scott	
CITADEL OF SERVITUDE	Aran Ashe	
BOUND TO SERVE	Amanda Ware	
SISTERHOOD OF THE INSTITUTE	Maria del Rey	
A MATTER OF POSSESSION	G.C. Scott	
THE PLEASURE PRINCIPLE	Maria del Rey	
CONDUCT UNBECOMING	Arabella Knight	
CANDY IN CAPTIVITY	Arabella Knight	
THE SLAVE OF LIDIR	Aran Ashe	
THE DUNGEONS OF LIDIR	Aran Ashe	
SERVING TIME	Sarah Veitch	July
THE TRAINING GROUNDS	Sarah Veitch	Aug
DIFFERENT STROKES	Sarah Veitch	Sept
LINGERING LESSONS	Sarah Veitch	Oct
EDEN UNVEILED	Maria del Rey	Nov
UNDERWORLD	Maria del Rey	Dec

Please send me the books I have ticked above.

Name   ....

Address   ....

              ....

              ....

              .... Post code.....................

Send to: **Cash Sales, Nexus Books, Thames Wharf Studios, Rainville Road, London W6 9HA**

US customers: for prices and details of how to order books for delivery by mail, call 1-800-805-1083.

Please enclose a cheque or postal order, made payable to **Nexus Books**, to the value of the books you have ordered plus postage and packing costs as follows:
  UK and BFPO – £1.00 for the first book, 50p for the second book and 30p for each subsequent book to a maximum of £3.00;
  Overseas (including Republic of Ireland) – £2.00 for the first book, £1.00 for the second book and 50p for each subsequent book.

We accept all major credit cards, including VISA, ACCESS/MASTERCARD, AMEX, DINERS CLUB, SWITCH, SOLO, and DELTA. Please write your card number and expiry date here:

....

Please allow up to 28 days for delivery.

Signature ....